RECKONINGS

KAREN E. OSBORNE

Black Rose Writing | Texas

The author grants the final approval for this literary material.

First printing

This is a work of fiction. Names, characters, businesses, places, events, and incidents are either the products of the author's imagination or used in a fictitious manner. Any resemblance to actual persons, living or dead, or actual events is purely coincidental.

ISBN: 978-1-68433-961-7
PUBLISHED BY BLACK ROSE WRITING
www.blackrosewriting.com

Printed in the United States of America
Suggested Retail Price (SRP) $20.95

Reckonings is printed in Garamond Premier Pro

*As a planet-friendly publisher, Black Rose Writing does its best to eliminate unnecessary waste to reduce paper usage and energy costs, while never compromising the reading experience. As a result, the final word count vs. page count may not meet common expectations.

To Bob, my friend, husband, partner, and love of my life.

Dear Liesl,

RECKONINGS

Thank you

Karen

RECKONINGS

CHAPTER 1
THURSDAY

Roxy sat in the cramped kitchen, the table and chairs taking up most of the space. On the other side of the drawn curtain separating the living and dining rooms, thirteen-year-old Max snored on the sofa bed. The refrigerator, covered with magnetic alphabet letters and family photos, made a low rumble matching the hum of the window air conditioner. Her fingers flew over the keys of the computer, a small, square laptop as old as her five-year-old twins. She paused and closed her eyes. It had been a month since her husband, Carl, told her he'd seen Spider Booth. A month. At some point, she'd run into him. Then what? She tried to force him out of her head and return her concentration to her writing, but he lurked on the edges of consciousness.

Jewel entered the kitchen, rubbing her eyes, her round belly small for eight months pregnant. "Morning, Mom."

Roxy nodded her response, her nerves ragged from thinking about Spider and her story at a critical point. A contest with a final submission deadline four days away added another sharp point of tension.

"Any coffee?" Jewel checked the pot. "First one up makes it. House rules." She sounded aggrieved.

"Hmm," Roxy said without acknowledging the complaint. She could see the end of her tale. Images swirled in her head like the snow in her story, momentarily blinding the protagonist and her rival.

"Mom, I'm talking to you."

1

Roxy, fingers hovering over the keyboard, pondered the perfect ending. What should her main character say at this crucial moment?

From the narrow center hallway, Cleo yelped a warning. Pharoah, the larger of the two rescue dogs, joined in. They both needed to go out. The twins bounded into the tiny space. Gabriella said, "I want oatmeal with strawberries. Do we have blueberries?"

Her smaller sister, Kia, said. "Can I have French toast?"

From the living room, Max's deepening voice yelled, "I'm sleeping. Be quiet. It's too early."

"Okay, guys." Roxy closed her computer. "Oatmeal for everyone. We only have bananas."

Her thirty minutes of morning writing was over. The contest winner would receive $1,000 and their story in the magazine—two helpful and spirt-lifting rewards.

"I want pancakes," Kia said, changing her order.

Carl was getting ready for work, and Roxy needed to do the same. She turned to seventeen-year-old Jewel. "Can you fix breakfast? I have to get dressed."

An audible grumble.

"Lots going on today." It was only 7:30 a.m. but weariness slumped Roxy's shoulders. "Just do it."

Carl called from the bathroom, "Next. I'm outta the shower."

"Max, it's your turn to take the dogs out." Roxy patted both animals on the tops of their heads. "You'll have to clean up any accidents if you don't move." She turned to her pregnant daughter, who was measuring oatmeal and milk into a pot and, ignoring Jewel's grumpy face, said, "Thanks, sweet pea."

Roxy walked into the now vacant bathroom and sat on the closed toilet seat, grateful for another few minutes of peace. She shut her eyes and rested her head against the wall. Spider's face reappeared. Her eyes flew open.

"Mom, are you almost ready? There's a line out here," Jewel said from outside the bathroom door. "You're taking forever and spent too much time on the computer. We're all gonna be late."

"Sorry. Five more minutes."

No one in her family understood the importance of Roxy's writing and especially her play, *The Monday Night Murder*. In nine days, the local community

2

theater was staging it—her family's ticket to a different life. They didn't have faith, or they couldn't imagine it getting them out of this tiny, one bathroom, two-bedroom apartment and into a new house and new jobs. Into the life Roxy dreamed about every day.

But Roxy believed.

• • •

Sweat slicked Roxy's face. She struggled to the car, balancing two piles of used clothes destined for New Hope Women's Shelter. Moisture-laden heat left her breathless and edgy. She felt every one of her thirty-six years, the toll of raising four children, and the cost of working on her feet, eight hours a day, at Frank's Beauty Salon and School.

A flash lit the sky. Thunder crashed. Windswept clouds masked and unmasked the August sun. To beat the impending storm, she picked up her pace. The folded and stacked armfuls wobbled as she hurried with her chin pressed against one pile, hoping the other made it to her Taurus intact.

The car looked as worn as Roxy. Chips and dents marred the paint. Tape patched the right rear bumper. She'd left her writing journal and the frayed copy of August Wilson's plays on the dashboard. Two child booster seats took up most of the back. A dog's chewing bone lay on the floorboards among a scattering of Cheerios.

After working all day and squeezing in her writing in the morning and during snatched minutes at work, Roxy spent the last hour going from store to store on Governors Avenue, Fieldcrest's main north-south thoroughfare—Gov Ave to its citizens—collecting donations from people she'd known for years. On the first Thursday of every month, owners, shoppers, and salespeople brought in their *gently worn* outfits for Roxy to deliver.

The trunk of Roxy's car, packed with toys from neighbors and her twins, also held outgrown athletic wear belonging to Max. Contributions from Jewel consisted of last month's editions of *Essence, Vogue* and *Elle* and an assortment of body lotions and face creams created especially for Black folks. Crisp twenties from her lifelong friend, Dallas, added to the donated bounty.

The women, children, and staff at New Hope appreciated the cash and gifts, but treasured Roxy's visits most. For free, she washed, set, and styled hair and gave squirmy children haircuts before heading home to her husband and their brood, exhausted but happy.

Today, the heat and dampness nibbled at her joy. Jewel's pregnancy and the stress of Roxy's play, its success essential, also weighed her down and clouded her mood. Thoughts of Spider nagging her all day sealed it.

From under the pile of clothes lining her right arm, Roxy pushed the key fob. Two beeps and a click. She wedged the clothes against the passenger side window and yanked open the door.

"Roxy."

Spider's familiar voice, one she hadn't heard in eighteen years, boomed from across the street. She peered over the car's hood. Another jagged flash sliced through the clouds.

"Hello." He crisscrossed his arms the way an airport marshal waves to signal a landing plane.

Roxy tried to steady her breathing and her shaking legs. Despite knowing she'd run into him ever since Carl mentioned Spider was back in town, she felt unprepared and quavered like a schoolgirl with an imagined monster in her closet. Except this beast was real.

Feet rooted in place and unable to move, she watched him dodge through the slow-moving traffic. How many times had she thought she spotted him in the mall or on the street? A blond man with a nipped waist, and the muscled arms of a competitive swimmer. But it was always someone else.

"Let me help." He grabbed a stack of the clothes; the back of his hand brushed against the swell of her breast.

Tremors shot through her. Her heart beat off kilter.

"Did Q tell you I moved back?" Spider used Carl's childhood nickname, short for his last name—Quinton. "Been here a month." He plopped the clothes on the passenger seat and straightened. "Give me the rest." He reached over. Tanned skin and blond arm hairs bleached white from the sun contrasted with her deep brown.

She clutched the pile to her chest. "What do you want?" Her words tasted bitter and hot.

"Is that how you greet an old friend?"

Spider, Carl, Dallas, and Roxy grew up together through high school. Spider disappeared after graduation. And now he was back–his hair thinner and his waist thicker, with squint lines spreading from the corners of blue eyes that probed hers. It was one of his superpowers–making others imagine he saw only them.

Roxy stomped around the car, swung open the driver's door, climbed in, and shoved the garments next to the others.

"Wait. Come on." He loomed over her.

"Get away from me." She grabbed the door handle.

"I met her." His voice became low and soft. "She's a beauty."

Roxy knew who he meant–understood the emotion in Spider's voice–but Jewel was not his child, no matter his assumption. "And stay away from my daughter." Roxy slammed the door and turned the key. The engine whined in protest until she pumped the gas and tried again.

Spider knocked on the glass, sending fresh panic ripples through her. She gripped the steering wheel. Another sharp rap. Without looking in his direction, she cracked the window. "What?"

"I'm going to be a part of Jewel's life, and you can't prevent me."

She swung the steering wheel hard and accelerated. He jumped. A biker swerved, cursing. Cars honked.

"I'll kill you first." The scream scratched her dry throat.

Tears puddled, making it difficult to see. At the light, she turned onto a side street and parked in front of a fire hydrant. Afraid to shut off the engine lest the battered auto not start again, she sat in the idling Taurus. She remembered rough hands pinning hers above her head on the scratchy Army blanket, the throb from the slap across her face, and the excruciating pain from his forced penetration. His words rang in her ears. "I should have done this a long time ago. You'll like it better next time."

She banged the steering wheel with the heels of both hands until the intensity of the pain shooting up her arms forced her to stop.

5

CHAPTER 2
FRIDAY

"Spider" Webster Booth was back in town. He'd seen Jewel. Roxy tried to focus, but fear jumbled her thoughts.

Carl, Jewel, and Roxy sat three abreast in folding metal chairs facing a cluttered wooden desk. Table lamps lit the room. An air conditioner jutted from one of the windows, its purple strips of cloth flapped from slats, infusing the air with lavender. Perspiration beaded on Roxy's nose and forehead. Carl stared straight ahead while Jewel fidgeted between them.

"You, okay?" Carl asked Roxy.

"Sure." They knew each other's every mood and tic. But today he missed her turmoil. She wasn't fine.

Behind the desk, the social worker, Annie Long, shuffled folders. What did the colors mean—yellow for unwed mothers, red for adoption applicants, and vanilla for unwanted babies?

Ms. Long's smile seemed practiced in the same way Roxy's twins responded to photo requests. "This is your decision, Jewel." She was an uptalker, making every sentence sound like a question.

"I've made it." Jewel jiggled her sneaker-clad foot. Crossed arms rested on the swell of her belly. "Adoption."

"Then let's get to it." With her left hand, Ms. Long opened a yellow file. A poised pen occupied her right. "Have you notified the father?"

"*No*. He doesn't have a say."

Carl gave Roxy a sidelong glance, a silent communication honed over eighteen years of marriage. We're a team, it said. Looking in the same direction.

Not this time.

Cool eyes appraised the family from behind thick lenses. A black ribbon struggled to hold the social worker's mixed gray hair in place. "Secrets rarely work out well."

Heat crept up Roxy's neck and cheeks.

"It's *my* life, *my* baby." Jewel was adamant.

Ms. Long placed both hands on top of the opened folder. "Telling the father changes nothing. You *are* in charge." She created a steeple with bony fingers. "Consider if it were you in the dark."

Jewel made a strangled noise.

Carl jumped in. "We're agreed. Adoption is right for everyone involved and who the father is... that's past mattering."

When they first learned about the pregnancy, Jewel was already four months along. Roxy had noticed the slight weight gain and found prenatal vitamins in Jewel's bag. They confronted her. "Yeah. So now you know," Jewel had said. "And why are you going through my stuff?" Carl begged her to name the baby's father. "Who did this to you? Did someone force himself on you?" The first question went unanswered, and the second received an emphatic, "No."

Carl reached over and put an arm around his daughter's narrow shoulders. "What happens next?"

"We'll be there at the birth." Annie Long jotted notes. "Make all the arrangements."

Roxy, flushed with guilt, twisted the delicate gold bracelet on her left wrist—her only physical remembrance of her mother. Aren't I responsible? Like mother, like daughter?

"Here's my card." Ms. Long rose from her desk and came around in front of Jewel. "Call me anytime if you have questions or want to talk."

Jewel slid the card into a pocket of her jeans. "What are they like?"

"The adoptive family?"

"Yeah."

"Decent people. They've been waiting a long time." Ms. Long's smile reassured. "Your daughter will be in a loving home, which isn't a given for Black adoptive children. So many languish. You and your baby are fortunate."

Were they fortunate or making a huge mistake? Roxy had other questions. How old are they? Where do they live? Are they church goers? How can you be sure they'll do right by her?

As if he sensed her thoughts, Carl threw Roxy a look. In a rare moment of verbal self-control, she stayed silent.

Jewel asked, "What if they don't like her?"

"What do you mean?"

"Say, she cries too much or something else upsets them. What happens to her?"

"They're going to love her." With her fingertips, Ms. Long smoothed the frown from her brow. "Parenting is hard no matter how you become one." Her mouth moved up and down in a quick smile. "They'll figure it out." Her uptalk made her sound less confident than her words.

Jewel persisted. "Can people give babies back?"

Ms. Long made an impatient sound. "There's a waiting period before the court finalizes the adoption. After the birth, you have a few days to change your mind, and they do as well."

Jewel chewed her lower lip. "Will I get to see her?"

"Most mothers find the earlier the separation, the better for everyone." She paused. No one spoke. "*But*, like everything concerning your baby, it's up to you. You can have an open adoption if the new parents agree."

They'd discussed the possibility. The law allowed parents to choose between knowing the adoptive family or not. Jewel had opted for privacy. Was she changing her mind?

Carl reached for Jewel's hand.

"There's time enough to decide," Annie Long said. "You have a few weeks before your due date and first babies are often late."

Jewel turned to her mother. "Was I?"

"No," Carl said before Roxy replied. "You were early and perfect."

•   •   •

Heat rose from the oozing asphalt. Thunder reverberated, and despite the sun blanching the sky, the air tasted wet. Yesterday evening, Roxy was confident of the storm and relief. Surely today.

The family walked toward their car, squeezed between a dumpster and the edge of a no-parking zone. Jewel stopped. "Do you guys think I should see her?"

"No," Carl said. His tone softened. "Ms. Long is probably right." Sunlight reflected off his patent-leather hair, still jet-black at thirty-six. He shifted from one foot to the other. "She's got experience. Take her cue."

Roxy's emotions bounced around as they had from the moment Jewel told them. Another child to raise. Jewel failing to graduate from high school and college out of reach. Carl, through all their discussions and arguments, never said how he *felt* about it. Only this was the right decision–the only *sensible* one.

Roxy envisioned the hazy picture the sonogram revealed. Carl wouldn't look. Roxy couldn't tear her eyes away.

"Whatever you decide to do," Roxy said, "is fine by me."

Jewel whirled, squinted her eyes, and jutted her chin the way her grandmother, Carl's mom, did. "I'm asking your opinion."

Roxy dug into her messenger bag for a tissue.

"Are you crying?" Jewel asked.

"I'm not."

"We agreed no crying."

Roxy sniffled, wiped her nose, and stuffed the used tissue back into her bag.

"So?" Jewel queried again.

How to answer when Roxy's head knew they were doing the right thing, but all the rest of her shouted stop? She searched for words that held no judgment. "If you're asking, do I want to see my granddaughter...?" For a moment, Roxy thought to lie, but the truth tumbled out. "Yes, I do."

Carl flung his arms into the air. "She's decided. *You* picked the social worker." His arms dropped and hit his sides with a thump.

"I'd tell your little girl I love her." Memorize her face. Whenever Roxy thought about the baby, she remembered her own mother walking out the front door and her father hanging his head with a sob. Was abandoning children genetic, caused by a defective gene?

"How can you love her? You're saying that to guilt me," Jewel said.

"Not true."

Carl angled into the driver's seat. "I gotta get to work. This is not productive."

They'd had this conversation countless times. Everyone agreed. Plus, the decision fit in with Roxy's bigger plan–a house with a yard and enough money for Carl to quit his job and get out from under his father's punishing rule at the salon and beauty school.

As if she had no control, the words swam out of Roxy's mouth. "Having this baby is going to be difficult enough without me making it tougher, but do you want your daughter wondering why her mother didn't love her enough?"

"You're supposed to be on my side."

"I am."

"Right."

"From the moment you fluttered inside of me, I loved you." At first, terror had overwhelmed her. She'd made stupid decisions–went to the beach with Spider, drank beer, and let him kiss her. The baby might be his, conceived during the assault. Then shame. Since she never told Carl about the rape, he believed Jewel was his. Roxy didn't know. There was no reason for a parental test because Carl assumed, and Roxy let it stand. But once Jewel moved inside Roxy's womb, none of that mattered–who or how. A protective passion swelled. It astonished her.

Roxy rubbed her own soft belly. "When you placed my palm on your tummy and your baby kicked, I fell in love with her, the same way I did with you, your brother, and your sisters."

The car engine whirred in agitation. Carl pumped the gas until the engine turned over. He leaned sideways and rolled down the passenger window. "Ladies, get in."

Jewel stared at her feet. "Sometimes, I get scared for her."

"We gotta bounce," Carl said.

Roxy's voice was barely a whisper. "Do you remember the story of my mother leaving when I was twelve?"

Jewel stamped her foot. "This isn't about you." She pivoted and opened the back door. "Everything doesn't revolve around your drama."

What's wrong with me? Why can't I stay quiet? "I'm sorry, baby. You're right."

"Okay then."

Roxy waited a few seconds. Let it go. Her Dad used to say, "You always travel one bridge too far." She seldom listened. "I remember the agony of being rejected by the person who should have loved me most."

"Argh." Protecting her soccer-ball belly with her hand, Jewel lowered her bottom into the cluttered backseat, swung in her legs, and slammed the door.

Roxy stared at the stony profile. Creamy bronze complexion compared to Roxy's brown, but not as fair as Carl. The same small ears close to her head. Soft, full lips, and wide-set eyes like Roxy's. But their color stumped everyone. Hazel—sometimes more green and other times gold-brown depending on the lighting or the hue of Jewel's clothes.

Roxy avoided mirrors. Her complexion was often splotchy, with permanent dark circles outlining her eyes, and her round belly was not due to pregnancy. Jewel was beautiful, but Roxy... She shook her head to clear the negativity that too often swamped her.

Carl was Jewel's father, no matter what. He loved her, raised her. And Jewel had a right to her own choices and secrets. Spider being in town didn't have to result in trouble, regardless of his assumptions or intentions.

CHAPTER 3

The pharmacy where Jewel worked stood several blocks north of Frank's Beauty Salon and School, the place where Carl and Roxy toiled as indentured servants, chained to the family business, not earning enough to start fresh somewhere else.

This was Jewel's second summer working for Governors Pharmacy and probably the last. A new CVS was opening in the now shuttered All You Can Eat Buffet across the street. For how long could the independent drugstore hold out? Fieldcrest, a town of sixty thousand, forty-five minutes north of New York City, was in economic decline and had been since the Great Recession of 2008. When the pandemic hit, it slid further. Frank's Beauty Salon and School managed to stay afloat by cutting staff and corners and, in Roxy's opinion, reckless borrowing. Since then, it crept along rather than rebounded.

"I can't get any closer," Roxy said. She parked next to a *No Standing, No Parking* sign. "This okay?" The store was a long block away.

"Sure." Jewel stared straight ahead. "Thanks."

"I'm sorry."

"You're trying to help." Jewel cocked her head to one side. "I get it."

Roxy prayed that her family, and especially Jewel, believed that. She darted a kiss on Jewel's cheek. "It's gonna work out." At least she'd do everything in her power to make it so. She retrieved a mini umbrella from the glove compartment and offered it. "Might rain."

"You wish." Jewel climbed out of the car. "What's up with Daddy?"

"Late for work is all." Carl had driven to the salon, four blocks away, and left them with a curt goodbye.

"He acted mad."

Several months ago, Carl's moods started swinging from unhappy to angry to back to his normal loving self, the man she'd counted on for eighteen years. Did it start when they learned of Jewel's pregnancy? Was he worried they'd have to raise the new baby? Or did he start changing when his father informed them of the renovations to the school and salon and the crushing loans he'd encumbered, leaving Carl feeling trapped, with no say in their future? She wasn't sure, but the wedge between them kept widening, a chasm of unspoken thoughts.

"Lots on his mind that has nothing to do with you," Roxy said.

Jewel had been Daddy's little girl all her life, but now the family dynamics were shifting. Whenever Roxy speculated about the father of Jewel's baby or the possibility of keeping her, Carl shut down the conversation.

"Okay," Jewel said.

Roxy waited for the unspoken *but*.

"He's all quiet these days. No joking around..." Jewel's voice trailed off.

"Work stuff. Not you."

Jewel nodded, but Roxy couldn't decode the gesture. The door thunked closed.

For a few seconds, Roxy watched Jewel walk away, spiral curls swinging, jeans hugging her hips and topped with an oversized Black Lives Matter shirt. Love and worry swelled. Yesterday, Spider said he'd seen Jewel. Tonight, over dinner, Roxy would ask Jewel about him. Casually. Guess who I ran into yesterday after work? Oh, you saw him too? What did you guys discuss? Roxy tried to guess the reason for Spider's interest in Jewel now. Back then, he knew Roxy was pregnant–acted smug but uninterested, as if he believed the baby was his but didn't want to step forward. Why show up now, and why connect with Jewel seventeen years later?

Roxy shoved her worries down. I'm no longer an awkward teenager. He can't hurt me or my family. I won't let him. She breathed in, filling her abdomen, and then let the air whoosh out.

The morning's visit with the social worker had been cathartic. Roxy needed to take her own advice–let it go and concentrate on her goal. In another year, sleeping in the living room would be untenable for Max. They needed a bigger home with a bedroom for Max and another for the twins, a room for Jewel... and oh, how Roxy longed for two bathrooms.

Her play was the answer. The local community theater offered a two-week run once she'd persuaded another childhood friend, Vicki Vega, to star in it. Acclaimed actor returns to her hood for an August gig. She closed her eyes, imagining what might come next. With favorable reviews by respected critics, off-Broadway or at least off-off-Broadway was possible. Surely, Roxy would earn enough for a down payment on a house and a fresh start. Regular people won the lottery, didn't they?

The blare of horns caused Roxy's eyes to snap open. She needed to get a move-on. A rap on the passenger-side window made her jump both from surprise and fear it was Spider again.

Mr. Dixon, an old friend of Roxy's father, peered in. "You'll get a ticket sleeping here." Eighty years old, Fred Dixon's ebony skin was as smooth as a thirty-year-old's. When he smiled, a gap showed where two teeth used to be.

Roxy straightened up. "Can I give you a lift?"

"Thought you'd never ask." The missing teeth added a whistle to his speech.

"Hop in." To make room, Roxy snatched her writing journal from the passenger seat and stuffed it into her bag. She rubbed the corners of her eyes and wiped her mouth with her hand. Rivulets of sweat moved down her sides and between her breasts. She glanced at her watch. She must have nodded off for a few earned minutes. Styling hair, keeping her commitment to write at least thirty minutes every day, the twins and Max's after-school activities, helping at the shelter, volunteering for the theater, and now daily rehearsals. Exhaustion dogged her. Every day. All the time.

"Shopped," Mr. Dixon said. He lifted two grocery bags, one in each hand.

She popped the trunk, clambered out of the car, and loaded the bags before helping him into the passenger seat and then settling in herself.

"I like the law banning plastic bags." He tugged the seatbelt across his thin chest. "Plastic is wasteful; takes years to biodegrade." He fiddled with the buckle.

Roxy bent sideways and snapped the belt in place. She smelled the pipe tobacco his doctor told him to stop smoking.

"Can't be too cool for me," Mr. Dixon said. "This heat makes it hard to breathe.

She started the car and cranked up the AC. "Am I taking you home?"

"If it isn't too much trouble."

She smiled inside. Mr. Dixon never wanted to impose but often did. She checked her watch again. She was due at the theater and then in Manhattan to meet with Vicki. Dallas had offered to go with her for moral support and "to keep the evil queen from tricking the lovely damsel." But Roxy could manage Vicki alone.

Fridays were Roxy's only real day off. Saturdays she worked. Sundays both the shop and school closed but family breakfast had to finish in time for church at ten and the command appearance at her in-laws for afternoon supper–a multicourse meal that began promptly at two and lasted well into the evening. While she loved Sunday service, the dinner with the Quintons was a struggle for both Carl and Roxy... some days worse than that. Frank Quinton was *not* a benevolent overlord. Fridays, on the other hand, were entirely hers and this one felt half over. A quick side trip would be okay. Time enough to make her appointments.

"Where're you off to?" Mr. Dixon asked.

Roxy put on her flasher and peered into her side-view mirror. "The theater." The car blended into the southbound traffic.

Once Roxy turned off Gov Ave, the congestion let up. Mr. Dixon yakked about paper and plastic, lazy salesclerks, the lack of rain, and the heat. Roxy caught every other word. She was worried about her upcoming meeting. Vicki was the pivotal cog to Roxy's plan succeeding.

"You listening?"

"Sorry."

"Is that movie star friend of yours really in the play?"

"Yes."

"How'd she get from here to there?"

Roxy sensed Mr. Dixon's scrutiny but kept her eyes on the road. Everyone was interested in Vicki-stories–the inside gossip only a close friend knew. *People* magazine filled that void for the never-gonna-meet-em stars. Vicki was different because she was one of their own.

"I remember her from back in the day–Puerto Rican, right?"

"Half. Her mom, like Dallas's folks, was Jamaican."

"Marty was kinda suspicious of her, but she did alright for herself."

Roxy's two best friends, Dallas and Vicki, puzzled her father, Marty Jackson. Vicki was Catholic and Dallas Episcopalian. "Can't tell the difference except for the Pope, her dad said. Too much sitting and talking if you ask me." The Jacksons attended Fellowship Baptist Church where folks sang praise and gospel songs, most on their feet clapping and stomping, for the first forty-five minutes of the service. But his biases didn't stop friendships. He always welcomed both girls and their parents into Roxy's home.

"Marty and I argued about sports, government corruption, and politics. He was a good man and raised you right."

"Did his best."

They drove in silence for several blocks. Roxy missed her father. Both her parents smoked, and it eventually killed him. Most days, Roxy felt like an orphan, but she hoped her mother was alive, well, and safe. Roxy forgave her mother a long time ago. Too hard carrying around all the grief and anger. She let it go. Would Jewel's baby forgive?

Mr. Dixon cut into Roxy's thoughts. "Ms. Vega come to those rehearsals of yours?" Whenever Roxy gave Mr. Dixon a lift, or helped him with a problem requiring online know-how, he checked in on how her play was doing.

"All through July." But not lately. Today's meeting was pivotal. Vicki had to return to the theater. Roxy reassured Mr. Dixon and herself. "From the time we met, freshman year of high school, Dallas, Vicki, and I counted on each other."

"The three amigos. That's what your father called you girls."

"Whenever I needed them, they both stepped up–Dallas with open arms and Vicki with a frown and a sarcastic remark, but both always said yes."

"Movie people, from what I hear, are unreliable. Don't pin your hopes on her."

If that was good advice, it was too late for Roxy to take.

"How's your oldest?"

"Fine, why?" She didn't mean to sound defensive. "She's great. Thanks for asking." The light turned red.

"Just wondering what she's doing these days."

"Working at the pharmacy until the baby comes."

"That so?"

The light turned green, so Roxy turned right onto West Cherry, toward Mr. Dixon's place.

"Saw her hop on the bus."

"Excuse me?"

"She caught the number five down the street from where you were napping."

"Jewel?"

"I'm old, not blind."

What was Jewel doing on a bus when Roxy had just dropped her off? She'd only closed her eyes for a minute. Roxy made a sharp U-turn.

• • •

From the antacid aisle, to greeting cards, to toothpaste, and back, Roxy searched. "Pardon me," she said to a young man in a blue work shirt, his name badge too faded to read. "I'm looking for Jewel Quinton."

Clustered pimples marred his cheeks and forehead. "She don't work here no more." He peered at Roxy from behind glasses as thick as Annie Long's.

"Since when?"

"Got fired 'bout three weeks ago. Had a fight with the manager. Kinda loud." He looked around as if worried someone might be in earshot. "It wasn't her fault. Guy's a dick."

Roxy hurried out of the store. She'd left the running car and Mr. Dixon at the same illegal spot and now a police car stopped alongside. Roxy broke into a jog, waving an apology to the officer, a man she'd known since grade school. With a mouthed, "Sorry," she climbed into the Taurus.

Mr. Dixon asked, "Everything alright?"

"She hasn't worked there for weeks."

"Kids."

"Where's she been all this time?"

"Saw her at Otto Sand's place with that Webster Booth—the one they call Spider. I hear, he's a developer buying up buildings near your theater."

Oh, sweet Jesus.

"She's grown in case you haven't noticed. Even with that belly, men will still sniff around her, pretty as she is." Mr. Dixon patted Roxy's hand. "At least that Booth fella is rich, or so folks say."

CHAPTER 4

Cramps gripped Roxy. Jewel with Spider? Yesterday, he told Roxy he'd seen her. But having coffee together at Sandman's?

Otto Sand, aka Sandman, was the local Godfather. He owned land, businesses, and buildings including an eatery and bar. When the banks said no to a loan, Sandman said yes. Except the cost was high.

Roxy's stomach roiled and acid rose in her throat. She willed the bile down, but it kept surging. Grateful that a neighbor helped Mr. Dixon carry and unpack his groceries, she searched for a nearby quiet spot. Fieldcrest was more working-class-suburban than urban, filled with narrow roads lined with low-rise apartment buildings and small, detached houses with one-car garages, and front and back patches of yard. Roxy crossed Gov Ave and turned south onto West Monroe. She noted only a few parked cars and no foot traffic. Unable to quiet her gut, she pulled over, opened the door, leaned out, and puked.

Mortified, she scanned the street again but saw no one. A pit bull, straining against his leash, growled. Somewhere in the distance an ambulance wailed. What if Spider said something to Carl or Jewel? She extracted a tissue, wiped her mouth, stuffed it into a corner of her bag, and snagged a LISTERINE Strip.

After several deep breaths, she picked up her cell and called home. The phone rang unanswered until voicemail kicked in. "You've reached the Quintons–Carl, Roxy, Jewel, Max, Kia, and Gabriella." Roxy hung up. She tried Jewel's mobile, but a recorded voice said her mailbox was full.

Panic pricked. She called Dallas at work only to get voicemail as well. "D, it's me. Check on Jewel when you can. I can't find her and I'm worried." Roxy knew Dallas would respond to the implied urgency.

Next, she tried Carl and left yet another message. Where was everyone? "I've got this funny feeling." Carl respected her intuition. "Jewel's not at work. Please call around for her." Like Dallas, sensing Roxy's anxiety, he'd track Jewel down.

Now what? Roxy's packed day, saturated with critical steps to move her program forward, was slipping away. Carl or Dallas will find Jewel. Spider didn't say anything. It is going to be okay, she told herself.

She twisted her gold bracelet back and forth, popped another LISTERINE Strip into her mouth, blew into her palm and sniffed. Satisfied, she shifted the car into drive and headed for the theater.

•   •   •

Only a few cars stood in The People's Theater parking lot. Roxy pulled alongside a gray BMW.

Apartment buildings, multi-family wood-frame homes and a Pentecostal Church shared East Linden Way on one side of the street. On the theater's side several homes stood to the east, their front yards thatched with rain-deprived grass. An empty lot and abandoned factory stood side by side at Linden's western end. As weary as it all appeared, she loved this block. It was a fighter. Owners swept in front of their homes. Pansies and impatiens potted in wooden planters edged front yards, their heads raised as if someone cared. Garbage cans had lids with only an occasional McDonald's wrapper or crushed Dunkin Donuts coffee cup spoiling the scene. And, of course, she loved her theater. No matter what else went wrong in her world, coming here lifted her mood.

The not-for-profit production company occupied a converted, ancient Victorian, its two pointy dormers rising like nosy neighbors watching from behind a sculpted hedge. The actual three-hundred-seat playhouse was a new structure artfully attached to the back of the Victorian. Low and square with a slant-roof and dormers that matched, it jutted out toward the empty lot next door.

The theater, three-years-old this summer, was the newest and unique among the dozen community playhouses in the tri-state region. Its mission, etched above the front door, said it all—*We Celebrate Unheard Voices*. The founder, Joe Dawes, built this one so local talent—writers, stage managers, set and costume designers, budding directors, and actors—had a place to grow and shine. From its inception, Roxy had carved out time to volunteer, doing the hair and makeup of aspiring and professional thespians, selling tickets, and helping with fund-raisers. The theater belonged to her and she to it.

After locking the car, she crossed the parking lot, climbed the four steps to the porch, and entered the spacious lobby. The front door thudded shut behind her. Carpet-covered stairs to the right led to the second and third floors. Straight ahead, a long hallway directed visitors to various rooms. The receptionist, a part-time employee, occupied the first one. No one was there.

"Hello?"

A deep bass responded. "In here."

She poked her head into the once-sitting-room-now-office, the second door along the hall.

"You're late," Joe said the minute she stepped into the room.

"Sorry. Family matters."

He stood and stretched a freckled brown arm toward her and shook Roxy's hand with a firm but not-too-hard grip. Back in the day, Joe boxed. Although he'd stopped, he kept fit by working out and coaching youth at the Y and the local Boys & Girls Club. He'd also served as a Big Brother for years, sending several kids to college via scholarships and his personal bank account.

"How are the rehearsals going?" he asked, sinking into his executive chair behind a cluttered desk.

"What does Larry say?"

Larry Frome, a long-time friend of Joe's and a respected director, had agreed to take on her play. From the theater's inception, Larry worked pro-bono, providing director and stage manager workshops, but this was the first time he'd agreed to direct one of the productions. Vicki's starring role required an excellent professional, not one of Larry's students. Joe pushed hard and Larry said yes.

"I'm asking you," Joe said, his words slow and flat.

Somewhere in the building a toilet flushed, rattling the old pipes.

"We're getting there."

Despite Joe's urgent desire for news about Vicki, Roxy had nothing concrete to offer. In late June, Vicki came to meet the team and discuss the project. The cast read aloud the entire play, getting comfortable with the dialogue and stage directions. Of course, she wowed the team, and for six weeks through July, she participated in every rehearsal. Then, in August, at the most crucial moment, she stopped with no explanation. Joe, Larry, and Roxy each called and left unanswered messages. With opening night a little over a week away, and its success hinged on Vicki, everyone was past worried.

Roxy said, "Vicki's return will get us back on track." Roxy's dad used a lot of railroad clichés. Light at the end of tunnel. The engine's moving while we're still laying tracks. Whenever they popped into her speech–unbidden–they made her smile inside.

Joe harrumphed and side-eyed Roxy. "Larry is getting antsy. Said this wasn't what he signed on for." He placed his hands at the back of his head, elbows jutting, and gave her a hard stare. "We have a lot riding on your promise to deliver her."

"As soon as I leave here, I'm training to Manhattan to see her. She won't let us down." Except she already had.

Joe still looked skeptical or just concerned, but he changed the subject. "Another friend of yours is here."

The hairs on the nape of her neck rose. "Who?"

"Spider Booth."

Roxy swiveled her head to see behind her.

"In the men's room." Joe rose and dragged a folding chair forward. "Have a seat."

She dropped her bag on the floor and sat down hard. Spider didn't belong in *her* theater.

"Sandman sent him over and a good thing too." Joe's brows arched up and down as he spoke. "You two are close, right?"

Speech deserted her.

"True, no?"

"A long time ago." Her voice rasped. "What does he want?"

"To help." He glanced at his computer screen. The laptop rested on a pile of folders that reminded Roxy of the social worker's office.

She cleared her throat and tried again, this time with more authority. "Why is Spider here? To help how?"

Joe's finger scrolled the Mac screen. "So, Vicki will be at tomorrow's rehearsal?" Joe's paprika freckles glistened with perspiration.

"Yes."

Her annoyance and fear must have come across because Joe faced her and put his arms up as if surrendering, making his biceps bulge against the short sleeves of his white shirt. "I believe you. But here's the problem. We invested a lot of money in hyping her. I mean all out, even though our cash is tight."

Roxy frowned. "She loves the play. She'll be back."

"Advance sales for opening night are coming along. Your people, right?"

"Yeah." Most of their students and customers and all their relatives committed. Dallas sold twenty tickets to her clients and friends.

"They're slow for the rest of the engagement." Joe stroked the wiry hairs of his trimmed, rust-red beard. "A two-week run is a long shot at this rate."

Events kept stacking up against her. Jewel's pregnancy, Carl's misery, Vicki's ghosting, Spider's return, and now the theater's financial woes. She had to find solutions. The play was her family's lifeline.

"I hate to tell you, but things are kinda dicey." He paused as if waiting for her to say something. "Get her back in the theater. We'll take some rehearsal shots and short videos. Invite select press in for an exclusive interview. Promote her like crazy with the last of our advertising budget, leading up to opening night."

Once again he paused, his gaze intense, as if willing Roxy to speak.

She twisted her gold bracelet.

"We're running out of time to make this happen."

At sixty, Joe Dawes was an institution, revered in the Black and brown communities. The remaining white population, local merchants, and politicians of all stripes also respected him. Over the years, the city had changed from mostly Italian, Irish, and Jewish to a far more diverse population with families from the West Indies, Dominican Republic, and Puerto Rico, shifting the makeup of neighborhoods and schools. Joe managed to connect with everyone. When he spoke, most people paid attention.

"I trust her." Vicki was her friend, but she also owed Roxy. Something Roxy hoped she wouldn't have to use.

"There you are." Joe popped up waving a welcoming arm. "Join us."

Roxy tried to breathe quietly instead of panting like one of her dogs.

Spider's voice boomed louder and deeper than Joe's. "Have to run."

"Stay a minute," Joe said. "Roxy, scoot your chair over." Joe came from behind the desk, lifted a second folding chair up and over Roxy's head, and placed it next to hers. "Grab a squat."

Still behind her, Spider said. "Two days in a row. Lucky me."

Joe said, "We're talking about Vicki and getting her here for tomorrow's rehearsal."

"She'll show." Spider sounded smug and confident.

Roxy sat rigid in her seat with her eyes front.

"Say hello to Q for me, Roxy." Then his tone changed to the softer one she heard on Thursday evening. "Give Jewel my best."

Bile once again filled her throat. She swallowed.

"See you at the board meeting, Joe," Spider said.

"Counting on it."

She heard his footsteps recede. The door creaked opened and then slammed shut.

Still standing over her, Joe said, "Not like you to be impolite."

"Was I?"

"He was kinda rude too." Joe sat back down. "So, no happy reunion between you two?"

The way Joe asked suggested he suspected something. Of course, that was ridiculous. Only Dallas knew. Roxy stood. "Why is he coming to a board meeting?" Her voice croaked. She edged around Joe's desk to the front window for a clear view of the parking lot. As if he sensed her scrutiny, Spider pivoted and looked up. Roxy jerked back.

"I have to keep our doors open. Bring in the money. That's my job. Your job is to get Vicki rehearsing again."

And to keep Spider Booth away from Jewel.

CHAPTER 5

The physical memory of Spider's stare digging into her back left Roxy chilled. She wrapped her arms around her shoulders and tried to focus on Joe. "How d'you connect with Spider?" She knew her voice held a note of accusation.

Without looking up, Joe shuffled the papers on his desk.

Before she could re-ask her question in a less judgmental way, Glenn Phillips, the Director of Philanthropy, walked into the office. Dressed in a well-tailored gabardine suit, he gave an agitated wave in Roxy's direction.

"Any word from Ms. Vega?" Glenn asked.

"Roxy's wrapping it up this afternoon."

Glenn lifted his chin in acknowledgment. Because he had no visible neck, the action made his upper body follow. Glenn's odd affliction made the muscles of his cocoa-brown face pull and tug his otherwise even features in different directions.

"Anything else?" Joe asked Glenn.

"We need $40,000 to make payroll and get this week's mailings and ads sent out." Glenn's twitches picked up speed. His eyes narrowed. "That's without touching the debt service."

Joe waggled a dismissive hand. "I'll call in some favors." He stood, towering over Glenn. "You go raise money."

Glenn said to Joe, "I have to pick up a few letters and a contract in the theater. Then I'll work on Wednesday's fund-raiser."

"Good." Joe lifted his chin toward Roxy and gestured to his office door. "Walk over with Glenn so he can fill you in on his fund-raising efforts. Plan a few visits–meet the writer, hear Vicki Vega stories straight from the best friend's mouth. Bring in some cash. Okay by you, Roxy?"

"Sorry?"

"Help with fund-raising?"

"Oh, sure, happy to," she said in a tone conveying the opposite. Spider's voice saying Jewel's name reverberated in her head.

Roxy and Glenn walked out the back door of the Victorian which housed the administration, fund-raising, and the sales staffs. Costume makers and set creators worked in the huge basement. They headed for the annexed auditorium.

"You still collecting clothes and money for New Hope?" Glenn asked.

"I was there yesterday."

"My wife gave me two bags from her book club. They're in my car." He handed Roxy a white envelope. "Plus, fifty dollars."

"Please thank her for me."

Glen pushed open the door to the theater.

"If I ask you something, will you tell me the truth?" Roxy asked.

"That's my problem. I'm always honest." He rubbed his chin as if he missed a used-to-be beard. "It's not a valued trait."

"What's Spider Booth doing with Joe?"

"Why are you asking?"

"We attended school together. He's not a good guy–least he wasn't back then." She remembered Fred Dixon's comment. "Plus, he's buying up land around here." She watched for Glenn's reaction.

"News to me." He coughed into his hand and scooped a bottle of water from his open briefcase. After taking a sip he said, "Sandman is talking him into investing in the theater and building a school next door on the empty lot like Dance Theatre of Harlem and Freedom Theater in Philly. As if that's going to work."

"I know nothing about them."

"Dance Theatre has a school teaching kids ballet, and an internationally recognized ballet company. No physical theater. Freedom Theater has a performance-space like ours, and it also teaches drama, and the kids get to act."

The idea impressed Roxy. "Like a magnet school?"

"I guess."

"Fieldcrest could use that."

"Yeah, well. I wouldn't count on it."

They'd reached the lobby, a wide uncluttered space except for the stack of posters leaning against the wall adjacent to the ticket and *Will Call* booths, each with pictures of Vicki in various television and movie parts. The signboards also contained the particulars of *The Monday Night Murder*, starring Victoria Vega, Tea Rose Washington, and Nick Pierce. Directed by Larry Frome. In smaller type, under the director's name, written by Roxanne Jackson Quinton.

In front of them, two sets of doors opened onto the ramps that led to patrons' seats. Bathrooms stood just off the doorway on the left. A snack-and-cocktail bar angled off the door on the right. A large vending machine selling soda, iced tea, and bottled water looked out of place in the elegant lobby. Dead ahead, a welcome sign and a potted plant decorated the table standing between the two sets of doors.

Mr. Smalls, the uniformed security guard, rose from behind the hospitality desk, his flashlight and walkie-talkie dangling from his waist. "Good day, Mrs. Roxy, Mr. Glenn." He tipped his hat. "How you folks doing?"

Roxy smiled at the old man. He smiled back–his eyes clouded from the abundance of beer Roxy suspected he drank. Several times she'd witnessed him consume three or four over ninety minutes. Joe had a soft spot for the older gentleman and kept him employed despite his condition. "We're doing well, Mr. Smalls. How are you? How's Mrs. Smalls?"

Unlike most days, she didn't register his reply. Nor did she continue the conversation or ask about his last meal or, as she often did, offer to get him something to eat. Her mind was on Glenn's deep frown, on the lack of money coming in, but mostly on Spider.

She trailed Glenn into the small office behind the ticket booth. "Can I ask you something else?" She did not understand why the theater was in financial trouble.

"Shoot." Glenn took off his watch and jangled it as if it had stopped working.

"You seem to bring in other money."

"Not lately."

"Aren't we doing a little better?"

"Define little." He lowered his overstuffed briefcase to the polished wood floor and grabbed some papers from a desk drawer.

"What's really going on?"

"You don't want to know."

"Please."

In a tight voice he said, "Our *great* director acts like we're on Broadway. He knows better. We're a small, struggling community playhouse. And what's he doing directing your play? No disrespect, but Fieldcrest is a long way from Broadway, and you do hair."

She tried not to sound offended. "He's enthusiastic about *The Monday Night Murder*."

"It didn't hurt that Vicki Vega agreed to join the cast."

"Unknowns get discovered." For years, Roxy had sent out her short stories and plays to magazines, literary agents, publishers, and contests. Like most writers, many more talented than Roxy, she received a flood of rejections. Some contained encouraging notes but still declined. Joe and Larry's interest in her play was a turning point. She thought about her latest short piece, *Thunder Snow,* and the upcoming contest. Her next acceptance?

"I'm not saying it isn't good." He tapped the face of his watch. "Hell, Laura Garrison invested and she's savvy."

"I heard. What's her story?"

"Local and affluent patron of the arts."

"More than The People's Theater?"

"Yeah, but she has a soft spot for our mission and she and Joe go way back."

Why didn't Roxy know this? Was she so absorbed in her life dramas, as Jewel accused, that she didn't pay attention to what was going on around her? "I'd like to thank Ms. Garrison in person. Can I meet her?"

"Come to the board meeting on Monday."

"You said Larry was doing crazy stuff. Like what?"

"Got an hour?"

"The highlights."

"Sets made off-site, and costumes designed at prices we can never afford. Besides, it's the exact opposite of our mission. We're supposed to use local folks and showcase *unheard voices*. And why is Joe going along?" Glenn rubbed his nose. He swung his round head toward her, forcing his entire body to follow. "Is the board asking questions? Of course not. Sandman loves mounting debt owed to him with interest."

On one level, the sets and costumes thrilled Roxy. She knew it was because of Vicki and Larry's reputations and not hers, but just the same. The best sets, the best costumes, a great actor, and director. How perfect was that? However, on a gut level, she recognized this was just like Carl's father, Frank, borrowing to renovate the salon and beauty school while putting the entire extended family in financial jeopardy.

"How bad is it?"

"I'm sorry to say this, but I'm not sure we'll make it past your opening. Fundraising can't keep up with bad fiscal management and that's the ugly truth. Why Joe asked Sandman to serve as chair of the board is beyond me. Talk about the proverbial fox minding the hen house." He shook his head.

Roxy's frown mirrored Glenn's as she tried to remember something he'd mentioned earlier. "Did you say we can barely cover the debt service?"

"Read the financial reports—eye openers."

"How much do we owe?"

"A couple of million."

"I thought donors like Ms. Garrison, memberships, advertisements in the Playbills, and ticket sales paid for everything."

"I wish." He lowered his voice. "Go to Monday's board meeting. You'll learn a lot, and most of it not good."

"Am I allowed?"

"No one will throw you out." He bent down, grabbed his briefcase, and stuffed the papers he'd retrieved inside. "Booth is the main event."

The nape hairs on Roxy's neck rose again. "What does that mean?"

He shrugged.

"I'll help you with the fund-raising visits."

Glenn moved toward the door by which they'd entered. "If you're not friends with any millionaires, it won't matter."

"Joe thinks so."

"I guess." Glenn held the door open for Roxy. "Let's get the donations from my car." He moved toward the main door.

"Are things really so gloomy?"

He stopped and swung around. "We're on a path. Sometimes the road you're on has no viable exit ramps so you keep going, even though there's a cliff ahead."

CHAPTER 6

Midday in midtown Manhattan. Heat radiated from sidewalks packed with white-collar workers and tourists, weaving in and out and brushing past Roxy as she tried to get her bearings. She adjusted her messenger bag across her chest and walked another block before spotting her destination.

The Four Seasons spanned 57th and 58th, close to Central Park on 59th. Roxy eyed the expansive glass entrance across the street just as the *Do Not Walk* sign flashed its warning. A foul smell twitched her nose.

"Spare some change?" A hunched woman with a too-familiar, rum-infused breath sidled up to Roxy. She dug out several quarters and dropped them in the woman's hand.

The panhandler muttered a thank you and inched toward a man waiting to cross.

"You're welcome," Roxy whispered to the woman's back. "May God bless and keep you."

Did Roxy's mother beg? For a few years after her mother left, occasional postcards arrived from Kansas City, St. Louis, and Chicago. The last one featured a picture of downtown Albuquerque. Then, right when Roxy needed her mother the most, the cards stopped. Roxy had sat on the Orchard Beach boardwalk, abandoned, bruised, and aching. Dried blood spatters dotted her thighs. Her tongue nudged the swelling of her lower lip from Spider's slap. At that moment, even though it had been years since she'd left, Roxy longed for her mother's comfort and reassurance.

She never told Vicki, her father, or Carl what happened. Only Dallas, who slipped out of her house and snuck her parents' car to pick up Roxy.

Old news. Stay focused on the dream and plan. Get Vicki back to rehearsals and on-stage opening night. Joe, Larry, Laura Garrison, and Vicki shepherd it to off-Broadway. Earn enough to buy a house and quit their jobs at the salon and school and find a new way to make a living and be happy.

With a slow turn and a determined step, Roxy strode across the street. A doorman welcomed her, held the door, and she entered the hotel. Chilled air surrounded her and dried her face. She took in the soaring ceiling and glass-edged marble staircase.

The doorman asked, "Checking in?"

Glass gleamed all around her and, unfortunately, reflected her wilted appearance. "Can you direct me to the lady's room?"

The bathroom, a line of stalls equipped with individual toilets, washbasins, and doors, appeared empty. Roxy locked the louvered door behind her and retrieved her cosmetic bag. She rinsed her mouth and splashed water on her face. Sweat, and now the water smudged, and streaked her makeup. She wiped most of it off with a tissue, then reapplied her eye shadow. The muted copper color enlarged her eyes and, in her mind, made the dark circles less noticeable. Refreshing her mascara and lipstick also helped, but the too-snug slacks and top clung. The walk in the oppressive heat from Grand Central Station on 42nd Street to 57th left her shoulder-length hair wild and frizzed. She finger-combed it and twisted it up into a knot then, not liking the results, let it fall along her cheeks.

Meeting with Vicki required optimism and confidence. Roxy turned her back to the mirror and squared her shoulders. Nothing more to do; it was now or never.

• • •

Despite the early afternoon hour, people packed the brightly lit lounge. No Vicki. Roxy hurried to a round table a couple just vacated and took a seat. In her head, she rehearsed her pitch for the umpteenth time.

She heard Vicki before she saw her.

"Meet me in one hour at the entrance on 58th," Vicki said to an unseen person.

A little taller than Roxy, Vicki was slim, with breasts much larger than she had before she'd landed her first part in a television show. In fact, almost everything about Vicki's appearance had changed. Her curly brown hair was now a shimmering auburn hanging smooth and straight down her narrow back. Arched eyebrows set off the once-brown, and now-amber eyes, thanks to contact lenses. The slightly crooked teeth of her youth gleamed straight and white.

Her throaty laugh followed whatever the unseen person said. Roxy stood and gestured.

A strapless sundress made swishing noises as Vicki walked across the carpeted floor on high-heeled sandals. She leaned into an A-frame hug and sat.

A waiter bustled over. "Welcome, Ms. Vega." He beamed at Vicki, who asked for a glass of "exceptionally good, very dry champagne."

In a signature move, she tossed her head and the column of hair slid into place. "Now, let's talk about Diana." She flapped her copy of the manuscript. "I still can't believe you wrote this."

"It took me over a year, and then all the rewrites."

Since middle school, Vicki and Roxy competed. Vicki always won. Ten times prettier than Roxy, she landed the lead parts in school plays while Roxy worked on logistics. As and Bs to Roxy's Bs and Cs. Long Island University accepted them both, but only Vicki attended. Thanks to Roxy's pregnancy, she didn't even make it to community college. The only time Roxy won was their junior year when Spider chose her to be his girl.

"Larry Frome hanging in there?"

"He really *likes* my play. In fact, he said it was sparse and compelling with nuanced insights into human nature."

Vicki laughed. "Don't sound so mad. I told you the day I read it how impressed I was, and I meant it. All the time, I kept thinking, Roxy is an author, and a talented one." She put the manuscript down on the table. "Remember the short stories you used to write and read to Dallas and me?"

"They weren't very good."

"We loved them. Lots of steamy sex that the three of us knew nothing about."

Roxy felt better. It didn't matter how many years slid by. They were still friends. They'd met the first day of middle school and quickly found they had a lot in common. Vicki's mother had died the year before from a heart attack. No chance to say goodbye. It was a strange but enduring bond—two motherless girls tended by the awkward love of old-school fathers.

Vicki's condescending tone resurfaced. "I'm glad Frome's still helping you. He's not *A-list*, but he's respected."

"He believes in the theater." Roxy paused. "Opening night is eight days away. We need you back on the stage."

Vicki didn't look or sound contrite. "The money people lined up yet?"

Several guests in the lounge sent surreptitious glances their way; others—tourists more likely than natives—openly stared.

"Larry is confident."

"Hmm." Vicki sipped her champagne from a slim fluted glass. Moisture stippled the outside.

"It's not guaranteed, of course." In fact, Joe had said it was a long shot, but he and Larry were working on it.

"We're talking community theater." She took a bigger swallow. "In *Fieldcrest*." Roxy tried not to show her reaction.

"Don't look like that." Vicki finished her drink. "Maybe they can pull it off, but if I were you, I'd enjoy the moment."

"Everyone loves you." Back in the day, Vicki preened when flattered—soaked it up and sought more. Not so much today.

"I have some ideas to make Diana more believable."

"Now?" Roxy's composure crumbled. "You never said during all those weeks of preparation."

"I'm saying it now. I hate the rape scene. It's gratuitous."

Spider's hot breath swept into Roxy's mind as her heart palpitated. She forced the scrap of memory away.

"We have three rehearsals left. Tomorrow, Wednesday, and then the final one on Friday evening."

Vicki signaled the waiter for another glass of champagne.

Roxy shifted her approach. "Your understudy, Tea Rose, is doing an excellent job, and Larry adores her."

"The local gonna-be?"

"With Lincoln Center credits and a recurring role in—"

Vicki put her hand up, palm facing Roxy. "Whatever."

"Joe has a photographer booked for tomorrow and Wednesday, social media plans leading up to opening night, and an exclusive press interview before Wednesday's fund-raiser." Roxy took a breath, her desperation easy to read. "We need you for all the events."

Roxy studied Vicki's expression and body language but couldn't tell if a yes or no was about to come.

CHAPTER 7

Over the years, Vicki and Roxy had stayed in touch via quick phone calls, Christmas letters, invitations to premiers in New York, and more recently through text messages and emails. The four of them, Vicki, Dallas, Carl, and Roxy, showed up for their high school fifteenth reunion, but Vicki didn't stay. In January, Roxy and Carl saw her in an August Wilson play at that Public Theater in Manhattan. Vicki sent two tickets (none for Dallas) with a note. *Be sure to stop by and say hello.* That's when the idea came to Roxy.

The dressing room, packed with actors, flowers, laughter, and wine, had sent shivers along Roxy's spine. This was her chance, what she ached for, her ticket to a different life. She'd pitched the play to Vicki.

At first, her reaction had been positive but uncommitted. "You did it. Wow. Good for you." Roxy pressed. "I've got a lot going on." Roxy pushed harder. Vicki's enthusiasm turned to annoyance. "I'll think about it, but probably not." Once again Roxy's words came out, even though she should have stopped. "One or two weeks, that's all I need." Vicki heaved her shoulders, puffed up her cheeks and exhaled. "*Fine.*" She eased her frown and smiled. "I'm proud of you."

Now, head and hair tilted to the right and a gentle sway to the left, Vicki sent the curtain of hair back into place. "I'll do the best I can," she said in the same manner that Roxy often spoke to her children. "I'll see," which meant fat chance.

Changing the subject, Vicki said, "I've snagged an exceptional TV project."

"What's it about?"

"Sci-fi but grounded." Roxy didn't know what that meant. "Anyway, they're filming in Boston, and I've got to be there. You see my problem, right?"

Someone came over and asked if they were using one of the chairs. Vicki gave him her cool, diva-no-teeth smile. The man backed off.

Roxy raised her voice and rushed through her appeal without taking a breath. "I do. I'm glad for you. But Joe, Larry, and the entire town are counting on you. Everyone is excited to see a movie and television star, our own Vicki Vega, back in Fieldcrest. The publicity—social media, flyers, local TV, and radio ads trumpeting your return to Fieldcrest." Hand to her heart, she gulped in air. "You must come tomorrow night."

Roxy didn't want to remind Vicki about her debt. They never spoke of it. She never used it, but now she was desperate. She had to do something and if that meant reminding Vicki of the unspoken obligation, then so be it. "I need you to promise you'll show up starting tomorrow." Roxy paused and leaned forward. "All our lives we've been there for each other." It was as close as she ever came to bringing up the incident.

When they were sixteen, Vicki got pregnant. She'd been crazy in love with a boy with spiky hair and a swagger. Once she told him, he spread ugly rumors about her. He said she'd slept with a dozen guys, which wasn't true. People whispered behind her back, something Roxy understood firsthand, having suffered from put-downs and snide comments most of her teenaged years. She was too dark skinned, too chubby, too nerdy. Prejudices held by many including other Black kids. And Roxy believed them. Let the cruel remarks chip away at her already shaky self-esteem.

Vicki, beautiful and popular prior to the smear campaign, crumbled. Roxy went to Spider. By then the school was 50 percent Black and brown. White families had fled north and east. Spider's father owned a local hardware store, and his mother was a nurse in the hospital. They were waiting for him to graduate before joining the white exodus. Captain of the basketball team and swimming squad, Spider was friends with everyone. "Can you make him stop?" Roxy pleaded. "Can you do something about the mean-girl clique?" People feared and adored Spider in equal measures. Just as he came to Roxy's rescue when kids were nasty to her, he did the same for Vicki, quashing the lies and snipes.

Roxy had accompanied Vicki to the clinic, paying for a taxi with her babysitting money. She sat in the waiting room and prayed. When Vicki came out with her eyes swollen from crying, Roxy asked, "How are you?" Vicki sat next to Roxy and laid her head on her shoulder. "Relieved. Sad." Roxy held her. She never judged or asked probing questions. At Roxy's request, Dallas "borrowed" her parents' car, even though she was too young to have even a learner's permit in New York. She picked them up at the clinic and drove them to Vicki's place. Roxy called her dad for permission to spend the night. Her parents still in the dark, Dallas returned the car and then asked them the same. The three friends watched old movies, consumed bags of popcorn and cans of cola into the night, and skipped school the next day, hanging out as far from Fieldcrest High as possible.

Roxy and Dallas told no one... ever. In today's world, who'd care. That wasn't the point. News of Vicki's abortion would have invoked the same level of devastation as Roxy's rape. In many ways, Fieldcrest was a small and conservative town.

Now, sipping the last of her champagne, Vicki studied her French manicure. Roxy wasn't sure if Vicki even heard her. After a few seconds of silence, Vicki said, "Okay, I'll be there. But Joe has to get me the publicity he promised—star gives back to her hood."

"It's all set."

"I've asked my publicist to lineup some charity events in the morning and afternoon of opening night."

Roxy knew part of Vicki's motivation for acting in the play was obliterating pulp magazine covers, headlining two DUIs and an unpleasant public incident with a married costar. Doing community theater in her struggling hometown along with some do-goods might burnish her image. Still, there were other ways to make amends. "Thank you. How will the TV show people take it?" Although Roxy's need for Vicki to show was overwhelming, she didn't want her friend to lose an opportunity.

"I have a bit of time." She paused. Swirled her wine in the glass. "It's not just the show. Kenny and I are working on a baby. At least, I am."

"Oh." Roxy tried to catch-up with the conversation-shift. "Congratulations."

"Too early, but thanks. My fertility doc says this is absolutely going to happen."

What was Vicki doing drinking while she was trying to conceive? When Roxy learned about Vicki's DUIs, she didn't believe them. Once again, the tabloid press was making something out of nothing. But maybe not. "You've been trying for a while?"

"Too long." She peered at Roxy from under lowered lids and lush lashes. "Ironic, right?"

Roxy reached for her friend's hand.

Vicki squeezed back. "Sex by appointment is *so* stressful."

"I'm sorry."

Vicki dropped Roxy's hand. "Don't get all sappy on me."

Conversation hum, clink of glasses and cups, and the faint scent of lemon filled the room.

"The treatments keep me close to home until each round is over. My life is nuts right now with an out-of-town show and trying to get pregnant at home. Your play..." Vicki shrugged and pulled back. "You have no idea what it's like to yearn so fiercely."

What could Roxy say to that?

"You were lucky. Q and you did it and bang–knocked-up."

Roxy made a face.

"Yeah, I know. Me too," Vicki said, her voice soft and a little sad.

"How's that lucky? I had to get married."

"You didn't *have* to marry."

Roxy ignored the implication. "Missed out on college."

"Women with babies go to school. You gotta crave shit. Make it happen."

Things were not ideal the first time Carl and Roxy made love. After saying no to Spider for a year, she wasn't sure why she said yes to Carl. Because of Spider's cheating, months before the rape, she broke up with him for the fourth time and started dating Carl.

It was mid-June, right before graduation. Carl had turned eighteen in April and received his driver's license. They'd been kissing in the backseat of Carl's car, a used Chevy gifted by his grandmother. Carl slipped his hand under her blouse and pushed her bra up above her substantial breasts. His erection noticeable, he whispered, "I want you so much. I love you."

She believed him. During all the on-and-off-again times with Spider, Carl picked up the pieces. She cried to him, and he comforted her, asking for nothing in return.

At seventeen, surely, she was the last virgin at school. "I love you, too," she told him. And she did, even though she still loved Spider.

Carl seemed happy but stunned. Although he was gentle, Roxy cried silently afterward. "Did I hurt you? I'm so sorry. We'll go slow. We don't have to do it again. I can wait."

Labor Day, four weeks after the rape, morning sickness hit hard, her nipples ached, and the stick turned blue.

"Gotta run." Vicki bent a finger toward their passing waiter. "I'm super busy. But even if I don't show up tomorrow, it'll be fine."

"It was a pleasure serving you, Ms. Vega." He flourished the bill in a black case with a pen jutting out.

Vicki clocked the check and then darted a look at Roxy.

"I've got it." Roxy snatched it up and flipped it open, inwardly gasped at the total and dug out her wallet. Not enough cash to cover the $60 bill plus a $12 tip. She slid her swollen-with-debt credit card into the provided slot. The waiter swept it away.

"The theater will cover it, right?" Vicki asked. "Joe better."

Roxy tried for a confident smile.

"It's the least he can do for me."

The waiter returned and Roxy signed. Vicki nodded to them both, kind queen to grateful servants, got up, and headed for the exit. Roxy grabbed the receipt and her card, slung her bag over her shoulder, and hurried after Vicki. Seventy-two dollars for three glasses of wine and the last still sitting half consumed. Damn. It took her hours on her feet to earn that much. Would Joe reimburse her?

A brick-red Lexus, which must have been waiting nearby, pulled up in front of the hotel. Dressed in a navy-blue suit, white shirt and navy tie, a man swung out and opened the back door.

"That's my ride." Vicki gave Roxy a quick, lean-in hug, brushed past the driver, climbed into the back seat of the car, and scooped the ends of her silver sundress in behind her.

"Rehearsal starts at six-thirty," Roxy said.

"I'll try. For sure, I'll be there on Wednesday. But don't count on more than opening night."

"I need at least a week. You promised."

Vicki poked her head out of the lowered Lexus window. "Fine," she said in an exasperated tone. "Meanwhile, work on the rewrite. The play will be stronger without showing the rape. It's essential the audience is aware. They don't have to see it."

When will I get that done? Roxy wondered.

"My assistant will send you my other notes."

Great.

The man walked around and got into the driver's seat. Roxy watched Vicki, compact opened, reapply her lipstick as the driver adjusted his mirrors and waited for an opening in the traffic.

Roxy's plan had to work. Laura Garrison, the woman sponsoring the play, probably knew publicists and influencers. Besides, Vicki loved the script and the character, Diana. She said so, did an amazing job in all the previous rehearsals, and half-promised to make it tomorrow. Things were going to work out. Roxy lifted her hand for a final wave.

Just as the car inched away from the curb, Vicki lowered the window again and yelled over the traffic-noise, "I forgot to tell you. Guess who called and asked to see me? You'll never guess. Spider."

CHAPTER 8

Tenements and urban playgrounds surrounded by graffiti-covered fences swept by as the commuter train, crowded with working people on their way home, rattled north through upper Manhattan and the Bronx. Some heads lolled. Snuffles and snores escaped. Many read *USA Today*, *The Wall Street Journal*, and *The New York Times*; others had tablets, computers, or e-book readers balanced on their laps. The spicy smell of someone's snack reminded Roxy she hadn't eaten since breakfast, and she'd upchucked most of it.

The forty-five-minute ride gave her time to write. She'd brought her journal intending to work on either the ending to her short story or her latest play about an alcoholic mother who walked out on her three children and wounded-vet husband only to return years later. Torn between it being a play or trying her hand at a novel, she focused on character development. Writing freed emotions for Roxy and eased aches and guilt. It let her spin out fantasies. Just as the play was her passport to a new house and freedom, it was also her chance at a career she never believed possible until now.

Roxy looked down on the blank sheet of paper and rolled her pen between her fingers. No words flowed.

She put down the pen, closed the notebook and retrieved the manuscript for *The Monday Night Murder*. Vicki wanted the rape scene out. Roxy flipped through the pages. For three weeks, she'd worked on it, writing and rewriting, trying to capture every nuance of that devastating hour of her life. Every time she watched

Vicki and then Tea Rose Washington, Vicki's stand-in, act it out on stage, Roxy knew she hadn't gotten it right.

With her black pen, she raked lines through directions and dialogue and stared at the mangled scene. Still, no new words surfaced.

A mechanical voice announced her stop. She stuffed her notebook and script back into her bag, queued up with the others, and stepped out the doors onto the platform careful to avoid the gap between the train and the station. Vicki's voice still echoed in her ears. "Guess who called." Roxy trudged down the littered steps, head low.

She reached ground level. Off to the right, she saw a stretched-out line of taxi's, their drivers standing by their vehicles, trunks open waiting for anticipated luggage. A sign pointed to *App Rides*. To the left, SUVs and new and battered cars lined up, double-parked with their engines running. As agreed, Carl was waiting.

For a few seconds, unbeknown to him, Roxy admired Carl's profile as he sat in the idling car. She loved his prominent nose and clean-shaven face. Even after eighteen years of marriage, he still made her pulse quicken.

He must have sensed her scrutiny because he raised his head and climbed out of the car. "How'd it go with Queen Victoria?"

"You sound like Dallas." Roxy swatted his arm in mock reprimand. "She promised to make rehearsal tomorrow night." Sweat seeped between Roxy's breasts. "To *try* to make it." She pressed the cloth of her shirt against the damp skin. "I see the car started."

Carl made a wistful sound. He kissed her cheek and opened the passenger door. She slid in. "B.J.'s gonna give me a hand on Monday. I gotta nurse the starter for as long as I can." B.J., Carl's older brother and Roxy's partner at the salon, was also handy.

The $72 worth of champagne and tip pricked her conscience. She should have left the bill on the table and ignored Vicki's meaningful look. "Thanks for checking up on Jewel." Both Carl and Dallas had left messages on Roxy's cell. "Is she home?" She clicked on her seat belt. Carl did the same.

"Fixing supper. Something vegetarian no doubt."

"I was afraid she might have run away." Packed up and disappeared the way Roxy used to fantasize about doing before she developed her survival plan. Take off like her mother. No explanation. Walk out the door. Roxy imagined a life in San Francisco or San Diego. Where did Jewel fantasize about?

"Why think that?" Carl gave Roxy a sideways glance and then turned the car toward the parking lot exit.

"She got fired."

"When?"

"Pretended to go to work for at least three weeks."

"Damn it. What happened?"

This is what they did. They worried about their children, and they fretted about the beauty shop and school. If everything was okay with Jewel, then Max landed in trouble or one of the twins was sick. If the kids were fine, the dogs required expensive medicine for something bad they ate in the neighborhood, or admissions for the beauty school were down, or too many instructors were out ill or on vacation or quit. Roxy could not remember the last time they talked about interesting topics or each other.

"We'll have to find out when we get home." She wanted to bring up Spider and share her dread about him seeing Jewel, but how to explain why this terrified her?

They drove in silence for a few minutes with only the radio offering conversation. A commentator discussed with a political pundit the upcoming elections. Roxy only caught scraps of content. As hard as she tried to fight it, her optimism about her play, and therefore their future, dampened.

Carl's voice, quiet but intense, cut through the radio noise. "I can't take much more of this."

"Of what?" She turned off the news and swiveled to face him.

"Living like this, under his thumb."

She knew, of course, whose thumb he meant. "Did your dad do something?"

"He's wrenching the life out of me."

"We're going to escape," Roxy said with passion. "Live better."

"Wishing doesn't make things true."

"I don't just wish."

For months, Carl hadn't been his normal self. Instead, he seemed depressed half the time and angry the other half. She thought it was because of Jewel and the baby. Frank had always been cruel. Roxy became numb to it. "Did he say something awful today?"

The car crawled through rush-hour traffic making its way east and then south, past the supermarket, the diner, and a string of mom-and-pop stores. They came to the corner of East Oak and Third and stopped at the light. Roxy's church, a towering brick edifice, made a stately presence on one corner. A once-gated community of condominiums, now a rundown collection of rental apartments, anchored the opposite side.

"Admissions at the school are down. Four new students this month instead of the twenty we need, and Saturdays and Wednesdays are the only lucrative days in the salon. The money isn't happening." Carl stared straight ahead even though they were at a stoplight. "Those stupid renovations eat up every dime."

"Did Frank talk to Sandman?"

"Either Sandman is not willing to renegotiate, or my father is too stubborn and proud to ask him."

"I don't know why Frank doesn't listen to you." She reached over. With a feather-light touch, she slid her hand down the back of his head and neck. Usually, he'd reach around, take her hand, and kiss her palm. She put her un-kissed hand in her lap.

"I gave him a list of ideas," Carl said in the same strained voice.

Some people's sharp edges softened as they aged. Frank Quinton showed no such signs.

"Good ideas to rev up business."

"I liked the specials and the contests," Roxy said.

"Yeah, well."

"Why not try some of them without his say-so?"

Carl shook his head. "We need to cut *big* expenses, especially in the salon, and generate real revenue."

"Like what?"

"We should rent out stations." This was an old argument, one with which Roxy was quite familiar. The salon was large enough for six or seven operators, but Frank refused to add non-salaried workers. Renting space brought in a cut of the stylists' business or a fixed payment or both. Plus, it expanded the customer base beyond their regulars. Carl's plan called for manicure and pedicure stations and turning the shop into a day spa. Once established, add a massage therapist. There was plenty of room. Frank refused. Carl said it was about control, stubbornness, and stupidity. The shop and school depended on volume. The level determined their salaries and commissions. Tips added to their bottom lines.

"Maybe if we try some small—"

"Big or small, his answer was *No*."

They reached their apartment building on East Peach Street. Carl pulled in front of the padlocked, wrought-iron gates that led to a no-longer-viable courtyard.

"It'll be okay." She waited.

He made a sound under his breath.

She wanted to explain *how* it would be all right. In addition to her prayers, she had a plan. But he'd think she was foolish. As far as Carl knew, her play was a hobby. It gave her pleasure, the way fishing and gambling pleased him.

Carl shifted toward her. In his left hand, he moved his lucky casino chip through his fingers and back again. "I hate this life. I hate our shitty apartment and I hate this fucking job. Look at this place." He lifted his chin toward their gray building. A group of kids hung out on the corner and leaned against an abandoned car with orange tickets decorating its windshield. "We're pissing our youth away and digging a hole so deep we'll never climb out. In four years, I'll be forty. What will I have to show for it? Jack shit."

With each sentence, hard as a blow, Roxy shrank back a little more.

In a calmer, flat voice, he said, "I'm gonna grab a couple of beers at Sandman's." He faced front again, the chip back in his pocket.

"What about dinner?"

"I'll wolf down something over there."

"The children are waiting for us."

He made another sound she couldn't interpret.

"What time will you be home?"

"Don't wait up."

Roxy stayed quiet. Finally, unable to come up with anything persuasive to say and afraid to ask the question on her mind, she slid closer to the door.

"This isn't about us," he said. "It's me."

How many men dumped women with the same line? If it isn't about us, what is it about? Do you hate me? Do you hate our children? Aren't we your life? "I was going to stay up late anyway. We can talk when you get home."

"No. You have to work tomorrow. Get some sleep. You look beat."

She smoothed her frizzed hair and tucked it behind her ears.

"I'll call you later. Kiss the kids for me."

Did Carl imagine running away, too? She twisted back around, stretched over, and kissed his lips.

"I gotta go."

Roxy climbed out of the car, closed the door, and stood on the curb as he drove away. She waited, but he didn't look back.

CHAPTER 9

Roxy understood Carl's frustrations. The work was demanding and the rewards slim. No matter how hard they worked, Frank ruled. Only the death of still-young Frank would set them free. Unless her play succeeded.

It might be too late. Carl didn't kiss her back.

She pressed the up-elevator-button, too tired to take the one flight of stairs.

When they moved in ten years ago, it had been a nice building, clean and kept up. They had two children then, Max and Jewel, and one dog, so two bedrooms and one bathroom worked. Behind the double, wrought-iron gate was an inner courtyard that gave Roxy a shady place to sit while the children and dog played. Two peach trees yielded fruit every summer. Carl, Roxy, and their neighbors picked them, and Roxy turned the family's share into peach pies and cobblers. Then the twins arrived, unplanned, and an abandoned mixed breed puppy via Max's arms. The apartment became claustrophobic. The building changed hands, the grass and flowers in the courtyard disappeared, and the concrete cracked. Neighborhood thugs used the courtyard for drug deals, so the owners padlocked it shut. Their rent increased. People moved out, but Carl and Roxy had nowhere to go.

The elevator jolted to a stop and Roxy got off. She trudged down the hall. Olivia, a neighbor who lived two doors down, came toward her.

"Hola, Roxy."

"Hi. You look beautiful."

"Gracias."

"Special occasion?"

Olivia thrust out her right hand. "Willie finally asked me." The tiny diamond winked in the pale hallway light.

"Congratulations. Your ring is lovely."

"Thanks." She wriggled a happiness dance.

"The last time we spoke you told me you'd left him."

"I said to Willie, 'I'm not getting any younger.' He said I was crowding him. Well, see what a few weeks of no sex can do?" She waggled her ring finger again.

"When's the wedding?"

"June, next year."

"Lucky man."

"He's waiting downstairs; I'd better run."

Roxy watched Olivia sway away. "Can I ask you something?"

Olivia stopped short and swung around. "Sure."

"How old are you?"

"Thirty-four. Why?"

"I guessed we're the same age. Almost."

"*No way.*"

Olivia didn't offend Roxy. Here was this beautiful woman, engaged for the first time, all turned out in a short, halter dress for a big date and only two years younger than Roxy, mother of four, beat and bedraggled, weeks away from being a grandmother. Why wouldn't Roxy's age surprise Olivia? "Have an enjoyable time and congratulations again."

Olivia walked back to Roxy. "Don't feel bad. You just need one of those glow-ups, like on YouTube." She frowned at Roxy's unadorned, blunt-cut fingernails, then lifted a fist full of Roxy's hair. "Start with a fresh cut and color."

Roxy grunted.

"No, really. Do it tonight and tomorrow you'll be a new woman."

Roxy felt and looked weary every day. No wonder Carl told her not to wait up.

"You'll have energy and a brighter outlook."

Olivia gave Roxy two thumbs up, made another one-eighty, and shimmied back to the exit.

Waking up a new woman with a better outlook sounded great if she could pull it off. She stood in front of her door. On the other side, she heard the colliding barks of the dogs and voices of arguing children. She ran her fingers through her hair before sticking the key into the lock.

Pharaoh, their German shepherd, greeted her first. He jumped up and barked an enthusiastic hello. Pharaoh was her dog. Cleo adored Carl, no matter what Roxy did to endear herself.

The apartment, divided by a long center hall, included a living room, kitchen, and bathroom on one side and two bedrooms separated by coat and linen closets on the other. Roxy put her bag down on the worn hall carpet and rubbed Pharaoh's head. After a few seconds, she eased him away.

"Mommy, Max is being mean to me," said five-year-old Gabriella.

"Well, hello to you too, missy." She held out her arms for a hug.

Kia pushed past her twin and leapt into Roxy's arms, her braids bobbing behind her. Roxy squeezed tight. Kia responded with wet kisses. Despite the chaos, it was good to be home.

"Max told us to get out of his room, but it's everyone's," Kia said in a rush. "Where's Daddy?"

It surprised most people to learn the girls were twins. Kia, tiny, wiry, fair complected, and bubbly was the exact opposite of tall, chubby, serious, Gabriella with Roxy's mocha skin. Both were cute and smart, just opposites.

"Tell *him* to get out," Gabriella said. "We were there first. He was in the kitchen eating cookies and now they're all gone."

The living room also served as Max's bedroom with the sofa his bed at night and family seating by day.

Kia wriggled out of her mother's arms. "He wants privacy," she explained, ever the peacemaker. "But it's time for TV. Can we watch in your room, Mommy?"

Max poked his head out into the hall. "They can't come in here."

"It's only six. Way too early for you to kick them out. And how about a hello and a hug?"

"Yeah," Gabriella said. "Way too early."

Max threw up his hands in a Carl-like gesture. It always startled her when their children mirrored their mannerisms, especially the ones she didn't like.

"Let them watch in your room," Max said. "I can't stand having them around all the time. They talk too much."

"Do not," Gabriella said. "*You* talk too much. Mommy, Max was on the phone ever since we got home."

"I thought he was in the kitchen eating all the cookies."

Gabriella gave Roxy a disapproving scowl.

Jewel stepped into the hall. "Come on, you two. How about a cool bubble bath instead?"

"Cartoons," said Gabriella.

"After, I'll read you a couple of stories."

"We want cartoons," Gabriella insisted.

"You can fix my hair," Jewel offered.

Both girls grinned.

Jewel said to her mother, "They were hungry, so I fed them. Your dinner is on a plate. I made spaghetti with lots of *vegetables*."

"It was good," Kia said. "I'm a veg-it-ter-rarian like Jewel."

Grateful, Roxy didn't have the strength to deal with the twins tonight.

Jewel asked, "Where's Dad?"

Gabriella squinted at Roxy. "Yeah, where's Daddy?"

Cleo yelped as if following the conversation and missing Carl as well.

"He had stuff to do." Roxy gave Jewel a pointed stare, one they often used when conversations were inappropriate for the kids to hear.

Jewel, still dressed in her Black Lives Matter T-shirt and jeans, stood just outside the kitchen. They faced each other in the center hall, Jewel at one end and Roxy at the other, with dogs, kids, bikes, helmets, and a skateboard in between.

Roxy held Kia's hand and walked toward Jewel. Gabriella and Pharaoh followed close behind. "Maybe you and I can talk later." She peered into the kitchen. Spaghetti-streaked dishes sat on the table, and pots and pans in the sink. She looked away.

"Talk about what?"

"Your job, for starters," she said and then hesitated. Her mouth, once again ahead of her brain, added "and Webster Booth."

For a few seconds, Jewel appeared caught. Then she shrugged. "Go on you guys and pick out a book while I run your bath."

The twins dashed toward the front and into the room all three girls shared. Roxy eyed the closed door to her bedroom. Now wasn't the time for this conversation, not with the children still up.

Exhaustion swamped her. "Call me when you're out of the bathroom," Roxy said to Jewel's back. "And thanks for making dinner. I'm gonna change clothes and watch the news." She paused. "And then you and I will talk."

Jewel disappeared into the bathroom. Max's music blared. "Turn that down. And clean up the kitchen."

The music continued at full blast. Not possessing the energy to insist, she let it go. She also knew she should help get the girls to bed, or at least offer. There was just so much Roxy could manage, and tonight the list was short. She walked into her bedroom and closed the door, slipped her top over her head, stepped out of her slacks, and stared at her image in the full-length mirror.

Since she was thirteen, her thighs had been fat, but now they looked huge. She touched what she liked to think of as a potbelly but had become a gut. Only her breasts still looked young and large without sagging.

She lay down on her back, closed her eyes, and unhooked her bra. For some blissful reason, Max lowered the volume. The running bathwater and the girls' laughter soothed.

•　　•　　•

Pharaoh let out a soft bark and Cleo scratched at the closed bedroom door. Carl must be home. Her heart picked up its irregular rhythm. She tugged on and patted her freshly cut and dyed hair. The red glowing face of the clock radio read 2:00 a.m.

"Mom, you awake?"

She tried to keep disappointment from her voice. "Come on in." She hit the TV off-button.

The swish of the ceiling fan replaced the television voices.

"What's up?" Roxy slid over to Carl's side of the bed. Jewel, now dressed in an extra-large *Sleepless in Seattle* T-shirt Dallas had given her, lay down next to her mother. The small mound of her swollen womb tented the cloth. Cleo jumped onto the bed and curled up at the foot. Pharaoh settled back down on the rug.

"When's Dad coming home?"

"Don't know."

"What'd you do to your hair? Turn on the light."

"You'll see it tomorrow."

Earlier, with the twins tucked into bed and Jewel and Max watching a movie, Roxy rummaged through the hair products in the cabinet under the bathroom sink. She found several old bottles of dye. One of them was honey-blond, a shade Jewel used on a wig for a part in a school play.

"Today it seemed like you'd changed your mind." Jewel's hands rested on her belly.

Roxy rolled over and brushed Jewel's hair from her face. "I'm on your side."

"But do you believe I'm wrong?"

Roxy's conflictions seesawed, sometimes hourly. Giving up Jewel's baby made life easier and Roxy's plan more achievable. But. How could they give up a child? Desert her?

"Whatever is right for you is good with us."

Jewel propped her torso up on her elbows. "Do you mean it? Because I'm not ready to be a mother."

"We love you very much."

"Well, Mr. Booth—he said to call him Spider—gave me a job in his company." Roxy sucked in her breath.

"He's teaching me real estate management."

She tried hard for a neutral tone. "Why didn't you tell me?"

"Because you'd freak." She side-eyed Roxy. "You're so determined I go to college." She sank back down on the bed and rolled over. "You missed out, and you don't want me to make the same mistake. Except, I'm not you."

"Pretending to go to work every day is the same as lying."

"I went to work. Not at the pharmacy, but still—"

"Where? What are you doing for money?" What has he asked you? What has he told you?

"Spider gave me some." She paused and then added, "Like an internship while I'm learning the business." She put her head on her mother's shoulder. "Don't be mad."

"But you *want* to go to college, don't you? For you. Not me."

"Commercial real estate management is a wonderful profession. Just ask Auntie Dallas."

"Why not go to her rather than to a stranger?"

"Spider isn't a stranger. At first, it felt weird. You know. Him paying me so much attention. But then he explained you and Dad and Auntie Dallas and even your movie star friend, are all tight since you were kids."

Roxy bit into her lower lip, determined to keep what she wanted to say unspoken.

"I'll save for college and help you and Dad out."

Tears filled Roxy's eyes.

"And don't worry. I can take care of myself."

"Of course, you can. You're smart and hard working." Still living at home, pregnant, fired, with a year of high school to go, but hey. "How'd the internship happen?"

"He's a nice man. And he likes you a lot."

Sharp memory pains crackled through Roxy's body. "He up and offered you a job?"

"Yup. Said he needed someone intelligent, and you were always good at stuff in school–used to help him pass his English exams–and he was sure I was smart too." Jewel inched closer to her mother. "This is a good thing."

Roxy slipped her arm under Jewel's shoulders and held her the way she did when Jewel was a little girl.

The fan stirred the night air, keeping the bedroom cool enough to sleep. It had dropped to seventy degrees outside, even though the threatened thunderstorm had not materialized. Temporary relief swept over Roxy. He had said nothing yet. Despite the heat, Roxy shivered. He didn't have anything to tell Jewel. He couldn't know because Roxy didn't. Besides, he'd never confess to rape.

"I need something better than the way you and Daddy live–a nice house and a real job. I'm sorry, Mom. You and Dad are great but..."

Roxy waited.

"Kids are too much trouble and money."

Jewel's words stabbed Roxy's conscious. "You deserve all those things."

"Some of my friends said I shouldn't have even told you. Just had it taken care of."

Thoughts of Vicki and Roxy at the clinic flashed through her mind. "I'm glad you didn't."

For a few minutes, both women stayed quiet.

Roxy said, "I love you. More than life itself."

"I love you too," Jewel said in a muffled voice, her face buried against Roxy's soft breasts.

Ten minutes ticked by before Roxy heard Jewel's sleep sounds. Carl hated their life, and evidently, Jewel loathed it as well. Somehow, Spider Booth was going to give Jewel a better one.

CHAPTER 10
SATURDAY

The laughing, storytelling voices of the Saturday regulars filled Frank's Beauty Salon. Roxy glanced at her watch. It was 5:30, a half-hour to closing, and they had five heads to finish.

"You seem a little shaky," said Angel from the booth next to Roxy's. He ran a comb through the white curls of Lilly, a tiny woman with a wrinkled face. "What time is the diva supposed to show?" Dressed in tight jeans and a sleeveless black shirt, Angel fluffed his customer's hair. "That okay for you, Miss Lilly?" he asked over her shoulder.

She shifted her head from side to side and nodded at his reflection in the mirror. "Very nice, thanks."

"Rehearsal starts at 6:30." Roxy checked to see who was next. "Denise, you can head for the sink."

Rising from one of the leather chairs in the waiting room, Denise ran her hand along the armrests. "Fancy. When did these come in?"

"This week." Roxy pumped a mist of hairspray around the head of a walk-in. "The last of the renovations and upgrades." At least Roxy hoped so.

"I like all the silver and black. Kinda upscale."

Roxy barely listened. From the minute she awoke with Jewel still in her bed, Carl weighed on her mind. He'd promised to call. The packed schedule of clients distracted her for only minutes at a time. One teacher at the school told Roxy that Carl had come in early, but so far, he hadn't called down or stopped in.

55

"B.J.," Roxy said to her brother-in-law. "Can you wash Denise for me while I check on Portia's color?" She patted the shoulder of the woman in the seat. "Please come again."

Angel said, "You open next week, right?"

"Seven days and counting." She glimpsed her reflection in the mirror with her new blond twists. The contrast made the dark circles under her eyes more noticeable, the opposite of her quest. Argh. So much for a new woman. It was the sort of stupid thing Roxy talked her clients out of right before their high school reunion or a big interview. What would Carl think?

Angel swept up clipped ends. "What are the odds your movie star friend will show? Hasn't she missed a bunch of rehearsals?" He made a neat pile. "Lots of people—not me of course—but folks are saying it's a publicity stunt. You're using her name to sell tickets and then at the last minute..." He snapped his fingers.

Roxy glared at him.

"Don't stank-face me. I'm the innocent messenger."

The walk-in stuffed a tip into the pocket of Roxy's *New York Yankees* shirt. "Thanks. Have a great weekend."

To Angel, she said, "Vicki understands how important this is. She'll be there. She's never let me down before, not ever." Of course, that was years ago, long before Vicki's first TV hit.

Earlier, as Roxy made pancakes for everyone and fended off questions about Carl and not-so-nice comments about her hair, she'd decided to display confidence no matter what. Carl needed hope. Roxy had to exude optimism.

She looked up. The once sunny day had turned storm dark, again. Lightning slashed. Rolling thunderclaps followed. Roxy flipped on the overhead lights. The way the weather kept teasing was maddening.

Frank's Beauty Salon and School was a landmark on Gov Ave. Named for Carl's father, the establishment opened twenty years earlier. Until a few months ago, it hadn't changed much. Then Frank borrowed who knew how much for renovations, merchandise for sale, and new furniture. The place appeared modern and prosperous thanks to outrageous debt to Sandman.

Roxy looked outside and again at her watch. She walked to the back of the shop to check on Portia.

The front door opened.

"Hey, Uncle Carl," said Zoe, the receptionist and B. J.'s daughter. "Aunt Roxy's in the back."

The rocking of Roxy's heart increased, beating in the off-kilter way that had plagued her for weeks. She darted a peek.

Carl peered into the new display cases filled with expensive Afro-centric jewelry his father purchased. "Any takers yet?"

"As if," said Angel.

"You have another five minutes," Roxy told Portia, a middle-aged woman with rose-brown skin who was getting her hair dyed one of the intense reds Roxy brought back from a Manhattan hair show.

As Carl came close, his familiar scent reached her. She loved all his smells. In the morning, it was aftershave, and a freshly ironed shirt. After a day working in the school, it was a subtle mixture of perspiration on warm, clean skin mixed with traces of shampoos, hairsprays, and conditioners.

The most important thing is to act natural. She wiped her hands on a stained towel.

The gray crewneck shirt was not what he had on the day before. Red capillaries spread across the whites of his eyes and stubble, sexy rather than unkempt, covered his cheeks.

"You finished early?" she asked.

"Yeah." He leaned forward and brushed her lips with his. "New do."

"Needed a change," she said, feeling foolish. Gabriella told her it wasn't pretty, and Max made a face. Only Kia said she liked it.

Carl tilted his head to one side. "Nice."

"Too short?" Too blond. Too everything.

He shook his head. "It was pretty before, but this looks great."

Roxy didn't believe him but appreciated his kindness. He often told her how beautiful she was. Said he liked her curves. But Roxy had a mirror and knew the truth.

"I'm heading over to Sandman's for a beer." He smiled at Portia, whose hair was still wet with dye. She'd been watching them and probably heard every word. "Going red I see, excellent choice." He turned back to Roxy. "Meet me when you're done, and I'll buy you a cold one."

"I have rehearsal tonight. Vicki is coming." Despite her intentions, her emotions crept in. Part of her frustration came from longing to join him, to talk and find out what was going on. But she also knew part of it came from anger. He should have called as he'd promised and apologized first thing this morning for not coming home.

"I'm going to Atlantic City." His tone now as chilly as hers was annoyed. "I was hoping you'd come."

"With *what* money?" She tried to keep her voice low. "You said you were going to lay off for a while." Carl's gambling was often the topic of their arguments, especially lately.

He didn't respond.

"We have children, responsibilities. I'll be at the theater until at least eleven." Rewriting the rape scene and the short story deadline flashed through her mind. "Or later."

"Oh, so *you* don't have responsibilities, but I do. You're off to the theater but I need to be the parent-in-charge." Carl heaved his shoulders. In a less heated tone he said, "I'm rooting for your play, but I need a break. You've been out every night for the last two months."

"And you were out all night." Crap. She took a quick look around to see if anyone else heard her. Portia lowered her gaze to her hands.

"I didn't want to wake you, so I spent the night at B.J.'s."

That couldn't be true. Roxy and B.J. had worked side by side all day, and he never mentioned it. He wasn't wrong, she had to admit, she *had* been out every evening, most times leaving him with the kids after a ten-hour workday. But she worked hard too.

As if he'd read her mind, Carl said. "We both deserve some fun."

Roxy still didn't reply. She remembered what he'd said the day before, about hating their life. What happened to them? Frank was always a tyrant, but they still laughed all the time and danced in the living room while the kids watched and clapped. What changed?

In the past, when she wore her Yankee pinstripes to work, that meant they were going to a game after work. Sometimes Carl treated her to a play, something affordable showing in a tiny theater in Greenwich Village, or a long-running hit selling tickets at discounted prices. Roxy would change in the bathroom, before they dropped the kids at their grandparents' and trained it to Manhattan.

"Great, the silent treatment." He walked toward the front. Over his shoulder he said, "I'll be at Sandman's. We're not leaving for Atlantic City until at least eight or nine so there's still time for you to change your mind."

"We?" Roxy stomped and caught up to him.

Carl lowered his voice. "Yeah, Spider's treating, so you don't have to worry about me blowing the rent money, if that's what you're thinking."

They were at the front door, and Roxy sensed eyes watching them.

"What does that mean, treating you?"

Carl faced her. "I don't take out my wallet for the entire night except for tips and a round of drinks." His dark eyes grew soft, the way he looked at her when he reached for her across their bed. "Come with us. He was a jerk back then but—"

"*A jerk* doesn't cover how he treated me."

"He's changed. I didn't trust him at first, but he's a good guy now."

"After one month of interactions you're sure of him?" It stunned all their friends when Spider dated Roxy, and even more so when she broke up with him for Carl. Back then there were some interracial couples at their school, mostly Black jocks with white or Puerto Rican girls. No white guys, except Spider, had a Black girlfriend.

"We'll have a fun time. Put stuff behind us."

Was that yearning in his voice, his eyes? What *stuff*, she wasn't sure. Did he mean with Spider or between Carl and Roxy? She longed for their relationship to be good again. She lifted her hand to touch his face.

He put his hand over hers and slid it toward his mouth and kissed her palm. "I miss you," he said. "Besides, Spider wants you to meet Nadine. Ever since he came back to town, he asks about you."

"He saw me." Roxy jammed her hand in her pocket.

Carl raised his right eyebrow, making an almost upside-down vee.

"On the street Thursday and again at the theater yesterday. Anyway, I gotta go."

His voice once again cool, Carl said, "Fine. You know Jewel or Dallas would mind the kids. Or B.J. We'd be back by midday tomorrow in time for dinner."

"And miss church?"

"One Sunday won't kill you."

"My customers are waiting. I'll see you at your parents' tomorrow."

He watched her for several beats. "I invited Spider and Nadine to Sunday dinner."

Roxy was thunderstruck.

"It's the least I could do."

"He's up to something."

"It's not like you to hold a grudge. It was petty childhood stuff, right?" He studied her face as if he were trying to understand. "People change."

Petty rape? Her cheeks burned.

B.J. called to Roxy from behind them. "Denise is waiting for you in your chair, and Portia is getting mighty red."

To Carl she said, "Have a good time."

Carl's eyes swept across her face as if trying to understand or ask her a question, but instead, he spoke to his brother. "Thanks for putting me up last night."

To Roxy, B.J. looked surprised.

"Yeah, sure thing, no problem."

The door closed behind Carl.

Her heart palpitated for a few seconds before settling back into a normal rhythm.

B.J. asked, "Everything alright?"

"Great," she lied, and from her brother-in-law's expression, she could tell he knew. She walked back with him. Trying for a conversational tone, she asked, "How about with you? What are you doing tonight?"

Like all the Quinton men, B.J. was handsome. Wavy black hair like Carl's, slim build, muscled arms from lifting weights, and a thirty-two-inch waist. He also sported a full beard and mustache.

B.J. hiked a shoulder. "Netflix and we'll order in. Same old, same old."

At the age of twenty-three, B.J. had wed an aspiring rapper. When that collapsed, without a year going by, he married a colleague of Dallas who ran her own real-estate business. Two years ago, she left him and headed west. Joanna entered his life last year. A teacher, she liked to read and listen to classical jazz. Roxy theorized that B.J. picked wives he thought he *should* love rather than women he *did* love.

"What'd you and Carl do last night?" She hoped she sounded politely interested.

"Nothing much." He lowered his eyes. "Shared some beers." B.J. returned to his customer.

Roxy washed Portia's hair. The soapy red water gurgled down the drain.

"I'd like a deep conditioner," Portia said.

Roxy nodded, grabbed the plastic bottle, squeezed, and began working the product into Portia's hair. Was B.J. covering for Carl? She was going crazy. She worked in the conditioner for another few seconds, massaging Portia's scalp with strong fingers. When she finished, she covered Portia's hair with a plastic cap to let her hair absorb the conditioner. "I can give you only ten minutes. It's closing time."

"I need the full thirty," Portia said. Her eyes widened as she pushed herself up and out of the deep chair.

"Sorry, but we close at six." Roxy's tone was abrupt because she was still thinking about Carl's lie, if it was one. Although Carl and B.J. covered for each other during their growing-up years, lying was a deadly sin in the Quinton household.

Portia made a grumpy noise.

"No charge for the deep conditioner."

Portia's expression brightened.

Over the last eighteen years, Roxy couldn't remember one time when she didn't know where Carl was. Often, she'd see him admiring other women—customers of all colors, sizes, and shapes gliding out with their hair freshly done. "Hey, if I didn't look, I'd be dead," he'd say with a laugh. Then he'd tell her she was the only one and more beautiful than whomever he'd admired, which wasn't true. "Checking out other women is just looking, not acting," he'd say with a smile. Nor did she have any reason to doubt him on that score.

Until now.

CHAPTER 11

The front door buzzed open, and Dallas Swan walked into the shop, her Air Pod Pros plugged into her ears and her hips moving in a silent dance. A wave of sultry August air trailed after her. The thunder had subsided, but the sky was still dark and the air heavy.

"Hey, everyone," Dallas said. She eased out one of the Air Pods. "What's this about *Elegant and Authentic African Jewelry* plastered on the window? Is this another one of Frank's money-losing ideas?"

"We're not allowed to speak ill of the overlord," said Angel.

"Did I? Let me look ashamed." She dropped her chin to her chest.

Angel chuckled. "When are you going to let me cut off those braids?"

Dallas gathered her tangle of braids to her small breasts. "If I did, Delilah, I'd lose all my strength." Dressed in a gold-and-purple African print dress she'd purchased in a market in Senegal, Dallas danced around Angel. Her gold bangles jangled and a bracelet with tiny charms winked from her right ankle. "How about letting me get you a new place?" She pulled out the other Air Pod, put both into their case, and slipped it and her phone into her GUCCI purse. "Some excellent condos are on the market not too far from you. I'll get you an outstanding deal."

"We have a no soliciting policy here," Angel said, laughing with Dallas.

Roxy shook her head and smiled at her friend as she gave Denise's hair a final pat and spray. "Thanks for checking on Jewel for me yesterday."

"All good?"

"I guess." With tiny movements, Roxy rocked her head back and forth, negating her words. "What brings you to our fair establishment this afternoon?"

Portia was back at the sink. Roxy rinsed out the conditioner. The creamy solution filled the basin with suds-like foam.

"Thought you could use a friend." Dallas twisted her braids into a low-hanging ponytail and snatched up a damp rag. "And you can always use a hand." She wiped down the neighboring sinks as Roxy finished rinsing Portia. "It's time for us to get outta here."

Denise yelled bye to everyone. Portia was the only customer left. The three women moved to Roxy's station, and she began blow-drying Portia's straightened hair. The round brush and heat created sleek curls.

"Are you still going out with the doctor?" Portia asked Dallas.

"Which one?" Roxy asked in an arched tone.

"Well," said Dallas, her chestnut brown eyes wide. "Dr. Last Month is long gone, and I plan to banish Dr. Dentist Friday Night by tomorrow."

Roxy chuckled. "What's wrong with this one?"

Dallas sat down in the swivel chair next to the one Portia occupied and swung first left than right. "He has visible nose hairs, which should be a punishable offense. Plus, he must be at least forty–way too old for me."

Portia's mouth hung open.

"I'm searching for a young one in his twenties. Cougar bait. Next time my internet ad is going to read, *Sassy Black woman with means of her own seeks handsome white gentleman with more means than she has.* I'm going to give chocolate a rest for now and expand my palate to include vanilla."

Portia gasped and gave Dallas a disapproving look.

Trying to stifle a laugh, Roxy said to Portia, "All done."

Portia nodded her thanks and hurried to the front of the shop.

"I think I scandalized Miss Thing."

"You are a wicked woman." Roxy wiped down Portia's vacated chair.

Dallas didn't appear remorseful. "Actually," Dallas said as soon as Portia was out of earshot, "there's something I need to talk to you about."

"Something fun?"

"I'll buy you a beer if you buy me a glass of wine. But not at Sandman's."

Roxy shook her head. "Can't. I've got rehearsal tonight with Vicki."

"Oh, that's right, Miss Vicki is coming," Dallas said in a staged Southern drawl. "Have you decorated her dressing room and arranged for acting lessons?"

"Stop being mean."

The door closed behind Portia. Zoe called from the front of the shop, "I'm locking up the register."

Angel said, "I'm out of here, people. Dallas, if I were interested in women, I'd marry you." He pulled open the glass door. "Ciao, everyone."

Zoe packed up her tablet, books, and phone. "Miss Swan, do you know anything about college admissions?"

Dallas sashayed her way to the front of the shop. "Some. How're you doing with the campus tours?"

"Good. I'm just worried about my applications, and Aunt Roxy suggested I ask you for help."

An awkward but efficient girl, Zoe was going into her senior year and considering some of the state's best public colleges. That's what Roxy hoped for Jewel, before...

B.J. walked past Roxy. "Hey, Dallas, thanks for helping. Did I tell you how much my cousin loves the place you found her?" Without waiting for a response, he asked his daughter, "Can I give you a lift?"

"Sure," Zoe said, blinking her dark Quinton eyes. Like her uncles, she had thick, well-shaped eyebrows and lashes. Unfortunately, she also had her grandmother's chin.

"Come by the office this week," Dallas said. "Email what you've done so far, and I'll take a look."

"Thanks, Ms. Swan. I'm down to three choices."

B.J. said to his daughter, "Joanna might help."

"*No.*" Zoe seemed to catch herself. "I mean, thanks, but I'm good."

B.J. kept trying to get his daughter and new wife together, but it wasn't working so far. Roxy understood. She remembered the first and only time her father brought home a woman. It had been a year after her mother left. Her dad had roasted a leg of lamb, one of Roxy's favorite meals, and let the thirteen-year-old Roxy have a few sips of beer. The woman bought cheesecake for dessert, another of Roxy's favorites. When her father returned from walking his guest to the door, he'd asked, "Did you like her?" "No," Roxy said. "It's not right. Mom is coming back." That was the end of that.

Zoe called out, "Night, Aunt Roxy. See ya, Ms. Swan."

B.J. grasped the canvas bag swinging from Zoe's shoulder and carried it to the door. They stepped outside. Roxy noticed the sun had re-appeared. The door banged shut behind them.

"Just you and me." Dallas put away the rollers in a caddy, matching them up by color and size. "Are you going to tell me what's got you so low?"

"What makes you think I'm down?"

"Aren't you?"

They knew each other the way couples do who have been together for years. Roxy sat down and swiveled around to face her friend. "Carl is going to Atlantic City tonight with Spider."

Dallas plopped next to her. "I'd heard he'd slunk back into town."

"Last night, Carl didn't come home."

"Ouch." Dallas stroked her friend's arm. "What's up with him?"

"He hates our life, and the way Frank treats him, but maybe he's met somebody."

"Are you kidding? You married a prince."

"Stuff happens."

"Is this what the twists and color are about?"

Roxy reached up and patted her do. "I look stupid?"

"Carl loves you, period, end of story. And your hair looks great. You looked good before, just stressed." She slid the now-filled caddy into a drawer and began gathering up combs and scissors. "I don't get why you can't see what Carl and your friends see. You're pretty and smart."

Roxy rolled her eyes.

Dallas offered an exaggerated head shake and finished putting away Roxy's tools of the trade. "What do you suspect rat-snake-evil-doer Spider is up to?"

"That's what I have to figure out. Carl believes he's a changed man, and Jewel likes and trusts him."

"Have to be a miraculous transformation."

"He's given Jewel a job."

"What?"

Sharing with Dallas always helped. "And yesterday, he was with Joe, who by the way, told me Spider's gonna save the theater."

"Busy little scorpion."

"He asked Vicki to call him."

Dallas scrunched her face. "Trouble is afoot," she said in one of her British movie voices.

"Could he be transformed from the boy we knew?"

"Creepy crawlers stay dangerous in my experience."

"Fred Dixon told me Spider's buying up property, and now Carl invited Spider and his wife to Sunday supper."

"Whoa." Dallas threw up her ballerina arms as her bangles collided. "This is a saga. Start from the beginning."

"Can we talk on the way to the theater?"

The two friends locked up the shop and headed for Dallas's minivan. Roxy had planned to Uber and then get a lift home from Tea Rose. She appreciated Dallas's car and company.

As they drove, Roxy told Dallas everything that happened on Thursday evening and Friday, including meeting with Vicki. "I don't know what to think," Roxy said when she finished her narrative.

Dallas appeared pensive. "There are a lot of clues here. We're just missing their meaning. You said Spider's joining the Quinton Sunday-meal-in-hell?"

Roxy nodded. They were in the theater's parking lot.

"If it were me, I'd ask him straight out, 'What are your intentions?'"

Roxy bit her lower lip. "What if he lies?"

"Probably will. No matter what, you'll learn something. Besides, you'll surprise the crap out of him."

Roxy laughed. "I might try it." She hugged her friend. "I've been going on about my troubles. You said there was something you wanted to tell me."

Dallas dropped her car keys into her GUCCI bag. "It can wait."

"No, tell me." She faced Dallas. "What's going on with you?"

"It's not that serious. You focus on your family. Keep Carl close."

CHAPTER 12

The director yelled at Tea Rose. "This is a rape scene not a date. What's the matter with you today?"

Tea Rose, a shapely Black woman with what Carl called, "Beyoncé legs," crossed her arms and glared at Larry.

"Back in fifteen everyone," Larry said. He slammed off the stage.

"What's wrong with him?" Dallas asked Roxy. They were sitting in the center mezzanine. A copy of the script, blacked-out lines visible, lay on Roxy's lap.

"The missing Vicki, I think." She twisted her bracelet. "Not sure."

"I thought Vicki ordered you to cut the rape scene?"

"I tried rewriting it yesterday on the train."

Dallas pointed to the script covered in black slashes. "Went well, I see."

"Larry likes it. At least he did. Now he hates everything."

"Let's blow this Popsicle stand," Dallas said in another of her movie voices.

The two women slipped out of their seats, walked up the aisle, and entered the lobby. The cast had been rehearsing for hours and were still on act one. Roxy eased a dollar bill into the vending machine slot and pushed the button for a diet iced tea. It banged down the chute. "You want one?"

"I've been clean and sober for a month. Don't tempt me."

Roxy twisted off the top and took a swig. Then she elbowed the exit door open, and the two friends stepped onto the parking lot blacktop. She stopped walking and took another sip. The sultry air still threatened rain. It left her skin sticky and made it hard to breathe.

"Did it help writing about it?" Dallas asked.

"I guess. I thought I was over it, but maybe not."

"Was murdering the Spider character in the play your first clue?"

Roxy laughed. "And the crying jags as I typed."

For months after the rape, Roxy couldn't bare Carl touching her. She blamed it on the pregnancy. Sleep was fitful and her appetite poor. The doctor pressed her to eat for the baby's sake. They labeled her depression hormone-induced—her body changing as the baby grew but Roxy knew better. The only thing that pulled her out was her fierce love for the little girl growing inside of her.

"Forgive the cliché, but it's a journey." Dallas put her arm around Roxy's shoulders. Both women stayed quiet for several minutes until Dallas asked, "Carl attend any of the rehearsals, yet?"

"No." Roxy raised her eyes to meet Dallas's frown. "I've kept the plot kinda secret, and he's so busy..."

The Monday Night Murder was both a mystery and a woman's story of revenge, forgiveness, and the possibility of redemption. During two acts, the protagonist, Diana, changes before the audience's eyes. At the end, the viewers are rooting for Diana, but they're unsure what will happen. The last scene leaves the storyline incomplete but with hints of possibilities. The rape of Diana is the driving force throughout the play.

"He's gonna figure it out," Dallas said. "I did the first time I read it."

"I intended to tell him, even back then. At first, I was too scared, and all mixed up. Who'd believe me?"

"I did."

Roxy squeezed Dallas's hand. A helicopter putted overhead and highway traffic from the nearby Parkway thrummed in the background.

"You were the victim."

"I didn't want to be."

"I get it," Dallas said. "But times have changed. #MeToo women are stepping out and demanding justice." She paused. "Back in the day raped Black women were silent, or ignored, or doubted. But now, more bad guys are going to prison."

"Not Spider."

"Unless you prosecute him."

Roxy thought about that. It terrified her. "It was a long time ago. Besides, how do I explain to Carl? I was his girl, but I went to the beach. I drank the beers."

"That doesn't make it your fault. You said no."

"I screamed it."

"That's rape and you know it. Diana, in the play, knows it." Dallas eased the bottle of iced tea from Roxy's grip and took a sip.

"What happened to the wagon you're on?"

"Too late now." She finished the tea and tossed the bottle into the recycle bin. In a soft voice she said, "Carl would have supported you."

At the time, Roxy's sadness confused both Carl and her father. Her dad asked, "Are you missing Mom?" Carl worried she was sorry they'd married, forced to because of the pregnancy. Their family doctor diagnosed postpartum depression. But Roxy knew the cause was both the rape-memory ripping through her body, and the heavy weight of her secret.

"Too late for me too," Roxy said. "My Grandma Jackson used to say, if you lie, you'd steal; if you'd steal, you'd kill."

"Guess she was right. Diana takes him out in the play."

Roxy tried to smile at Dallas's joke, but her mouth only twitched. Tears puddled instead. "Getting married fast seemed the best way."

"I know."

Roxy felt grateful for her steadfast friend. She'd stayed by Roxy's side through everything, served as Roxy's maid-of-honor, and comforted her during the rocky pregnancy.

The helicopter's phat-phat-phat faded. Dallas turned toward the dark Victorian. "What will he think on opening night?"

"I have to figure something out before then."

"The truth might still work."

"I need to find the right time, the right way." She'd dug a deep hole. "After I determine if Spider's changed and what he's planning."

"How's that going to make it easier?" Dallas asked.

"My head aches. Can we talk about something else?"

"Burying their heads in the sand never works for the ostriches."

"Please?"

Dallas's expression mirrored the kind a mother gives to her misbehaving children.

"You said you had something to tell me."

"It can wait."

"No, tell me. At least the headlines."

"Zay crap and Tapp-and-Glory drama." Detective Xavier "Zay" Adams was Dallas's on-and-off boyfriend since high school and Tapp and Glory, her overly involved and protective parents. "Long tale requiring several glasses of wine."

"Okay, but soon. Promise?"

Dallas smiled. "Let's get back to your saga."

"I've gotta figure out what Spider is up to."

Dallas paced around for a few seconds. "You said he's buying land."

"According to Mr. Dixon."

"Really? That's your source?"

Roxy made a face.

"Fine." She threw up her arms, making her bangles jingle. "We're in this development boom."

"Boom?"

Dallas waved her hands. "Too strong a word, but our real estate *is* recovering, especially in the Westwood section where my folks live."

"Why us?"

"Proximity to Manhattan, undervalued properties, and lots of green space."

"Crummy schools, rising crime, and shops declaring bankruptcy every day. I don't get it."

"We're missing something that others see." She paused and tugged on her lower lip. "Spider still has friends in this town."

"Mr. Dixon also heard Spider is wealthy."

"If it were me, I'd put a consortium together for high rent condominiums or a commercial/entertainment complex, so people didn't have to travel to White Plains or Manhattan. I'd pull together a group like this, but I don't have the chops. The theater, since it's just east of Westwood, is in a perfect location if gentrification happens."

They had their heads close together the same way they conspired when they were teenagers. Roxy smelled Dallas's lipstick mingled with breath mint.

"How much money do you need to buy up blocks and build? A gazillion?"

"Not a lot of your own money. That's what the consortium is for." Dallas tapped the tips of her long fingers together. "Sandman and Spider have the juice to pull it off."

"Like a multiscreen movie theater, Whole Foods, and up-scale housing kinda thing?"

"Exactly."

"All legal?" Roxy asked, already disappointed in the answer she expected.

"Yeah."

She needed to prove Spider was a bad guy and get him outta Carl and Jewel's lives. "What happens to the homeowners?" Roxy remembered her conversation with Glenn Phillips. Did Spider promise Joe the magnet school in exchange for Joe's support?

"They make money if they're smart and sophisticated and get raped..." Dallas stopped. "Sorry, but you know what I mean. If they're not savvy or just folks, they get ripped off."

That sounded like Spider, but not like Joe. Was Spider duping him? Or was Joe helping Spider do the right thing? "How do we find out the truth?"

"Sleuthing."

"Spider is presenting at the theater's board meeting on Monday. I'm going."

"Wow. This sounds like it's moving fast."

"Can you come too?"

Dallas shook her head. "I have book club Monday over dinner, and we're meeting in my house. Maybe take my dad as your date."

Tapp Swan was the smartest and most educated man they knew. Degrees from Columbia and NYU, he ran his own management consulting firm before selling it a few years back.

Roxy, an idea pricking the back of her mind, said, "I think I should go alone, but keep me posted if he hears anything else."

Dallas nodded. "Will do. Plus, I have a few ideas, but they're not fleshed out. Let's meet on Tuesday and compare notes."

"Grab that glass of wine and a beer and talk about you and Zay too."

"Sounds good." Dallas consulted her watch. "So, where *is* Miss Congeniality?"

"There's still time for her to show."

"Right." Dallas lowered her head into her hands, and then lifted it again and stared at Roxy as if she were addled. "You need a new plan because that selfish diva is not coming through. She was the Wicked Witch of the West as a girl, and she's only gotten more adept at it with time."

The three amigos had never been a natural threesome. Dallas and Roxy were best friends, and Roxy and Vicki were besties. The three hung together, but Dallas acted suspicious of Vicki or jealous or both, and Vicki avoided Dallas when Roxy wasn't around. Still, Dallas helped Vicki the night of the abortion.

"I'm not giving up on her yet," Roxy said.

Dallas looked pointedly at her watch.

"Not tonight," Roxy conceded. "But she has big plans for Wednesday."

•   •   •

Dallas dropped Roxy in front of her apartment building, hugged her goodbye, and drove off. Instead of going in, Roxy walked three blocks north to Lemon deep in thought. If Spider was up to something illegal or improper, and she uncovered it... She crossed the street and still pondering Spider's moves, meandered along North Second Avenue. At the corner of Second and East Juniper, Roxy stopped.

Proof of Spider's nefarious ways would make confessing to Carl much easier. He'd forgive her and hate Spider. Charity work and good publicity for Vicki, via Laura Garrison, followed by excellent reviews that caused Vicki to stick with the play for its two-week run. Then a new house with enough room for the new baby, and Jewel in Westchester Community College after Carl and Roxy explained everything to her, together. Upset at first, but she'd understand, just like Carl. In about a year, they'd leave Frank's rule and start their own business. By that time, her play might be a movie or a television miniseries. Vicki hadn't been in a movie in a while. The play might be the perfect cinematic vehicle after her new show.

Roxy walked down East Juniper to First. The dream had to stay alive in her mind and heart; she had to keep it front and center. There it was. The faux-stucco house on the corner with a *For Sale by Owner* sign askew on the postage stamp lawn, among a row of houses so close to the next that neighbors could lean over and touch the deck railing. An air-conditioner protruded from the second-floor window.

Purple, red, and yellow pansies spilled over the sides of two ceramic pots on the dollhouse front porch.

The house was perfect. Within walking distance from Elm Park and the elementary school where the twins were starting in September. A sugar maple shaded the deck that was just big enough for the grill, round table, and six chairs. Welcoming lights glowed from all the windows. Not for the first time, Roxy wondered about the seller's asking price–she had no clue. How much could she earn from her play? Another unknowable factor.

She stood staring at the home, imagining her family crowded on the deck, laughing, and sipping cool drinks, Carl grilling burgers–veggie for Jewel–and the neighbors waving hello. Careful not to intrude or scare the family, she didn't walk around and sneak a peek at the backyard. Instead, she conjured images–a swing set for the twins, and another picnic table. If only her dad were still alive, he'd be so proud of Roxy's success–the play, the house, Carl's new business, and Roxy's life as a full-time writer. Another play and perhaps a novel on the shelves of the local Barnes & Noble and the independent bookstore in Westwood.

Roxy's reverie faded. Most days, she didn't admit to herself that part of her dream was a writing life. It felt too crazy, too out of reach. In fact, her entire plan and imagined life felt frail no matter how concrete she tried to make it in her mind.

By the time things came together for her, new people would own the corner house, and right now, few options existed. B.J. and Joanna had money. Joanna's parents, both dead, left her some cash and property, but Carl might be uncomfortable asking his brother for help. Dallas earned well and her parents were affluent. Roxy didn't finish the thought. Dallas gave them so much already–babysitting, business from her clients, money to the kids. And Tapp, Glory, and Roxy were not lend-money-close. Besides, debt was crippling and important to avoid.

The lights blinked off on the first floor. Roxy squinted at her watch. 10:15 p.m. The rape-scene rewrite and the short story for the contest loomed ahead. She walked back home, passing quiet dwellings, some with sagging porches and chipped paint and others recently constructed and squeezed onto tiny lots.

She had to believe. Vicki would show. The play would succeed, and there was another home–an affordable one–in her future.

CHAPTER 13

The apartment was quiet with no barking dogs, TV pitches, or arguing children. Three night-lights gave the central hall a soft glow, backlit by the bright light coming from the kitchen. It was good to be home, even if it wasn't the little stucco. She dropped her messenger bag between Gabriella's unadorned, and Kia's pink-and-purple, big-girl bikes.

Roxy stepped into the kitchen. "Hey."

"Hey, yourself," Jewel said.

Roxy plopped down next to Jewel at the Formica table, jammed in one corner, each of the six chairs almost touching the next one. Several coloring books and a scattering of crayons covered one end of the table. Roxy put the loose crayons into the box.

Arrayed in front of Jewel at the other end of the table sat a bowl of soapy water, nail polish remover, emery boards, paper towels, a bottle of base paint, and another of forest green nail polish. Jewel covered her pinky fingernail with quick strokes.

"I need a beer." Roxy stretched over and opened the refrigerator door. "Did you have any trouble getting the girls to bed?" Colored magnetic alphabet letters clattered to the tile floor.

"They asked for you." Roxy heard the unspoken accusation that underlined Jewel's words.

"Thanks for feeding everyone and getting them to bed." She kissed the top of Jewel's head. What would she do without her girl? "I appreciate you."

"No prob." She moved on to her next nail.

74

With practiced ease, Roxy picked up a red B and an orange X and put them back on the door next to family photos stuck on with ladybug magnets. She spent too little time with the girls. The play and work sucked up every second; she needed to do better. "Maybe next weekend we can do something fun together?"

"Isn't your play opening on Saturday?"

Roxy hit her forehead with her palm. "Too much going on. So, on Sunday then. We'll skip dinner at your grandparents and head for Long Island and Jones Beach. When was the last time we did that?"

Jewel made a skeptical frown and an exaggerated eye roll.

"Interesting nail color."

Jewel, moving on the next finger, didn't respond.

Peering into the refrigerator Roxy asked, "Where's all the beer that was in here yesterday?" She stood, shoved aside cartons of orange and apple juice, a plastic container of yesterday's spaghetti, Jewel's fat-free yogurts, and a carton of milk. "Where's Max?"

"Walking the dogs."

Roxy spun around. "It's ten thirty at night. What were you thinking?"

Without taking her eyes off her manicure, Jewel said, "What were *you* thinking? Was I supposed to walk them? Where's Dad? Where were you?"

"You watch your tone, young lady."

"I fed *your* kids, *again*; cleaned *your* kitchen, *again*."

"Oh. You don't live here rent free? You don't eat the food? You buy your own clothes?" What happened to no problem?

"I'm nine months pregnant in case you forgot."

How could Roxy forget that? "Look, I'm sorry. I shouldn't have said that but—"

Jewel jumped in before Roxy could finish her sentence. "Besides, what are you so worried about? He's only going around the corner."

Roxy inhaled. From behind the orange juice, she retrieved a can of Bud and several slices of pizza stored in a Ziploc bag. She closed the refrigerator door with her hip. After freeing the pizza, she put the slices in the toaster oven, bending the edges so both fit. She set the temperature to 400 degrees.

When Roxy was little, her mother used to sit at the kitchen table with her just like this. The ashtray overflowed with menthol cigarette butts, and multiple beer cans formed a ragged chain on the table. "You take everything too serious, Roxy.

Don't you get it? You have no control. Trouble comes in six packs, no matter what you do. You might as well let life carry you where it will."

"You're right," Roxy said to the top of Jewel's bent head. "They're my children, not yours. I'm grateful for your help. And, certainly, you shouldn't walk the dogs at night either." She popped the lid of the beer can and took a sip.

Jewel kept her eyes on her task.

"But Max is thirteen years old and shouldn't be out this late at night, not in this neighborhood or any neighborhood."

"Try telling that to Pharaoh."

"Why didn't you go with him?"

"And leave the twins by themselves?" She shook her head. "You'd be fine with that?" She made a sucking noise. "Right."

Roxy decided to ignore her daughter's attitude. Jewel had legitimate complaints, but she was still dead wrong. "The dogs will either hold it, or pee on the rug, or you let them loose and hope they come home."

"You'd make me mop up the dogs' piss."

Once again, Roxy chose to ignore Jewel's disrespectful tone. Instead, she stayed on message. "Max can't be in the street alone at this time of night. Any trouble happens and the police might only see the color of his skin."

"Ten thirty isn't so darn late. Geez."

She sounded just like her father. Roxy took another sip of her beer and then put it back in the refrigerator. "Yesterday, I noted three chilled beers. You're not drinking, are you?"

"I had company."

"You're making me crazy."

"This is why I'm not having any kids. I mean after this one. Why I'm not keeping it—"

"Her. The baby isn't *it*."

"Keeping *her* and why I'm getting a place of my own."

"Who was here?"

"What? I can't have friends over?"

"To drink?"

"He's legal. Not some teenager." Jewel screwed the cap on the bottle of nail polish and blew on her nails.

"He?" They'd asked her a thousand times about the baby's father, begged her to tell them. They just had this conversation with Annie Long, the counselor. "Is *he* someone special?"

Jewel made an *I-get-what-you're-trying-to-do* face.

Roxy waited.

"Spider says I should keep *her*, but he doesn't have any kids, so what does he know? Believes family is everything. Well one day with this crew and he'd get over that idea."

"You've discussed the baby with him? He was here drinking beer with you?"

"You're not listening."

"I'm going to find Max and then you and I will finish this conversation." She scanned the room for her bag and then remembered she'd left it in the hall.

"When my nails are dry, I'm going to bed."

"You wait for me, understood?"

Roxy stalked into the hall, retrieved her bag, and rummaged through it until she found her keys. "I'll be right back."

Why was every evening ending like this? Where was Carl to help? She pulled open the door. It slammed behind her. Everything was spinning out of control with Jewel and Carl going nuts on her.

Roxy took the stairs, moving fast, and exited the front door. She had to get them out of here. Where might Max take the dogs? There was a small park about five blocks south but even he knew better than venturing too far from the house after dark. Pharaoh's bark answered the question.

"What are you doing here?" Max asked, pulling on Pharaoh's leash. Cleo continued sniffing the sidewalk.

"Searching for you." She bent over, petted the top of Pharaoh's head, and then looked up at her son. When had he grown a mustache? It was only a faint black line of fuzz, but it hadn't been there this morning, had it?

"What's wrong?"

"Nothing. How was your day?"

Rap music increased in intensity as a car of teenagers eased by, driving only five miles an hour. A horn honked.

"Hey, Ms. Q." A young man, his baseball cap askew, waved from a shiny Corolla.

Roxy recognized him as a friend of Jewel's. She waved back. Laughter warmed the air. The neighborhood had changed, but it wasn't dangerous. The mayor cracked down on the gang bangers and drug dealers. After that, the area stabilized and now it was coming back, just as Dallas had predicted. Roxy was just on edge.

"Mom, can I ask you something?"

Max barely reached Roxy's shoulder two months ago. Now, they were the same height. At this rate, he'd pass her by Christmas. "Sure."

"Are you and Dad getting divorced?"

Roxy stopped. "What a thing to ask." Both dogs raised their heads with ears perked. Roxy lowered her voice. "Of course not." The dogs went back to sniffing the ground.

"How come he doesn't come home anymore?"

She tried to keep her voice light. "Your father is home every night, just not tonight and last night. Everyone needs a break."

"Okay." His tone held the same skepticism she'd witnessed on Jewel's face.

"This is not something you need to worry about." She put her arm around him. "Things are kinda tough right now, but it's gonna get better." She gave him her best smile. "You'll see."

"If you say so."

They reached the apartment building. Roxy used her keys to open the lobby door and all four of them pushed in.

"Sometimes adults have problems, but that doesn't mean they don't love each other or they're splitting."

They clattered up the steps to the second floor. At the landing, Roxy peered sideways at Max, trying to gauge his reaction. His lids were half closed, and his mouth set in a tight straight line.

"What's happening at camp? Having fun?"

Max grunted. They walked down the hall in silence.

"Who visited Jewel today?" She tried to sound nonchalant.

"Ed."

They reached their door. "Ed who?"

"Ask her."

"I'm asking you."

"Her boyfriend. Acts like it or hopes to be."

"Do I know him?"

Max made an exaggerated groan.

"I get it. Ask Jewel."

• • •

Weariness pressed down on Roxy. She ached for bed. Her dad used to say no matter how late it got, stay up until you talked it out. Her mother used to laugh, take a deep drag on her KOOL LIGHTS, and call him Professor Shrink. His advice didn't work for them.

Roxy's stomach rumbled. She returned to the kitchen.

"I made you some tea," Jewel said. She put the pizza slices on a paper plate.

"It's late."

"Skipping meals isn't healthy." She placed the plate on the table. "Wonder where I heard that."

Roxy patted her midsection. "Do I look like I'm starving? My belly is almost the same size as yours." She took the mug of hot tea, splashed in some milk, and added sugar. She sipped. "Ahh."

"You're welcome."

Water from the shower serenaded them.

"Remember when we couldn't get Max to bathe at all?" Jewel poured a mug of tea and like her mother, splashed in milk and stirred in sugar. "Now, I can't get him out of the bathroom."

"Why is Spider is helping you? What's it to him?" Did Jewel hear the tremor in Roxy's voice or detect the fear that squeezed her chest?

"I think he wishes he had a daughter."

Roxy almost spit out her tea; she covered with a cough. "What makes you say that?" The shower stopped. "He and his wife are still young enough to have a daughter of their own."

Jewel crinkled her nose. "She's nice in a prissy way."

"You met her?"

"Don't get so upset."

Roxy took a quiet breath and squeezed her hands together. "I'm not, just curious."

"She helps Spider with the business. Anyway, I got the impression they can't have kids." Jewel slurped her tea. "Lucky her."

"Has he come on to you?" The scary question came out in a rush. Maybe this wasn't about Spider thinking Jewel was his daughter. What if he was hitting on her the way he treated every pretty girl he met back in high school? Jewel hardly looked pregnant.

"That's disgusting. He's Dad's age." Jewel got up from the table and gathered her nail-care paraphernalia. "I'm going to bed."

With closed eyes, Roxy rubbed her temples.

"You should get some rest too. Are you sick or something?" Jewel asked.

"I'm fine, stressed. And thanks again for taking care of Max and the girls. I shouldn't have." She paused. What part of the conversation was wrong or inappropriate?

For several seconds, Jewel stood in the kitchen doorway. Roxy peered at her. A thick cascade of auburn hair framed a face pinched in concentration. When she was born, her hair was light brown and straight. As she got older, it became darker with big loopy curls. Carl suggested she got it from his maternal grandmother, who was mixed race. Roxy let that stand.

Once again, words swam out of Roxy's mouth before she took time to think things through. "Who's Ed?"

"Max has a big mouth."

"It wasn't his fault. I made him."

Jewel turned down the hall toward her room. "I'm gonna kill him."

For some time, Roxy sat in the kitchen staring at the refrigerator door, absently twisting her gold bracelet around her wrist. No Carl two nights in a row. No Vicki for the past three weeks. Ed. Who the hell was he? Jewel palling around with Spider. Both Jewel and Carl. Max worried about a divorce. She covered her mouth with one hand and held her head with the other. Perhaps her mother was right. Roxy had no control of anything in her life.

She closed her eyes and let out a low groan.

CHAPTER 14
SUNDAY

Roxy, the twins, and Max rounded the corner. They walked to and from church every Sunday, except during downpours, snowstorms, or bitter cold. As they approached their building, Dallas hopped out of her minivan. She waved. Her bangles glinted in the sunlight.

"Hey, you," Roxy called. Dallas spent Sunday mornings having breakfast with her parents before they went to church. "What brings you to this part of town?"

"News and lots of it," Dallas said in a rush.

"Hi Auntie Dallas." Kia jumped into Dallas's embrace.

"You too, Miss Gabriella." She held both girls close.

Max smiled, tipped his head hello, but didn't come in for a hug.

"Where's Jewel?"

Roxy noted and appreciated that her friend didn't ask for the missing-in-action Carl. "Under the weather."

They all climbed the stairs to the apartment. Pharaoh's bark welcomed them home.

Roxy said, "Can you check on Jewel while I get this crew settled with snacks? We can rendezvous in my bedroom in ten."

Ten minutes later the two friends sat side by side on Roxy's bed. Pillows propped them up.

"Tell all," Roxy said, eager to hear Dallas's news but worried it wasn't good.

"This morning I had breakfast, as usual, with Glory and Tapp." Dallas called her parents by their first names when she spoke of them but never to their face. "After criticizing my clothes and pressing for marriage news even though I'm not even dating someone acceptable much less steadily, we had a pleasant breakfast."

Roxy laughed. For the Swans, a thirty-six-year-old daughter should bring home a man with a specific résumé. Like Tapp Swan, he should possess at least two degrees—undergrad and one from a graduate professional school like medicine, law, or an MBA—and be a man of color, preferably Jamaican but American would do. Raised by both parents who attended church every Sunday, he should demonstrate impeccable table manners coupled with an excellent vocabulary, hold doors for ladies, own income-producing property and/or a large stock portfolio, and possess a substantial bank account. The financial requirements were the one point on which Dallas and her parents agreed.

"While I was there, Spider-the-terrible called me."

Roxy straightened up. "What?"

"He asked if I'd meet him for coffee and I agreed. That's why I'm here to warn you before you walk into dinner with the Cranks without my intel."

"What did he want?"

"Patience milady," Dallas said, holding up her hands for silence. "Tapp overheard my conversation and gave me some info. According to him, it's all the talk at City Hall. Folks are excited about the money Spider's promising to bring in." Dallas smoothed her sheath along her thighs. She slanted her eyes toward Roxy.

"Tell me straight. I'm a big girl."

"Tapp said, and I quote, 'This town needs investment from people willing to take a chance. Even though I'm not part of the inner sanctum, it looks to me like Booth's the knight we've been waiting for.'"

Roxy willed deflation away. "What happened at your meeting with Spider?"

"Despite what my dad said, I went with my armor on. He'd sucked in Tapp and the big dogs at City Hall, but he'd have to prove himself to me."

"It's okay, Dee-Dee." She sensed her friend's nervousness about meeting Spider and Roxy's reaction.

Dallas took an audible breath. "After a bit a sparring, he offered me a gig."

"Oh."

"Yeah. He came across sincere using his super-power–that looking deep into your eyes making you believe you're the only person he cares about in the entire world. He worked that one with significant effect, I'm ashamed to say, even though I recognized the move."

"What's the offer?"

"Find a house and office space at twice my commission."

"Whoa."

"I told him he can't bribe me because we're on to his evil plan. I offered to recommend other realtors."

"And?"

"He said he believed in investing in friends as if that described our nonexistent relationship."

Roxy heard a commotion outside her door, which reminded her it was time to get to her in-laws. Max and the twins were squabbling. Their voices escalated which each passing minute. She scooched off the bed. "I have to change for dinner into something more comfortable. Can't be late." She zipped through her choices in the closet. "Where are they looking?"

Dallas rose as well. "Within the city limits but on what he called, 'the nicer outer edges.' He likes north Westwood."

"And the office space?"

"That's the most intriguing part and why I said yes. He intends to buy a building close to The People's Theater."

●　　●　　●

Every Sunday afternoon found Roxy and her family at the home of Frank and Celeste Quinton. From two o'clock until at least seven, the clan gathered, ate, and talked, the women in the kitchen and the men around the table, or in the basement shooting pool or out in the yard smoking cigars. Antiquated and ridiculous as it was, it had been like that from the first day of her marriage.

On a corner lot in the northeast part of town, not too far from The People's Theater, the two-story brick house boasted cultivated gardens, one in the back and one on the side. Peach trees–almost every yard in Fieldcrest had at least one–azaleas, and rose bushes as tall as a person, their scent deceptively sweet, bloomed from early spring until well into the fall. Deceptively sweet because there was little sugar in the potent brew of Frank Quinton's household.

Coming from a family of two, Roxy initially found the Sunday dinners were a treat. Roxy loved belonging to a big, raucous family who argued, laughed, and hung together in times of trouble. B.J. welcomed her and the sisters and cousins were kind. They all knew her most of their lives. Roxy wished they'd included her father but wasn't sure how to bring it up. None of the Quinton clan extended an invitation, not even Carl.

It only took a month of dinners, however, to change her mind. Frank was mean. She'd sensed this over the years, but up close it was hard to miss. Carl dreaded the gatherings and soon, Roxy did as well. Going home to her father reminded her she had something special in her dad's devotion and unconditional love.

There were, however, pleasant aspects to Sunday afternoons. Today, Roxy stood for a few seconds on the walkway, closed her eyes, and breathed in a plethora of mingled aromas—roses, turned and watered earth, and peaches ripening on the big tree in the yard's corner. Once Carl and Roxy had their own spot, she'd plant a garden in honor of her father.

He loved growing vegetables and flowers but never had a yard. Instead, he volunteered in the community patch managed by the church. Most everyone loved her dad. A quiet man, clumsily raising his daughter, he was devout and loyal and had more friends than he knew. She missed him every day. Not in the same way she missed her mother, wondering where she was, why she'd left, if she was dead or alive; she missed her father in a happier way. He loved her without complications or parentheses of explanation.

The conversation with Dallas left Roxy on edge. Maybe Spider and Nadine wouldn't show.

The twins darted by, playing their version of tag, a game that required ducking and hiding between Roxy and Max's legs. In a rare moment of tolerance, Max laughed and helped Gabriella avoid the quicker Kia.

"Roxy."

She spun around, almost dropping the reusable bag holding two fruit pies she'd purchased as their contribution to the meal. It had been a long time since she baked pies from scratch.

"Daddy." Kia took off, her braids swinging. She flung herself into her father's arms.

Carl caught and lifted her. "How's my girl?"

"Did you bring us something?"

"Sure." With his free hand, he fished into the pocket of his lightweight sports jacket and slipped out two casino chips. "One is for you, and one is for your sister." He leveled his gaze on Gabriella. "Who doesn't seem glad to see me."

Gabriella took Roxy's hand.

"You can cash it in with me for something special," Carl said extending a chip to Gabriella. "An ice cream or a jump rope."

Kia hugged Carl and whispered in his ear loud enough for everyone to hear. "She's mad at you."

Still holding Roxy's hand, Gabriella reproached her father. "You didn't come home."

Carl reached down and picked her up with his other arm. "I'm home now."

She hung stiffly along his side, her back arched away from him his chest. "Two times."

He stretched his neck forward and kissed her forehead.

"Hey Dad," Max said. His changing voice cracked.

"Hi Son. Where's Jewel?"

"She's got a fever or something." He looked toward Roxy as if seeking confirmation.

Carl raised his eyebrows in an unspoken question to Roxy.

"Nothing serious." Then, with a glance toward Max to let him know he'd gotten it right, "Tomorrow, if she still has a temp, I'll take her to the doctor."

Carl said to Max, "Do me a favor and take your sisters inside." He eased both girls down onto the brick path.

"And take the pies into the kitchen for me," Roxy said, handing them to Max. "Make sure your grandma sees them and tell her they're from us."

"Aren't you guys coming in?" Max took the package from his mother.

Roxy and Carl responded simultaneously. "In a few minutes."

Max tucked Kia under his arm. She spread her arms wide. "I'm an airplane."

Trailing behind, Gabriella gave her father one last glare before following her siblings inside. The door closed behind them.

"You're looking pretty. New outfit?"

In an offhand way, Roxy said, "Just a new way of wearing some old clothes."

"I like it."

Roxy was glad she'd taken the time to fix herself up. Despite her fever, Jewel rose to help with the kids and give Roxy some make-up and dress pointers. "Jewel's doing."

In fact, Jewel had offered her concealer. "Dot here, and here," she instructed. "Now put on your foundation." She insisted Roxy cinch her waist with a wide belt over a cotton top with cap sleeves and a flowing A-line skirt. "Let's get you looking pulled together," Jewel said. "For when you see Daddy."

Roxy examined her reflection in the full-length mirror. The concealer downplayed the under-eye dark circles and foundation gave her mocha skin a velvety glow. The coppery gold color of the top complimented her eyes. Jewel's gold hoop earrings went well with the short blond twists. In the end, she agreed with Jewel. She wanted to look good for Carl.

Carl said, "I'm sorry."

She waited to hear him out. Was he sorry for something he'd done or something he was about to say?

"I've been acting kinda nuts."

Physical relief washed over her. She'd been holding her breath, waiting to hear he was leaving or worse. Instead, he opened his arms and she slipped inside, burying her face against the soft fabric of his jacket.

"Just so you know, I spent the last two nights at the Spring Street Motel. Alone. Thinking."

She looked up at him, seeing a few dark hairs he'd missed when shaving. Then she pressed harder into him, sank as deep into his arms as possible. "Stuff we can talk about?"

The front screen door opened and banged closed. "What are you two doing out here?"

Roxy stepped out Carl's embrace to face her father-in-law. Not as tall as Carl nor as handsome, Frank still carried his sixty years well. Clear eyes, smooth skin, the same ebony waves but with silver streaks at his temples. Frank kept fit. Dressed in gray slacks with a navy blazer and a white, open-collar shirt, even his bearing was formal.

"Hey, Pop," Carl said in a level tone. His arm circled Roxy's waist.

"You're late."

"We'll be there in a minute. Roxy and I are..."

"Your mother's been asking for you both." Frank leveled his dark eyes on Roxy. A fat cigar worked around his mouth as he spoke. He took a drag. "She needs help in the kitchen." Curls of smoke painted the air.

Roxy watched Carl stiffen, his lips became a tight line and his lids lowered, not unlike Max's expression the night before. She'd become immune to Frank's waves of misery but for Carl they were harder to ride. He took his arm away.

"I'll be there in a few," Roxy said.

Blocking their path, Frank said to Carl, "You've been gambling. The girls showed me their casino presents." Accusation and contempt colored every word.

"It's none of *your* business."

"Don't you disrespect me." Frank removed his cigar from his mouth and waved it in the air. "It will be my business if you expect me to bail you out again."

Roxy reached for Carl's hand. "Come on. Let's go in."

At first, he hesitated, but then he let Roxy move him past Frank. Just as Carl's hand touched the doorknob, Frank said, "And you wonder why I don't let you take over the business. You'd gamble away everything I built."

Carl spun around, his face a mask of anger and pain. "You were a shit father, and you still are."

"Oh, poor you. No hugs from daddy. No attaboys. Yeah, well. I gave you your *life*."

Carl balled his fists at his side. "And you think that's enough?"

"Plus, a roof over your head, food to eat, an education, and a trade." He lifted his chin in Roxy's direction. "You came crawling home with a knocked-up girlfriend. I gave you honest work and a way to support your family." With each sentence Frank's voice rose in volume.

"I work hard." Carl's volume matched Frank's. "Roxy, B.J. and me *are* the salon and school. When's the last time you brought in a dime or let us grow the business?"

Frank leaned in close, his nose almost touching Carl's. "Go on blaming me for everything that's wrong, but at what point are you responsible for your own life?"

Roxy wanted to step between them. Make them stop before they both said things they couldn't take back, but she feared it was already too late. Over the years, whenever Frank lectured, cursed, and accused, Carl backed down first and kept the peace. After all, Frank held Carl's livelihood and inheritance in his hands.

Frank said, "You think I can't see what a mess you've made. Gambling away your paychecks and not taking care of business. Jewel pregnant just like her mother. Well, it's time for you to unfuck your life by yourself. Don't come crawling to me."

What made a father treat a son like this? Roxy often wondered who'd hurt Frank as a child. Carl wasn't the only one he stomped on, but the others didn't push back. "Please, let's go inside." She tugged on Carl's balled fist.

For several seconds, the three of them stood. Frank and Carl frozen in a stare-down. Roxy darted her eyes from one to the other. Frank blinked and took a step back. She sent up a silent prayer of thanks.

The front door swung opened. "Dad, come on, Uncle B.J. challenged us to a game before dinner," Max said.

Without turning toward his son, Carl put his arm around Roxy's waist again. "Rack 'em up. I'll be right there."

"You okay, Dad?" Max asked.

Roxy said, "Everything is fine. Go back in." She watched Carl's breaths lift his chest and ease his shoulders. He looked down on her.

"Yeah, let's join the family," Carl said.

They left Frank alone in the yard.

CHAPTER 15

The voices of the female cousins, wives, and girlfriends butted against each other the way elbows and knees bump on a crowded dance floor. Adjacent to the eat-in-kitchen was a large dining room with a table long enough to seat all the adults. Some of the men already sat drinking beers. Beyond the dining room, in the front of the house, was an equally large living room with a never used but functional fireplace.

"You alright?" Joanna, B.J.'s wife, peered at Roxy. "Celeste says serve the munchies now." Married to B.J. for a year, she often acted awed or overwhelmed by Sunday dinners.

"Yeah." Roxy searched for free counter space.

"You seem a little ragged," Winnie, Carl's cousin, said in her usual blunt manner. At thirty, Winnie hadn't smoothed her own sharp edges, but she and Roxy were close, at least as close as Roxy was to any of Carl's family except for B.J. Although tactless, Winnie was never mean.

"I'm fine." Of course, she wasn't. The horrible scene with Frank in the garden left her shaken. She vowed to erase the worry from her expression. "But I thank both of you for asking." She tried for a reassuring smile. "Joanna, can you help me get this platter together?" Roxy placed fruit salad, shrimp cocktail and sauce, stuffed mushrooms, cheese, water crackers, and small forks and toothpicks onto a wooden serving tray.

"They're moving through the beer at a Quinton pace. I'll bring out more." Winnie, her wavy Quinton hair dyed the color of mud with orange swirls, angled past Roxy in the direction of the dining room. "A handsome white guy just arrived. Are we expecting company?"

Roxy wiped her hands on the apron tied around her waist. She peered out the archway between the kitchen and dining room, past the tables and the overstuffed furniture in the living room, to the front door. Spider. A tall woman in an expensive-looking, lemon-colored suit stood next to him. Great. Just what she needed. She'd forgotten they were coming.

"Do you know him?" Winnie asked, waggling her eyebrows.

But Roxy didn't laugh. "Spider Booth. He left town when you were twelve so you wouldn't know him, but the family does."

"Should I take the bread out of the oven, Aunt Roxy?" Zoe asked.

"Can you give Joanna a hand?" Stepmother and stepdaughter, Joanna, and Zoe, found it hard to communicate or cooperate. "If you finish the platters and take them out, I'll get the rolls ready." Determined not to look again, Roxy opened the oven door and took out each sheet of fragrant bread.

Celeste, her mother-in-law, interrupted Roxy's thoughts. "They're waiting." A stout woman with features that matched her personality, Celeste Quinton only gave orders in the kitchen since Frank dominated every other room. Half the time, Roxy felt sorry for Celeste. One hundred percent of the time she prayed her daughters grew up to be nothing like their grandmother.

"Hors d'oeuvres are ready," Joanna said. She and Zoe, each with a full tray, walked Celeste out of the kitchen.

Spider's bass soared over the other conversations. Roxy readied the rolls in four matching breadbaskets and covered each with a thick cloth napkin to keep them warm. Her hands shook.

"Coming?" Winnie asked.

Roxy handed the bread to Winnie. "Thanks. I have to work on the mac and cheese."

"May I help?" asked an unfamiliar voice.

Roxy spun around, her hand massaging her rebellious stomach the way Jewel often rubbed her baby bump. In front of her stood a chesty woman, her woodsy perfume clashing with the kitchen aromas.

"I'm Nadine," the woman said. "Webster's wife." She used Spider's given name in a manner that seemed to Roxy as point-making.

Winnie, who had bustled back into the kitchen, gave Roxy a quizzical look. "Nice to meet you," Winnie said to Nadine. She gathered wine glasses and put them on a silver tray. "Want to help?" She thrust the tray into Nadine's hands and continued placing glasses on it. "This is messed up—women waiting on the men like this." Winnie screwed up her face.

Nadine pursed her lips.

Roxy had to suppress a laugh. Welcome to my world.

"What the heck," Winnie said. She grabbed the tray from Nadine. "Don't buy into this oppression. The next thing you know, you'll be a regular, cooking, serving, and washing the dishes. Run while you can."

"I'm Roxy." Still chuckling inside, she walked over to Nadine and offered her hand. "Don't mind Winnie. Please, take a seat at the table. You're a guest."

"You and Webster dated in high school? Are you *that* Roxy?"

Nadine didn't look like Roxy imagined. Of course, any woman of Spider's would have curves. What surprised Roxy was Nadine's ordinariness—pale skin, watery blue eyes, and unremarkable hair in a short bob.

"Guilty," Roxy said, trying for a light tone. "Long time ago."

Nadine's mouth moved as if she wanted to say something else but was having difficulty forming the words.

Carl's sister, Yolanda, poked in her head. "The natives are restless. How's the mac and cheese coming?" She spoke in an educated accent, not Bronx or Fieldcrest like the rest of the clan.

"Meet Nadine Booth," Roxy said.

The two women shook hands. Kindred spirits from what Roxy observed. Both dressed in expensive-looking suits and decorated with jewelry Roxy believed was real rather than costume.

"You have a daughter, don't you?" Nadine asked Roxy.

Roxy's heart picked up speed. "Three."

Yolanda said, "Roxy and Carl have a brood and they're about to be grandparents, if you can believe that."

"I met her," Nadine said. "She's lovely."

Roxy tried to get a handle on the conversation. Why was Nadine asking about Jewel when she'd already met her and knew who Roxy was? Why the deception?

Nadine seemed lost, as if undecided what to do next. She looked around for a few seconds. "I guess I'll join the others." She swept out of the room.

Yolanda glanced at Roxy. "Spider's wife?"

"Yeah." Roxy tried to puzzle out an explanation. After popping the loaf pans of mac and cheese in the oven, and setting the timer for twenty minutes, she stirred the chicken gravy. Meat juices swirled around.

"I bet she's a lot older than we are, in her mid-forties at least," Yolanda said.

The Quinton women quoted others during family discussions. Roxy tried not to supply any fuel, so she stayed quiet.

"Kind of stern looking too," Yolanda added. "I mean for a man like Spider."

"And what type is that?" asked a familiar male voice, deep and smooth, and, like Yolanda's, devoid of its once working-class accent.

Roxy sucked air into her lungs and breathed out.

"No men in Celeste's kitchen." Yolanda clicked her tongue at Spider. Roxy heard Yolanda leave but didn't turn around.

"Not going to say hello? You raced away the other day, almost ran me down and avoided me at the theater. Can't do that forever."

He put his hand on her shoulder. A light touch that seared her skin. She shrugged it off.

"You changed your hair."

The wooden spoon still in her hand, she faced him. Gravy dripped onto the tile floor.

Spider grabbed a paper towel, stooped down, and mopped up the spill. "You're looking mighty sexy." He grinned at her.

The compliment felt dangerous and insincere. Roxy stayed quiet and concentrated on her task.

"Clingy tops, cutoff shorts, and bathing suits..." He twisted around, eyed the wastebasket, and tossed the stained towel in as if it were a basketball. "Your best looks."

Blood thudded through her and pounded in her ears. She prayed he didn't sense her anger or panic.

"Carl had a hell of a run last night. Won big. His game was on fire."

For months after the rape, she couldn't be near him without getting sick. Eighteen years was a long time.

"I told you, I'm going to be a part of Jewel's life."

Roxy took another deep breath and exhaled slowly.

"There's no need for us to be enemies. I'm trying to help you. Carl wasn't *lucky* last night." He came closer and once again loomed over her. "High-stakes private game and Carl won. Do you understand what I'm telling you? He raked in the money because I made sure of it." He took two steps back. "Just like you, I want Jewel and the baby to have everything they need."

With her right hand gripping the handle of the pan, Roxy continued stirring. All it would take was one fling of the contents in his face, burning his smug mouth and staining his tan shirt and slacks. Then she'd raise the pan and bring it down hard on his head. She turned toward him. "You stay away from her."

For several beats, they stared at each other. Spider's eyes narrowed and darkened to slate. Roxy's nerves quivered, but she didn't lower her gaze.

When he spoke, his voice was calm. "I'm on your side."

"You know nothing about us."

"Jewel told me you've urged her to keep the baby. I agree."

"You have no right."

"You know I *do*. She's beautiful—a perfect mix of you and me."

"You leave my daughter alone or I will pierce your heart with a jagged knife."

Spider's jaw muscles bunched. Roxy braced herself for the remembered slap.

Instead, he said in an even tone, "There's no need. You'll see. I'm here to improve your lives."

• • •

Eleven adults and seventeen-year-old Zoe sat around the dining table. The crocheted tablecloth was over a hundred years old, passed down from mother to daughter to son. The children, hosted by great-grandma MeMa, sat at the kid's table that Celeste set up on Sundays in the living room. To protect the carpet, she covered it with a laundered painter's drop cloth.

Roxy tried to relax, or at least not show anyone how rattled she felt. She lifted her wine glass. It tipped and red wine splashed onto MeMa's heirloom.

"Oh, no." Roxy scooted back. "So sorry."

"Don't worry about it," Frank said, his voice thick with annoyance.

She soaked a napkin with soda water and dabbed the stain. So much for not revealing her worries.

"It's been through worse. A little spilled wine–pish." His brittle laugh contradicted his words.

Carl appeared to bristle at his father's tone. She gave him a quick nod, letting him know she was fine. Cooled emotional fires left behind smoke and embers, but other than the twitch around his mouth, Carl looked relaxed. Earlier, she'd heard him laughing with Max and B.J. She noticed him avoiding contact with Frank, joining a different circle or activity whenever his father came close. Frank's harsh words–unfuck your life and stop blaming me–rang in her ears. Amidst the vitriol, there was a message worth heeding. They needed to get out of the mess they were in.

Deep in thought and still working on the stain, Roxy sensed rather than saw Spider's cool eyes trained on her.

Seated opposite her and next to Carl, Spider said, "I'm sorry Jewel isn't here. I was hoping to see her. Did she tell you about her new job?"

"She's sick. Isn't that right, Uncle Carl?" Zoe scooped a mouthful of mac and cheese into her mouth.

"We appreciate your help," Carl said. Roxy raised her eyes to meet Carl's. He gave her a pointed stare before turning back to Spider. "She'll be sorry she missed you."

Zoe tried again. "What kinda job?"

"A good one," Spider said to Zoe. To Carl, he asked, "How ill?"

The conversation became a low hum in her brain as Roxy pretended to eat. Chicken and gravy, rolls, string beans, carrots, and baked macaroni and cheese left streaks of food and oil as she moved them from one side of her plate to the other. Jewel must not work for Spider. Was Roxy being selfish? Suppose he wanted to help and wasn't trying to make trouble? Besides, if she insisted Jewel quit Spider's job, what acceptable explanation could she offer Jewel or Carl?

Roxy came back to an earlier decision–to find out Spider's actual plans. If she was right and he was up to no good, she'd discredit him in both Jewel's and Carl's eyes before she told Carl the truth. She remembered Spider's meeting with Joe and his plan to connect with Vicki. She'd have to discredit him in their eyes as well. Dallas suspected he was part of a land-deal consortium. Perhaps there was more to it, something illegal. She wiped her mouth. An idea formed. Detective Zay Adams worked for the county police department. When they were kids, he was the older man in Dallas's life. Today, he was a sometime boyfriend between the doctors, lawyers, and dentists Dallas dated. Besides all the known criminals, Zay knew many people who worked and lived on the edges of wrong. He might help her.

Roxy put down her napkin. "I'm going to check on Jewel," she said to Carl and the table at large. They had left Jewel home with the dogs, Roxy's cell phone (Jewel's carrier cut off service due to lack of payment), and some vegetable soup. Just as Roxy was about to stand, Spider rose holding a glass of wine.

"May I make a toast?"

The table quieted.

"Thank you, Carl and Roxy, for inviting Nadine and me today and the Quinton clan for once again making a place at your table."

Spider sounded sincere, even to Roxy's ears.

"As you know, we've moved back to Fieldcrest. What you might not know..." He looked at Roxy. "... is that we're here to stay. This is where I come from, where I belong. This is home."

Everyone raised a glass except Roxy.

"Welcome back," Frank said. He took a swig of beer. "Now let's finish up here and get desert going." He pointed his bottle at Celeste. "The Yankees are playing."

"Roxy," Spider said.

Not wanting to appear rude to a guest in front of her in-laws, she paused.

He lifted his glass to her. "To family."

CHAPTER 16

Roxy felt guilty saddling Zoe, Winnie, and Joanna with cleaning up. She doubted
Yolanda, would help. Nevertheless, now was the best time to go. Unable to reach
Dallas on her cell or landline, Roxy decided to find her. She needed to do
something, anything.

Winnie and Joanna sliced the fruit pies Roxy bought from the local bakery.
Under her grandmother Celeste's supervision, Zoe poured coffee into china cups
and brought them out on a tray to the dining room.

"Thanks for covering for me," Roxy said to Winnie. "I'm worried about Jewel.
I'll be back within the hour." Although she hated lying, she had no choice.

Roxy slipped out the back door onto the brick patio. The L-shaped yard
abutted another house in the back, a second house to the east, and the road on the
west side. She hurried down the steps and ran into her brother-in-law.

"Escaping?" B.J. lit a cigarette.

"I thought you'd quit."

A chain-link gate connected two sections of the hedge-camouflaged fence. On
the other side was the sidewalk and street. Roxy glimpsed the roof of the Taurus
over the foliage.

"I did. Three hours with my family drives me to this." He waved the lit
cigarette in the air, then put it to his lips and inhaled. In a steady stream, he sent
the smoke back out through his nose. "Between my father's put downs, Zoe's sneers
at Joanna, my sister's scoffs at Zoe, and my mother's sarcasm for everyone, a

cigarette seemed the least of the evils." He took another drag. "Where're you heading?"

Maybe B.J. could help. After all, Spider had been drinking beer and wine with him all afternoon and something might have slipped. "Three hours with Spider drives *me* out the door."

B.J. didn't take the bait.

"I've got to check on Jewel. And you shouldn't let the crazies ruin your health."

He flicked the unfinished cigarette into an empty flowerpot. "It's kinda strange that Spider is now Carl's bud. What's up with that?"

Thank goodness. Someone else saw how wrong this was. "What do *you* think it's about?" A question Roxy asked herself when Carl first told her he'd run into Spider. The entire family had been at the kitchen table having a rare weekday meal together. Roxy bubbled with news. A call from Vicki's assistant confirmed Vicki's two-week run and the first few rehearsals were great. Although the little ones didn't understand, they caught Roxy's excitement and clapped and cheered for her. "Spider is back," Carl said, slamming down her mood. "He's invited B.J., me, and some of the guys to play poker."

Why was Spider in town, and why would Carl and B.J. hang out with him? Even though Roxy never told them about the rape, they both knew how Spider treated her. When she mentioned this to Carl, he said, "That was a long time ago. Who cares?" Now it all felt like a chess match with Spider the master.

B.J. clicked his lighter on and off. "Carl used to say he hated him."

"Really?" As a girl, she'd always known Carl cared about her, loved her, in fact, for as long as she loved Spider. He proved it. When she told him she was pregnant, he stepped up without hesitation. Of course, he assumed Jewel was his, and she probably was... is.

"Sure. He loved you, and you fell for the biggest hound in school. He knew Spider cheated on you all the time and hated it. So why are they friends now?"

"You gambled with him, right?"

"Once, yeah."

"So, I could ask the same question about you."

Carl and B.J., eleven months apart, ended up in the same grade after B.J.'s fourth grade teacher held him back. It wasn't until the sixth grade that someone besides Carl realized B.J. was intelligent. Turned out he was dyslexic. From the time the brothers turned ten and eleven, they made a pact. Had each other's backs, no matter what. Fought each other's battles. Shouldn't that same loyalty apply to Roxy?

As if reading her mind, B.J. said, "I love you like a sister, but I'm not your husband."

Roxy's voice hitched. "Something's not right."

"I get why you're upset." With his right hand, he cupped Roxy's shoulder. "But the guy comes off pretty positive." He squeezed and dropped his hand. "People can evolve, as they say."

"I suppose."

It was only four o'clock. The sun was still high in the sky and the humidity no less oppressive. An ancient oak offered shade but did little to cool them.

Roxy took an unsatisfying breath. "He and Carl are not in the same league. Spider is a rich tycoon." She knew why he hung around with Carl but what else was going on?

B.J. waggled his head. "I heard Spider and Sandman are into some land deals together. Not Carl's kinda thing."

"Of course not."

"Besides, Carl can take care of himself."

One of Frank's favorite stories was the day Carl pummeled his quicker, older brother. When they were young boys, B.J. often teased Carl. When wrestling, B.J. punched and kicked, besting his baby brother every time. The year Carl turned ten, however, he'd had enough. The way Frank told it, he dragged Carl off B.J. while Carl's fists kept wailing. Both boys received Frank's belt and banishment to bed without super. They never fought each other again and their brotherhood pact cemented.

Roxy watched a yellow-and-black butterfly picnic on the roses, flitting from flower to flower. The rose bushes swayed in the damp breeze. She considered her next words. "I ran into Spider at the theater. I'd hate to see Joe getting involved in anything shady." She studied B.J.'s reaction. "Do you know what kind of land deal?"

"I keep my stuff private and don't poke around in other people's dramas."

"True enough." Even though the two families rarely socialized outside of Sunday dinner, Roxy appreciated her partnership with B.J. at the shop. From everything Roxy knew, B.J. didn't repeat gossip or the confidences he heard from their customers. "I'm not being nosey. Joe might be in trouble. Can't you share who told you about the land deal?"

B.J. shifted from one foot to the other and back again. "I don't even know if it's true."

"What did the *person* say?"

"Miss Lilly." One of their few white customers, an older lady with wrinkled skin and a head full of white hair. She booked with Angel, but if he wasn't free, she liked B. J.

"Really?" Roxy's tone matched her skepticism.

"My point. She's not like that."

Roxy tried one more push. "Jewel is waiting for me. I'm worried about her, but I can't leave without hearing this. I need to give Joe a heads up."

B.J. made a huffing noise. She waited.

"Miss Lilly said Spider and Sandman were trying to buy up good people's houses, trick them out of their land so they can build a development," B.J. said, all the while shaking his head as if discounting his words. "When I acted surprised, kinda doubting her, she explained her husband and Sandman play cards together—have for years—and he overheard a telephone conversation."

"Oh."

"See, I told you it wasn't worth repeating. I mean, her husband hears a private conversation and then repeats it to her, and she whispers in my ear. Who knows how many changes they made with each telling?"

"Still, it could be true."

His second cigarette burned down to a nub without B.J. smoking it. He squeezed the tip and ground it into the bottom of the same flowerpot. Then he scooped both butts out and held them in his hand. "No sense getting my mother into a state." He gave Roxy a sheepish grin. "What are you gonna do?"

Roxy's mind raced. She had to speak with Detective Zay Adams. Vilifying Spider might not be as difficult as she first thought. "It's probably nothing, like you said. I'll keep my eyes and ears opened and give Joe a subtle warning."

"I'll let you know if I hear anything else."

"Appreciate it."

"Perhaps it won't be a bad thing. Fieldcrest needs a boost. It'll help us too, at the shop and school. Suppose they're working on something to save this tired city?" He shrugged. "Just saying."

She gave him a quick peck on his check. "Thanks for trusting and helping me. I'll be back in an hour in case anyone asks."

She hurried out of the yard and climbed into her car. Because Jewel's phone was dead, Roxy had given hers to Jewel in case she got sick in the bathroom or something. Now Roxy had no way of finding Dallas other than driving to her home or office and hoping she was at one of them.

For the first time in days, Roxy's energy surged as she puzzled through Spider and Sandman's connection. Spider's interest in Jewel had nothing to do with a land deal. She guessed Carl was a way to get close to Jewel. Not for the first time, Roxy feared Spider was going to blackmail her—force her to look away as he developed a relationship with Jewel. If she didn't, he'd tell Jewel he was her father. Which he wasn't. Nor for sure. The real estate takeover was something else. Frank had borrowed a hefty sum of money from Sandman, leaving the school and salon swamped with debt. Not illegal. Sandman's fans saw him as a good-guy Godfather. Behind his back, his detractors claimed he was greedy and underhanded, but no one ever accused him of being crooked. So, what were they doing together?

She turned on the engine and it started with the first click. The sun-cooked air inside stifled her. She rolled down the windows and blasted the muggy air out with the air conditioner fans. Sweat coated her face and neck. Still pondering, she pulled out from the parking space and headed for Dallas's house.

At the first light, her mind left the road and focused on her questions. There had to be a connection between what Spider was doing and the theater. Glenn told her they owed millions. To whom or what institution? Dallas suspected a promise to build his school in exchange for cooperation around the land buy-ups. People respected Joe. They listened to him. Sandman served as chair of the board of trustees of the theater and the conduit to the anonymous donor, the theater's largest benefactor. Was Spider the anonymous donor? That sounded far-fetched but then again, she shouldn't rule anything out. When Roxy asked Glenn, the Director of Philanthropy, if Laura Garrison was the largest secret benefactor, he'd said no because she gave annually under her own name. It was confusing, but Roxy had to figure it out.

One avenue of inquiry was the connection between Spider, Sandman, and Joe. Another was how Vicki and Dallas fit in. Why offer Dallas double her commission? Was he trying to bribe Dallas, so she'd help him get to Jewel? And his call to Vicki was strange. Plus, he intimated that he'd get Vicki to show up for Saturday's rehearsal which didn't happen. More threads to unknot.

Roxy's family and Joe declared Spider a changed man and the future savior of Fieldcrest. That, she didn't believe.

Her head throbbed with questions and suppositions, her mind going over the pieces of the jigsaw puzzle in a loop. She needed someone to help her get at the truth.

CHAPTER 17

Dallas lived on West Obama and Fifth, a wide street of private, semi-attached homes, most owned by families of Caribbean descent. Each had a strip of grass separating a footpath and driveway. Five steps led up to the front doors. Aluminum awnings provided shelter from rain and sun. Dallas's home stood out from the rest. Instead of grass, she planted beds of basil, thyme, and sage, each thriving despite the draught. A curving bay window jutted out over the driveway and miniature herb garden. Most of the homes had screen doors and, behind the screens, wooden doors painted the same color as the rest of the house. Not Dallas's place. Hers, painted a deep purple, had a wreath of dried roses, eucalyptus, and crab apples hanging from a bright red sash. The welcome mat had SWAN printed in large letters.

Roxy rang the bell and waited. She pressed it again and then banged on the door just in case. Hearing nothing, she peered through the bay window but saw no lights. Roxy headed for Dallas's office. Her business often meant working weekends. When she left Roxy earlier in the day, Dallas mentioned going shopping, but how long might that take?

Five minutes later, Roxy reached the real estate storefront. Seeing Dallas's minivan in front, Roxy parked and jumped out. A "Welcome, We're Open," sign hung from the front door. Bells jangled as Roxy entered.

"Hey, you," Dallas said. She came from behind her desk with a grin on her face. Shed of her church dress, she wore a blazer over a T-shirt that topped a pair of jeans. She'd swept up her braids in a cloth wrap and gold hoop earrings hung from her lobes.

"I went to your house first..." Roxy gave Dallas an inquiring look. "I figured you'd finished shopping and might be home."

"Groceries bought and stored. Doesn't take much to feed one."

"I came here half-hoping not to find you working on a Sunday afternoon."

Dallas's laugh was soft. "A client kept buzzing me all morning. His thumb drive is full."

"What does that mean?"

"No room in his brain for any additional information."

Roxy chuckled.

"I came in to deal with his issues." Dallas slid over two leather sling chairs. "Rest yours." She sat. "How did you escape from Ma and Pa Crank?"

"Not easily." Roxy settled into the offered chair. It had been a while since she'd been to the office. "New wall hangings?"

"I swept them up at this great African mask market in Harlem."

Five fierce masks hung intermingled between Dallas's college and graduate school diplomas, real estate license, and several awards from local women's organizations and the mayor's office.

Roxy asked, "What do they signify?"

"The hell if I know." Dallas kicked off her platform sandals. "I use them to ward off deadbeats trying to stiff me."

Roxy slipped out of her shoes as well. "And too-ardent suitors?"

Now Dallas laughed with more gusto. "I just liked them."

"Darn." Roxy jumped up and grabbed the office phone sitting on Dallas's desk. "I need to check on Jewel." She dialed her home phone. "She's not feeling well."

"Hello," Jewel said, her voice sounding sleepy.

"How are you?"

"A little better. When are you coming home?"

Roxy smiled at Dallas and gave a thumbs up, letting her know Jewel was fine. "In a couple of hours."

Dallas tugged on Roxy's arm. "Tell her I'll be there within the hour."

Roxy mouthed her thanks to Dallas. "Auntie Dallas is coming by."

"Can she bring me some vanilla Häagen Dazs?"

Covering the phone with her palm, Roxy mouthed the request to Dallas.

"Anything for my goddaughter."

"Sure," Roxy said into the phone. "Meanwhile, drink lots of water and don't forget to take an aspirin every four hours to get your fever down. We'll be home soon." She hung up. "Thanks. I think she's lonely."

"More like relieved. She's probably not even sick. Has a boy over there."

Roxy made a face. "You jest, but there may be some truth in those words." She plopped back into the chair and tucked her feet under.

"Get out."

"Ed somebody."

"Our little girl has a boyfriend? Is it someone other than the baby-daddy?"

"You know who the baby's father is?"

"Whoa, Mommy. I have no idea."

Dallas loved Jewel. She cared about all of Roxy's children, but Jewel was her favorite. The day Jewel was born, Dallas was in the delivery room with Carl. She became Jewel's godmother, played with her in the park, took her to Disney World for her tenth birthday, and, for several of her younger teen years, to the nail spa once a month. They were pals.

Roxy lowered the volume and pitch of her voice. "I'm not sure who Ed is, but right now, he's the least of my worries."

"I'll probe a bit. Gently, of course," Dallas said.

"Max seems to have info." Roxy shoved the conversations with Max and Jewel aside. She had to focus. "Have you met Laura Garrison?"

"Sure, why?"

"She's sponsoring my play."

"Now I like her even more." She shot a broad grin at Roxy.

"What's she like? I read about her in the local paper, but there wasn't a lot of info."

Dallas looked up toward the ceiling. "Hmm. Private. Smart and elegant. Married money and made more. My kind of woman."

"Well connected?"

"Yep. Arts, business, and political folks of all stripes. Well-liked by everyone. Kinda like Joe. Where's this going?"

"I want to meet her. Vicki's bailing on me and I'm hoping Ms. Garrison can help bring her back."

"Not the wicked witch again. Forget her."

Roxy made a disapproving face. "I can't. Everything hinges on Vicki appearing opening night and being magnificent."

"How's Laura going to help?"

Roxy hadn't worked it all out yet. "I need Vicki for at least one week. It's critical, and she's gotta come to the last rehearsals. We're running out of time."

"How many more?" Dallas asked. "Opening night is damn close."

"Two. I'm desperate."

Dallas puffed out her cheeks and shook her head. Her earrings swung and glittered in the light. "Rumor has it, Laura and Joe had a thing. Not sure when this was and who was married to whom, but the tale ends with Laura breaking his heart."

"Isn't she white?"

"Yeah, so?"

"Nothing." Roxy felt silly. It was just that Joe was so pro-Black and brown. It surprised her. "What else can you tell me?"

"Laura has tons of connections in Manhattan too including Lincoln Center."

"I need a favor."

"An introduction?"

"No. I've got that covered. Remember, I'm going to the theater's board meeting tomorrow and she's a member." Roxy paused for a half-second. "Spider is up to no good."

Dallas didn't come back with one of her sharp comments.

"What?"

Dallas said. "It's possible."

"Probable."

"Tell me what you're thinking."

"I mean something more than hanging out with Carl and bothering Jewel and buying land near the theater."

Dallas stayed quiet.

Roxy plowed on. "I heard from a reliable source." She stopped. "I heard from a semi-reliable source that Spider and Sandman might be involved in a shady land deal—something illegal."

"Where'd you hear this?"

"From B.J. who got it from one of our customers." Roxy's voice went down an octave. "Who heard it from her husband, who overheard a private conversation." She knew she appeared as embarrassed as she felt.

"Uh-huh." Dallas pursed her lips and rolled her eyes.

"It's worth checking out. I need leverage."

"I'll do more sleuthing tomorrow."

All afternoon Roxy had tried to decode Spider's behavior, but she needed facts and now Dallas had a stake in the outcome. If Spider were for real, Dallas could make a lot of money. Her father said that Fieldcrest needed a knight. Was that who Spider was? "Actually, I was hoping you'd ask Zay to look into it for me."

"Oh no." Dallas feet landed hard on the floor.

"He can unearth intel fast. If it's true, that Spider is here to save us, let's find out."

"I'm not asking Zay Adams for squat."

"This is life and death stuff, Dee-Dee," Roxy said, using the childhood nickname they'd made up the summer they became blood sisters. Ro-Ro and Dee-Dee, sisters forever, in life and death. They'd sliced their fingers with a knife, something they watched in an old, corny western, and pressed their bloody fingers together, all the while making disgusted sounds. "Why not?"

"This is real life, and nobody is dying."

"I'd ask him myself," Roxy said. She interlocked her fingers. "But you know he won't do it for me." She cocked her head to one side. "For some reason, I'm not one of his favorites."

"Oh, because you called him names, and accused him of taking advantage of me and—"

Roxy raised her hands in surrender. "No need to recite the complete list."

"I can find out what you need without Detective Adams."

Roxy leaned forward. Her long skirt gathered around her bare feet. "It *is* life and death. He believes Jewel's his daughter." She sucked in her breath. There, she said it aloud, almost stated the whole thing to the one person who already knew the truth. "I can't tell Carl or Jewel it's a possibility until I discredit Spider."

Dallas eyes, round and bright, stared into Roxy's. "This is a hot mess. Tell Carl about the rape and do it before another day goes by."

"I can't."

"He'll forgive you for not telling him earlier, and he'll understand your pain and actions."

"What can I say to him?"

"The truth." Dallas sounded exasperated.

Roxy hadn't noticed it before, but soft classical music played in the background. Usually, Dallas swung her hips to reggae or R&B, her iPhone air pods plugged into her ears. Street sounds mingled with the strings and horns. Roxy tried to gather her thoughts, to find a way to explain her rationale and plan to Dallas. "All these years have gone by..."

"He loves you and the kids." She crossed her arms. "He loves Jewel."

Roxy's throat and cheeks burned. "Here's the thing. If I can show Carl what a sleaze Spider is, then..." She hung her head. "It's all I've got."

Dallas's voice rose with indignation. "What happened wasn't your fault. We've had this conversation."

Roxy lifted her head. "I know."

"Do you? Because I'm not hearing conviction."

"I'm trying."

The two friends stayed quiet.

After several seconds, Dallas asked, "What if Spider's the real deal?"

"At dinner today, Spider said he's here to help. He gave Jewel a job and made sure Carl won money at a high-stakes poker game."

Dallas squeezed Roxy's shoulder and then dropped her arm. "Did you ever do a paternity test with Carl's DNA?"

"No."

"I just thought that maybe early on—"

"Carl is her father. Period. DNA or not." Tears formed in the corners of Roxy's eyes. She studied the pattern of the rug underfoot, it's blue and green swirls almost moving like ocean waves. "Please help me."

Dallas, standing over Roxy, said, "Zay called. Asked if he can come by tonight."

"That's great. Bring it up then."

"Said he had something important to tell me."

Roxy heard the catch in Dallas's voice. "Like what?"

"He's leaving town? Has cancer? Let's stop dancing around and get married?"

"What do you want?"

"Zay isn't the answer."

"For you?"

"For your investigation."

Roxy ran her tongue along her lower lip. She waited.

"I'm not comfortable."

"I get it." Asking Dallas to get Zay involved wasn't fair. Those two had a complicated relationship and Roxy shouldn't make it harder.

When Dallas was sixteen, they'd met at a party thrown by a high school senior and his older brother. Dallas, Vicki, and Roxy had dressed at Roxy's house while her father worked overtime. No one to see them shimmy into skinny jeans and off-the-shoulder tops, clothes forbidden by their respective parents. Vicki helped them apply makeup—mascara, blush, and lipstick—so they'd appear older, mature, and sophisticated.

Roxy remembered how dark the foyer was, with no supervising adults in sight. The smell of marijuana, booze, and body heat hung heavy in the air. The three teens made their way to the basement where the tunes rocked the floor. Vicki lit up, but neither Dallas nor Roxy knew how to inhale. Instead, they sipped a fizzy drink that made Roxy's head throb.

They stood on the edge of the dancing, wriggling their hips to the beat. Then they saw him.

Walking with a confident swagger that none of the high school boys had achieved, he kept his eyes on Dallas. Small even teeth except for the two eyeteeth slightly crooked and pointing inward, hooded eyes, and a quick smile that softened an old-man expression, Zay Adams was everything Dallas's parents rejected for their only girl.

Back then, Dallas had to climb out the window of the third-floor apartment because her parents were old school. No boys, no dates. Group activities only. She and Zay snuck around. He attended John Jay College studying law, drove a sleek Camaro, and had a full-time job in his father's machine shop. When he took Dallas to clubs, no one asked her for ID. She was with Zay.

When they found out, the adult Swans went crazy. Under pressure, Dallas broke up with him. Her parents sent her to Jamaica for the summer. When she returned, Zay had moved on.

Roxy knew all this but was desperate and her emotions a jumble. Perhaps Dallas was right, that getting dirt on Spider wouldn't make it any easier to tell Carl and Jewel. There might not be any dirt. Spider could be a good guy, and then she'd have involved Dallas and Zay for nothing and left Carl and Jewel hating Roxy for the rest of her life. On the other hand, if Spider was bad news, if he was going to hurt her family, the theater, and the community, she *must* expose him, whether or not it saved her.

"I need your help," Roxy said again.

Dallas made a funny sound in her throat, a cross between a groan and a cough. She leveled her gaze on Roxy. "Of course, I'll help you, but this is a bad idea."

Roxy slumped into her seat. She was fresh out of better ones.

CHAPTER 18

The drive back to Roxy's in-laws took fifteen minutes. Sunday afternoon traffic was light. Roxy found a parking spot a block away. The gate to the backyard stayed opened on Sundays, allowing grandchildren to play in and around the house. Today, probably because of the heat, the yard was empty. Roxy snuck in the way she'd left.

Winnie glanced up from the dishwasher. "How's Jewel? We were getting worried."

"Better, just tired; her godmother is with her now." Roxy grabbed a set of heavy-duty rubber gloves and pulled them on. She plunged her hands into the soapy water. "Why do we buy into her ridiculous notion that dishes require washing before putting them in the dishwasher?"

"Because it's her home, not ours," said Joanna. She wrapped leftovers and squeezed them into the refrigerator. "Besides, she'd go insane."

"Remember last Thanksgiving when we tried to use paper plates?" Roxy chuckled at the memory. "I can still see her purple face."

"We were mean," Winnie said. She took off the apron she wore over a pink halter dress. "What's your take on Spider's wife? She didn't utter a word the entire afternoon."

Joanna said, "I liked her.

Winnie said, "I don't know about her, but he's a dream. Rich, handsome, funny... What's he doing with Nadine? She's not the most attractive woman." Winnie wrinkled her nose. She'd inherited a small, straight one from her grandmother on her mother's side and, along with her light complexion and long hair, acted like she was *it*. Roxy liked her despite the affectations.

Joanna said, "B.J. told me you and Spider used to be sweethearts when you were kids."

Roxy loaded the dishwasher with the now-clean dishes. "A zillion years ago. I have no idea who he is today."

• • •

Carl, Dallas, and Roxy watched from the bedroom doorway. Jewel sat propped up on a pillow in Roxy and Carl's room. The ceiling and floor fans moved the warm air around. Half-empty glasses of water and iced tea sat on the end table on Roxy's side.

The twins rushed in and climbed on the bed.

"Are you sick? Is the baby being born?" Kia asked snuggling next to Jewel. "Can I touch your tummy? Is she moving around? Does she have the hiccups today?"

"I let her hang out in here. Hope that was okay," Dallas said.

"Sure." The little house on the corner popped into Roxy's mind. She pictured everyone in his or her own bedroom, each with a flat screen television and an air-conditioner in the window or central air like her in-laws' house. Two baths and a powder room. A basement turned into a playroom.

"I'd better get going," Dallas said. "Zay's coming over tonight."

Carl asked, "When are you going to marry that man?"

"Have you met me?" Dallas asked with a laugh. "A bumblebee sipping nectar from all the flowers."

"More like a wasp if you ask me." Carl joined in the laughter.

Dallas turned and gave him an eye-roll. "Watch it, big boy, my sting is lethal."

"Thanks for all your help. Can't imagine what we'd do without you," Carl said.

Dallas made a mini curtsey. "You're welcome."

He gave Dallas a quick hug and then turned to Roxy. "I'll get the twins to bed."

Dallas whispered, "He's in a positive mood. Dinner at the Cranks went better than expected?"

Roxy understood Dallas's question. "Yeah, Carl and I are good."

"Ooh-La-La. Sounds like some loving is on the agenda tonight."

"You're so bad." Roxy hugged her friend. "You won't forget about asking Zay."

"I've got this. Enjoy your evening."

•   •   •

As soon as Max vacated the bathroom, Roxy rushed in. What she craved was a cool bath, but that would hold everyone else up. Instead, she showered, letting the tepid water bring down her body temperature. It *had* been a good day despite the row in the garden and Spider's presence. She'd learned something. Information she could use to make it easier to confess. Zay was an experienced detective. Surely, he'd uncover whatever was going on. What didn't happen today, was anything that got her closer to her house. She hated that their future rested in other people's hands. What was *she* going to do about Vicki? Frank's words stayed in her head. It was time for Roxy to take more control.

She slipped off the shower cap, wrapped a towel around her torso, shuffled to their bedroom, dropped the towel, and climbed into bed.

Carl entered and closed the door. "Finally." He stepped out of his slacks, hung them on a hanger, and then unbuttoned his shirt.

Roxy watched from the bed, naked under the sheet. "It keeps getting harder to get the crew into bed."

"Did you check on Jewel?" he asked.

"Uh-huh. She said she's fine but I'm going to take her to the doctor tomorrow."

"Maybe you should get a checkup too." Carl tossed his shirt into the hamper by the closet door. "Check out why you're so tired."

"Stress–the play and everything."

"I'm sorry."

This was the second time today Carl had apologized. Was he offering sympathy or was there something more? "For?"

"My part in your worries." Carl slid under the covers next to her.

On most Sunday evenings they made love–something Roxy looked forward to. For a sweet hour of foreplay, sex, and afterglow, she stopped living in her head. Troubles, kids, work, the play–all melted away. She became only nerve endings and joy. Times, however, weren't usual. He still hadn't mentioned the money he'd won. She inched closer and put her head on his shoulder.

With a light touch, she caressed Carl's chest. After her mother left, Roxy had slid into a depression so deep the school psychologist met with her weekly for several months. Roxy cried through the sessions. Her father was so sad. If she moped around all the time, it made him gloomier. During one session two months in, Ms. Dash asked, "When you think about your grownup future, what are you doing?"

"Writing plays," Roxy said, half expecting the woman to laugh. She didn't.

On more than one occasion, Ms. Dash told her, "Negative thoughts and energy bring negative results. Believe in your dreams, and work toward them every day, no matter the odds."

Pastor Went urged her to believe in herself the way God believed in her. Every time Roxy lost her way, which was often, the psychologist's and minister's voices lifted her back onto her path. She wished she could give Carl some of that.

"How did rehearsal go yesterday?" Carl shifted under the sheets and covered Roxy's hand with his own. "Did Vicki show?"

"Fine." She didn't want to talk about Vicki or the rehearsal or anything else.

Carl clicked off the lamp on his side of the bed then rolled onto his back.

Roxy moved her hand down his chest, her fingers playing with the soft hairs, inching along his stomach, and stopping at his dense pubic hairs, thick and curly. After a few teasing seconds, he lowered her hand until she wrapped it around the base of his penis and ran it along from bottom to top.

"I'll let you keep doing that, but only for another hour." An old joke between them.

Tiny droplets of semen oozed out. Carl moaned and rolled over, pressing Roxy onto her back.

"Your turn," he said, his voice husky. He kissed her. She rose to meet his mouth, her back arched. They kissed with swirling, probing tongues. His lips moved down her neck. Tiny kisses gave her shivers. She loved this part. His fingers rubbed her clit while his kisses moved to her breasts. He sucked each nipple.

Stroking her clit and still sucking her nipples, he repeated movements they both knew worked well. Her vaginal scent filled the surrounding air. Roxy arched against his fingers as he sank two inside her. Her groan of pleasure matched his in volume and intensity.

Carl straddled her. Using one hand, she helped him enter, guiding the tip while she stroked its length.

"That okay?"

"M'm, M'm, Good," she said, another old joke.

Together they moved back and forth in a steady push-pull; his hands gripped her buttocks. Roxy reached an almost painful pitch, on the edge of, but not quite. The exquisite intensity left her breaths ragged and her mind empty.

Carl moved faster, harder, and then a last thrust. He cried out softly, always mindful of the children. "I love you," he said into her hair.

She kissed his lips and cheeks. "I love you so much," she said with fervor.

For a long time, they lay curled up, spoon-fashion. Carl breathed slower, quieter, and Roxy knew he'd fallen asleep. Making her movements small so as not to wake him, she inched away from the curve of his body. The sheets, damp from their perspiration, bunched under her. She rolled over onto her back.

The whir of the ceiling fan mingled with Carl's gentle snores creating a usually comforting music. Hearing Carl declare his love was something she needed. Reassurance. She hugged herself. Today and tonight were both good.

She closed her eyes and tried to sleep. Although exhausted, rest eluded her. Images of Spider and Jewel swirled in her mind. As much as she tried to stop them, they wove and danced, sometimes intermingled with scenes from her play.

The clock on her nightstand read 12:20 a.m. Roxy swung her legs over the side of the bed, stood up, and put on her robe, an aged-thin-to-ragged cotton leftover. She padded across the narrow hallway, clutching the robe around her and into the bathroom and washed up. She shuffled into the kitchen, trying to be extra quiet so as not to wake Max. Only drapes separated the kitchen and living room where he slept. She groped her way to the gas stove and switched on the burner under the teakettle. Click, click, click. Blue flames leapt up and spread along its base. A cup of chamomile tea would soothe her.

She sat in the dark kitchen and waited for the water to boil, trying to think and act with positivity, hold on to her dreams and plans. Ms. Dash's voice echoed in her head. "You can be anything and accomplish everything you set your mind to doing." Pastor Went's voice, a prayer. "God believes in you."

CHAPTER 19
MONDAY

Jewel and Roxy sat in the OB-GYN waiting room. Pink-and-blue-stenciled stuffed animals decorated the walls. Pregnant women with swollen bellies, some with young children perched on their diminished laps, filled every seat, with only a few older women sprinkled around. It was 9:00 a.m.

"I don't get why you were sleeping in the kitchen," Jewel said.

"I *don't get why* everyone was so upset about it." Roxy mimicked Jewel's expression and tone.

"Because we all think you and Daddy are getting divorced." Jewel pulled out the iPhone Dallas gave her for her birthday. Earlier, Roxy had paid the overdue bill and now the smart phone was in full working order.

"At least Max does." Jewel inserted the ear buds and appeared to focus on selecting her playlist rather than speak to her mother. "Are you?"

Of course, the kids were frightened. A crowded waiting room wasn't the best place to have this conversation, but Roxy had to put an end to her children's anxiety. "Your father isn't leaving us."

All her muscles ached as if she'd been working out. Last night, after her tea, she put her head down on the kitchen table for a few minutes and the next thing she knew it was morning.

She pressed her fingers against her temples. "Things are rugged, but everything is okay with us."

That was true last night but not this morning. The list of problems was getting longer and the stakes higher. Roxy hoped she sounded more confident than she felt. She glanced over at Jewel to see how she was taking Roxy's reassurances. Jewel didn't appear to be listening. "We're fine," Roxy said, her voice louder.

"If you say so." Jewel's thumbs flew over the keyboard of her phone.

"I do."

Jewel raised her head. "He doesn't come home, and you sleep in the kitchen... sounds all good to me."

"Sarcasm is a poor substitute for actual conversation." Roxy couldn't believe she'd said that. It was one of her mother's favorite quips to Roxy's father. Was that why they broke up? No honest discussions. Did they trust each other? Roxy's lack of openness with Carl filled her with shame. She had to right things.

"Jewel Quinton?" A woman in a bright pink smock stood at the doorway between the waiting and exam rooms. Jewel waved her hand. "I'm fine too. I don't know why you've dragged me here."

"Persistent fever—101."

Jewel struggled up. "Hold my stuff." She removed the ear buds, slid her phone into a pocket of her backpack, and gave the bag to her mother.

Roxy gave her a look.

"*Please.*" And then, sounding alarmed, "You don't expect to come in with me, do you?"

"Just when it's time to speak with the doctor, after the exam." She took Jewel's silence as agreement.

Roxy sat back and closed her eyes. The day had started rough. Carl appeared as much hurt as worried when he found her asleep in the kitchen with her head resting on her arms. She'd offered a silly explanation, excused herself, and checked on Jewel. The fever remained. When she shared this with Carl, he was almost nonresponsive. By the time the twins and Max were up, his chill had turned icy.

Roxy picked up *People* magazine, supplied for waiting patients, and thumbed through it, looking mostly at the pictures, and only reading their captions. She clocked Jewel's backpack on the seat next to her. Snooping wasn't right. Jewel was old enough to enjoy her privacy without concern. But who was Ed? And what was going on between Jewel and Spider? Roxy had a responsibility to ensure her daughter's safety. She dug into the side pocket and tugged out the phone.

Clicking on contacts and then on search, she typed in Spider's name. Nothing came up except his address and phone numbers–cell, work, and home. No email address, which seemed odd. Perhaps he preferred texting. Argh. Get a grip. He hadn't told Jewel anything, so Roxy was worrying too much. She pondered for a minute, holding Jewel's phone. Ed popped back into her mind. The baby's father? After clicking on the message icon, she keyed in his name. A stream of texts emerged. She tapped the latest one before realizing her mistake. A blue dot indicated Jewel hadn't read it yet. Damn.

"Mrs. Quinton?"

Roxy jumped. The phone bounced off the chair and onto the carpet. The magazine slid to the floor. "Coming." She stuffed Jewel's phone back into the backpack, swung her own bag over her shoulder, and lifted Jewel's in her right hand.

"This way, please."

The nurse had a Boston accent, reminding Roxy of their vacation three children ago. Vacation–a foreign concept these days. The last time the family went anywhere together for more than a long weekend was before the twins were born.

Flushed and guilty, Roxy followed. "Is everything alright?"

"The doctor will explain," the nurse said in a soothing voice.

Roxy followed her down a narrow hallway, past several small exam rooms on the right and left of the corridor. When they reached the doctor's office at the end of the hall, the nurse ushered Roxy in with a wave of her hand.

Jewel, seated on an upholstered chair, raised feverish eyes.

A woman, who looked barely older than Jewel put out her hand and introduced herself. "Dr. Melanie Clinton. I'm covering for Dr. Wu, who is not in today."

"Oh." They'd been working with Dr. Wu for the entire pregnancy. A small Asian woman from Hong Kong, with bright black eyes and ivory skin, she used an American first name–Wendy. Dallas recommended her, and Roxy trusted her.

"Please have a seat."

Roxy slid into the chair next to Jewel. Sweating palms left a damp handprint on her slacks.

"Jewel has a virus, and it's nothing to worry about, not serious at all."

Without waiting for Roxy to respond or ask a question, the doctor continued. "She needs bed rest and lots of fluids." She paused, clasped her hands, and leaned forward. "I am, however, concerned about the size of the baby. She's big for such a slight woman."

Roxy's heart rocketed in her chest.

"We're going to monitor her. Dr. Wu may recommend inducing labor or consider a Cesarean."

"When will she be back?" Roxy asked.

"She's ill."

"What if something happens?" Jewel asked.

"I'll be your physician or one of my colleagues. Please don't worry."

Roxy slowed her breathing and straightened her shoulders, trying to appear calm for Jewel's sake.

"Meanwhile, let's schedule an ultrasound ASAP," Dr. Clinton continued.

"Too big for what?" Jewel asked. "I don't understand."

The doctor smiled in a way that reminded Roxy of Vicki–barely tolerant. Dr. Wu was warm and patient. Roxy did not like Dr. Clinton.

"A precaution. The baby looks and sounds healthy."

"Mom?" Jewel's eyes dug into her mother's.

Blood pounded through Roxy's veins filling her eardrums and making so much noise, she was sure everyone in the room heard it as well. She forced a smile. "It's going to be okay. I promise."

•

No one spoke during the ride home. The doctor had been vague about the implications of a "too big" baby. When they peered at the ultrasound, they saw a healthy girl floating in Jewel's amniotic fluid, her tiny heart beating.

When Jewel was born, fear gripped. Roxy didn't have younger siblings or cousins. None of her friends had married or made babies yet, so she had no one to ask questions. Her father appeared more frightened than she was. When she asked Carl questions, since he had a younger sister, he listened but offered no comforting answers. She never felt more alone.

Jewel interrupted her thoughts. "How do you like the name Iris?"

"Huh?"

"For the baby–Iris Quinton?"

Roxy signaled and then pulled the car over. She couldn't drive and have *this* conversation.

"Have you changed your mind?" Roxy asked. Until this moment, Roxy believed she was ambivalent, wanting Jewel to keep the baby but also afraid of the emotional and financial cost. But now, hearing the baby's name, Iris, wiped away all doubt. She fought to keep her tone level. "Tell me what you're thinking."

"Don't get mad."

"Why would I be mad? This is—"

"Spider believes it's wrong to put the baby up for adoption."

"Spider?" Her mind flashed back to the conversation in Celeste's kitchen. It was clear he had a plan of his own for Jewel and her baby that he'd already put in motion.

"Sunday, after Auntie Dallas left, he called to check on me."

"I see."

"You don't. That's what you mean."

"This is sudden."

"I can change my mind."

"Of course." The joy Roxy felt seconds ago, vanished.

Elbows resting on her thighs, Jewel propped her head up with both hands. "I know I screwed up."

"I had you young." Roxy kept the sadness and shame out of her voice. "Teenagers make mistakes. Everyone does."

"I feel bad for the family."

"For us?"

"The adoptive couple."

Roxy pictured a not-so-young man and woman counting the days and setting up the nursery. "This decision has to be right for you. Not them or me and your dad and certainly not for a total stranger, who you only just met."

"I'm trying to figure out my life." She lifted her head and eyes, peering at Roxy under half-mast lids. "I'm tired all the time and angry and cry a lot."

Grownup life is hard, and you are in it too soon. "Normal reactions at nine months." Roxy remembered weeping and yelling through April and May. Thanks to Dallas and Vicki, Carl missed most of it. By the time he returned from the beauty school and his job, she greeted him with a smile and a late supper.

Roxy reached for Jewel's hand. "Let's talk more tonight and go by the church and sit awhile. Seek guidance."

"That's what you would do."

"Yes."

"That's not me."

Silence fell between them. Roxy imagined all the dueling emotions in the car like two rivers merging, their currents moving in different directions. She spun the wheel left, leaving the curb, and pointed the Taurus toward home.

They parked in front of their apartment building.

Roxy said, "It's okay with me."

"That I keep her?"

"Uh-huh." Despite Spider, Roxy's happiness resurfaced. This was a huge and scary decision, but it felt right. Still, the choice had to be Jewel's and hers alone. In the end, Roxy wanted to do right by Jewel and the baby.

"Anyway, I'm not sure." Jewel started to cry.

Roxy reached over, leaning across the gearshift console, and held her daughter close. "I understand. We'll figure it out together."

Jewel snuffled and lifted her head. "Do you hate your mother?"

Whenever Roxy brought up her mother, Jewel accused Roxy of being self-absorbed. "Everything is always about you," she'd said.

"No. I wish I knew why she left." She sucked air deep into her lungs and let it out. How to explain? "At first, I missed her so much I made bargains with God-if you send her back, I'll do my chores without Dad asking, I'll get all As at school. Later, in my teens, I became angry. What kind of mother deserts her child? Now, I wish her well. Hope she's alive and happy somewhere. She left the summer I turned twelve."

"Did you ever see her again, or hear from her?"

"A note came in the mail a few days after she walked out."

My darling girl, this is not your fault. Always remember I love you. Your father will explain. Be good. Study hard. Say your prayers every night. I'll keep you in mine.
With all my love,
Mom

"Did your father explain, like she said?"

Roxy laughed—a quick burst of a humph. "He was as confused as I was and as devastated."

"Why do you think she ghosted like that?"

"No clue. Postcards arrived from different places and then nothing." Roxy snapped fingers. "She vanished."

"Did you ever look for her?"

"I begged my dad to find her, but he said she'd decided, and he had to honor it. I must have cried myself to sleep for a year."

Jewel said in a quiet voice, "I don't want Iris to think I don't love her, like you said." She rested her head on Roxy's shoulder.

Roxy handed a crumpled stack of tissues to Jewel. Soon, clogged-air nose-blowing replaced the sounds of weeping.

"I don't know what to do."

"You'll figure it out. Whatever happens next is up to you, not Dad or Spider or me." She bit her tongue, rejected the warning in her head and added, "or Ed."

Jewel looked up. "What?"

CHAPTER 20

The sweet scent of hair spray filled the air as Roxy finished her customer's up-do, a practice session for the young woman's wedding. Hand mirror held high, the customer eyed her hair from every angle, twisting this way and that.

"Can you pull out a few curls around my face?"

Using the tail end of a narrow comb, Roxy freed several curls as both women watched via the wall mirror. Brides were the toughest, but Roxy loved it when she got it right-women glowing like queens.

"I'd like it softer around my face."

Dallas's reflection came into view as she approached Roxy's station.

"I've got news," Dallas said. She turned her attention to Roxy's customer, cocked her head to one side, index finger and thumb on her chin. "You're beautiful. Your hair looks stunning."

The bride-to-be beamed.

"So, we're all finished here?" Roxy asked the twenty-something woman, suppressing a laugh. Dallas was shameless.

Jingling bracelets accompanied the click of Dallas's shoes pacing the tiled floor. "Just be another sec," Roxy said to Dallas. "You can pay Zoe," she said to her customer. "See you on the big day."

The minute the young woman was out of the seat, Dallas walked Roxy to the back of the salon where they stood close together in the dark hallway near the bathrooms and the spaces used for eyebrow and lip waxes. Balanced on a card table, the coffee machine gurgled next to an open box of now stale doughnuts, their iced heads shining pink and orange under a hanging light bulb.

"Zay has intel."

"Good news?" There was something about Dallas's tone that worried Roxy.

"We're to meet on his lunch break, which is now. Can you get away?"

"That was fast."

"He has lots of databases at his fingertips."

"Give me the headlines."

"We have just enough time to get over there," Dallas said, already moving toward the front. "Angel be a sweetie and cover for Roxy. Something important has come up."

Angel glanced up from a magazine and swiveled around in his seat. "Like there's any business to cover." He made an amused sound. "You got it. No stress."

Mondays were usually one of their slowest days but this one was dead. Roxy followed Dallas to the front door.

"Thanks, I'll be back in..." She gave Dallas a questioning look.

"A half-hour or less," Dallas said.

•   •

Detective Zay Adams was as tall as Joe Dawes and as skinny as anyone Roxy had ever known. Because he had a big head, Carl used to call him the Black Q-Tip but never to his face. They were sitting in Subway, the fast-food restaurant around the corner from the beauty shop. Dallas and Roxy sat on one side of the bolted-to-the-floor table and Zay on the other. He bit deep into a turkey sandwich oozing with yellow-brown mustard. Roxy barely touched her ham and Swiss. Dallas gulped down the last of her water.

"So?" Roxy shredded her napkin.

"According to my sources," Zay began. "Booth is going to be at the theater's board meeting tonight presenting a financial blueprint for developing the entire block including a drama school for underprivileged youth."

Roxy's heart sank. "It's legitimate?"

Dallas nodded her head. "He's giving them an interest-free-crazy loan."

Fear crept up Roxy's spine. It sounded like good news for the theater and good for Fieldcrest's children. Where was the evil?

As if picking up on Dallas's attempt to comfort Roxy, Zay added, "I haven't finished digging."

Dallas, her liquid brown eyes wide, said, "Spider is getting accommodations plus Joe's support for the rest of the project."

"Like what?"

Zay answered. "No details yet."

"But you're not sure–I mean, you didn't find out if there is anything underhanded?"

"Nope." Zay popped the last bit of sandwich into his mouth. "I gotta tell ya. Fieldcrest's time is now. This could be what we need."

"Traitor," said Dallas. Her voice was tight, and the word sounded heavy with emotion.

Zay stared at Dallas for several beats. Then, tilting his head way back, he drained his cup. "All I'm saying is that it sounds legit to me." He paused. "And right on time."

Roxy sagged in her chair.

"We've just begun to investigate." Dallas looked pointedly at Zay.

"Just saying." Zay kept his eyes on Dallas. "He might be legit."

If that were true, reasoning with him and helping him understand that being a part of Jewel's life would destroy her family might make him back off. She intended to go to the board meeting to meet Laura Garrison, corner Spider, and find out more. She'd checked and found out the meeting started at four. "Thanks, Zay." She turned to her friend. "I appreciate both of you taking the time."

"Sure," Dallas said.

Zay waved Roxy's thanks away, watching Dallas, as if waiting for something.

Roxy stood up. "I have to run to the john. Be right back." She'd give them a few minutes. The tension between Dallas and Zay was palpable.

Coming back to their table, Roxy eyed them. They appeared to be sitting in a loud silence.

"I've got to get back to the station." Zay's eyes darted toward and away from Dallas like a nervous teenager.

"Thanks again," Roxy said, watching her friend but Dallas gave nothing away.

All three gathered their belongings and stepped out onto the sidewalk just as thunder rolled through the afternoon sky. The wet heat caused beads of sweat to pop out on Roxy's forehead. She swiped them away with the back of her hand.

"Well," Zay said, "I guess that's that."

Dallas stared straight ahead.

Zay waited for another second and then walked away.

Thunder rumbled again. The sky grew dark with the swiftness of a storm-driven wind. Black clouds blanketed the sky. Roxy glanced at her friend. Dallas slapped her hands on the tops of thighs, her bracelets laying a track over the drumbeat.

"What happened last night?" Roxy remembered Zay had something to ask Dallas. "What did he say?"

The music of bracelets and thigh slapping stopped.

Roxy shifted gears. "Sounded like you two were a good investigative team."

"Did it?"

"He seemed kinda hurt. Did he propose and you told him no?"

"I'll tell you later." She sounded as gloomy as the sky.

"You keep putting me off. I want to help."

"You have your own troubles, little lady. Let's stay focused on you."

Roxy put her arm around Dallas. "No. Talk to me? What's wrong?"

"Damn," Dallas said. "Rain, already. All these rumbles and clouds that swoop in and then disappear. It's getting me agitated."

"Dee-Dee."

"Really, I'm fine."

Roxy didn't believe her, but she let it drop for now. Dallas would share in her own time and own way. Meanwhile, Dallas was right. Roxy had a plateful of her own troubles.

CHAPTER 21

Rectangular tables placed in a squared-off U filled the small room. The twenty people in attendance sat behind tent cards lettered with their names. A projector on a portable table stood at the mouth of the U and a screen on a stand stood several feet behind it.

They were in a space that had served as a living room or library when people lived in the Victorian. Folks stood in clusters, chatting, more men than women and most in business attire but some dressed more casually. A man with a gray ponytail held *USA Today* and sipped coffee from a Styrofoam cup. On one side of the room, pressed up against the wall, another rectangular table covered with a white tablecloth held a coffee urn, cups, a bowl of fruit, a platter of small sandwiches, and another plate with assorted cookies.

Roxy searched the room for a friendly face. She saw Glenn Phillips sitting in a seat against the wall. She walked over and sat down on a metal folding chair next to him.

"Hi. Taking you up on your invitation."

His face muscles twitched in what she hoped was an "I'm glad you came" expression.

"We have to sit at the children's table, I gather," she said, referring to the chairs behind and away from the board members' padded seats. She watched Joe Dawes dart from one people-cluster to the next like a job applicant trying to network. An elegant woman sat opposite Roxy. In her sixties, she had dewy skin that glowed with health rather than makeup. Joe slowed, then sat down next to her. The smile she gave him looked familiar and welcoming. For several minutes, he bent his head toward hers and spoke into her left ear. At one point she jerked back, her face scrunched as if doubting something he'd said or just surprised. She scribbled notes on a leather-bound pad. There was something arresting about her, a quiet dignity Roxy envied. "Who's that?" Roxy asked Glenn.

"Laura Garrison."

"Oh." Her hair was shiny silver and smartly styled. Roxy recognized an expensive haircut when she saw one. A pair of diamond stud earrings flashed as she moved her head.

"Here's the agenda." Glenn proffered a piece of paper.

Glenn was making her anxious. Both of his legs jigged up and down, his heels drumming against the wood floor. In fact, there was distinct electricity in the room like the charged air outside. Maybe Roxy was imagining things. She glanced at the agenda and saw the item listing Spider. Even though that was why she came, her breath still caught in her throat.

The People's Theater
Board of Trustees Meeting
Monday, 4:00 p.m. to 5:30 p.m.

Agenda Item	Amount of Time	Time	Information	Discussion	Decision Vote	Presenter
1. Approval of the minutes	5 min	4:00-4:05			X	Otto Sand, Chair
2. Financial and Fund-raising Reports	10 min	4:05-4:15	X	X	X	Otto Sand, Glenn Phillips
3. Strategic Plan for School	60 min	4:15-5:15	X	X		Joe Dawes, CEO, and Webster Booth, guest
4. President's Report	15 min	5:15-5:30	X	X		Joe Dawes
5. Adjourn		5:30				Otto Sand, Chair

Roxy scanned the room but didn't see Spider. Despite the cooled air, she was already perspiring—eager to hear what he had to say and dreading being in his company again. It was 4:10, and the meeting had yet to start. Joe sat down next to Otto Sand, aka Sandman, his tanning-booth coloring making his white skin as brown as Joe's. Both wore light-gray suits and white shirts so similar it seemed planned.

Using a cloth handkerchief, Joe wiped his brow. Bits of lint dotted his forehead. She found Joe's confidence unshakable and yet today, face glistening, he appeared as nervous as Roxy. When his gaze landed on her, he studied her for several seconds. Roxy waved. Glenn had said anyone could attend. Joe nodded back with narrowed eyes.

"Let's start," said Sandman, his baldpate illuminated under the florescent lights. "Any changes, comments, or questions to April's minutes?"

"There's a typo on page two," said a woman in a red suit. She pointed it out and Sandman noted it. The board approved the amended minutes.

That's when Spider made his entrance.

Dressed in a cream-colored suit and matching open-collar shirt, he nodded to Sandman and Joe and then took a seat at one of the open spaces. Everyone checked him out with sidelong glances or fleeting sweeps except Laura Garrison who continued to make notes. Spider didn't appear to survey the room.

The financial and fund-raising reports were next. Roxy forced herself to focus. The news was grim. Debt, poor fund-raising results, and slow ticket sales except for *The Monday Night Murder* opening night. Despite depressing numbers, the board members appeared upbeat in an anticipatory way, waiting for the report to end. During the presentations, several people sent covert glances her way—or at least it seemed that way to Roxy. Once the chair of the finance committee and Glenn finished the reports, they sat. Joe sprang up.

"Thank you, Mr. Chairman," he said, his voice filling the room without a need for a microphone. He didn't mention Glenn. "These are trying times. I am pleased, however, to announce we have a solution. A financier who believes in our mission, vision, and work has offered a proposal. I've invited him to this meeting to share his ideas for your consideration. I am honored to introduce returned native son, Webster Booth."

CHAPTER 22

Spider rose to enthusiastic applause from several people in the room, their facial and physical animation willing good news to counter the dismal financial reports. Those who didn't applaud shuffled papers, shifted in their seats, and stretched their necks around their neighbor for a clearer view. Glenn, once again sitting next to Roxy, snapped the point ejection button of his pen on and off with a steady clack.

Back in high school, Spider caused the same levels of disquiet. The clique Roxy belonged to was small and outside the mainstream but comfortable–Carl, Dallas, Vicki, one of the basketball players who had a thing for Vicki, and another boy, geeky but sweet. Spider, on the other hand, didn't belong to a group. He glided from one to the other–Black, brown, white, and others–always welcomed. Captain of the swim and basketball teams, he also ran track and belonged to the debate club. Tall and lean, he'd saunter over to their table in the dining room, spin around a chair next to Roxy, straddle the seat, and ease down. His tray stacked high with burgers, fries, juice, and some chocolate-oozing desert. She sensed eyes watching from around the room–envious, incredulous more likely–partly because she was Black, but mostly because she was chubby, plain, and quiet. At least that's how Roxy saw herself then and now.

"Movie tonight," he'd say as a statement. She'd nod yes, as if he'd asked her a question. He made her feel thin, pretty, and smart, not because he paid her compliments, but because he'd chosen her. Now, eighteen years older, he was still in command of his audience.

With a nod from Spider, someone switched off the lights. Spider pressed the projector's *on* button. A PowerPoint slide wavered on the screen behind him.

"This is a breakthrough moment in Fieldcrest's history," he began. "In the weeks ahead, you will hear and read about the first, major new residential development project in at least two decades. Tonight, in this historic room, you are about to become privy to a dazzling redevelopment plan well before the public. A project that will revitalize our city. An endeavor that will not only keep The People's Theater around for generations to come but will, in fact, make it a region-wide destination."

Spider paused, reached for a glass of water, and took a sip. All Roxy heard was the breathy sounds of rapt attention.

The next slide revealed a soaring tower with balconies on each floor, large windows, and an open garden on the roof. "This is what we need to bring the middle and upper class back to the heart of our city while making room for our humblest citizens."

The thrust of the proposal, as Spider explained it, was building a mixed-use tower on the street next to the theater, their back yards touching. The project included retail space, indoor parking, 150 luxury condominiums and up to 150 market-rate rental apartments, twenty percent of them reserved and priced for lower-income families. Next to the theater, the plan called for a vast playground, fitness center with a sliding-fee membership, and a water park that transformed into an ice-skating and hockey rink in the winter. Even the proposed retail space encouraged diversity. Spider expected upscale stores like Whole Foods and ethnic specialty stores offering Caribbean and Latin groceries and a community health center providing quality healthcare at affordable prices. Success, explained Spider, required a partnership with state and local governments, non-profits, philanthropists, corporate leaders, and private investors.

Once again, Spider paused. The next group of images concerned financing. The consortium backing the project, led by Spider, included Otto Sand and other names Roxy didn't recognize. With each click of the remote, Spider pointed out how the theater benefitted from, as well as contributed to, the project. A series of slides provided architectural renderings of the two-block development. Sketched families, pets, trees, and flower-edged walkways helped everyone imagine the renovated area.

Spider looked around the room. No one shuffled papers. All eyes focused on him.

"For years, Joe Dawes, a true pioneer and visionary, held a dream close to his heart," Spider said. "With your help and guidance, he realized a portion of it—this magnificent theater that is for the people. There was more, however. Joe envisioned a school where children from all over the region could learn about the power of stage acting and playwriting, expressing one's most inspiring, scary, romantic, thrilling ideas and doing it in a manner that moved others." He clicked the button on the remote slide-changer, and a new image came up, a representation of a building sitting next to The People's Theater. Lush landscaping with a brick path connecting the two buildings complemented the Victorian-like facade.

"As you can see," Spider said, a laser pointer highlighting the sketched entranceway, "children from all over the county, southern Connecticut, and the north Bronx will find a home here. They will learn to write and act, set design and production, stage management, costume making, lighting, and directing from the finest professionals. The school will have the latest technology and our children will have access to all the tools they'll need for success. We'll offer classes to adults and children alike in entrepreneurship and business management, helping to lift our city into the global economy. To attract and keep the best, we will set aside low-income apartments for our teachers. Joe Dawes will bring in an outstanding head of school and create a separate board of trustees."

Spider gave his audience a warm, broad smile. "The most important aspect, however, is..." He paused, then one by one, made eye contact with each board member. "Your children—our children—will excel and our city will flourish for generations to come."

The awed second of silence that happens after virtuoso performances hung in the air. Roxy, her eyes wide, held her breath. Applause erupted and swept her up.

As the clapping waned, Joe jumped up, came around and pumped Spider's hand. Then, creating an arc with his own clapping hands, he started another round. Feeling guilty about her earlier enthusiasm, Roxy folded her hands in her lap.

"All of this," Joe said gesturing toward the architectural rendering, "for an affordable loan with generous terms."

Everyone began speaking at once, peppering Joe and Spider with questions. "What's the projected completion date?" "Is the mayor in favor?" "How can we help?" "Are the development contracts in place?" "What did the environmental impact report state?" The two men, as if in a well-rehearsed play, fielded each one with confidence. "We'll displace families who live on the two blocks now. What happens to them?" a man asked. Spider assured him the consortium planned to buy their homes and help find them new ones, better ones. In addition, they'd be at the head of line for one of the new affordable apartments if that was their desire.

After thirty minutes of the Q & A, a woman raised her hand. The tent card in front of her read Sheila Brown. "This is all quite impressive," she began. The unstated *but* clear. "How are we securing another loan when we're already in so much debt?" She rose to her full height, towering over everyone seated around the table. "And, sir, how will we manage the debt service when we can barely keep our doors opened now?"

Joe made a small bow. "That's a fair question and I'm glad you asked it." To Roxy's ears, his tone conveyed the exact opposite.

He turned toward Spider. "Sheila is an accountant and one of our newer board members." Smile in place, he shifted his gaze back to room, clicked to change the slide, and pointed to an image labeled "revenue projections." The multi-colored lines, each representing a different revenue stream, all pointed up including philanthropic donations. "We are fortunate Mr. Booth, and his partners, have great confidence in our future success." Joe stepped aside to enable all a clear view of the graph and, glancing around the table, he added, "As you can see from our analysis, we anticipate a strong fiscal picture."

Still standing with her thin shoulders pulled back, Sheila continued to press. "I see it, but I'm having trouble believing it."

A few people bobbed their heads. Roxy watched Laura's expression trying to gauge her reaction. She appeared to be listening but showed no emotion.

"What collateral are we using?" Sheila asked in a more challenging tone. "There isn't anything left to mortgage." She sat down as the head-nodders murmured.

This time Spider answered. "You're securing the loan with the land and buildings you own. You don't have to pay for the first six months and then at very low interest rates." He stared down the dissenter. "This is about the children of Fieldcrest and their future. The money will come."

This time church-like vocals akin to Amen accompanied the applause.

Roxy glanced at the questioning woman to see if she'd speak up again. Her expression remained skeptical, but she made no additional comments.

Glenn Phillips stood up. "Excuse me," he said over the buzz. "That pays for the building. How do we pay for the additional staff, faculty members, the productions and programs, and everything else?"

Spider turned to Glenn. "Mr. Phillips?"

Glenn nodded, his body moving in tandem with his head.

"Current benefactors, Mr. Sand, and I will help you raise the monies needed. We have powerful and moneyed people collaborating with us."

Joe glared at Glenn and appeared to include Roxy in his disapproval.

"In my experience," Glenn said, sounding almost angry, "you've based your projections on hoped-for donations rather than reality. We learned that from the first loan we took when we built the theater." Taking a page from Spider's book, he made eye contact with everyone. "If you all recall, it didn't work then. Why will it work now?"

What Glenn said was true. As he had explained it to Roxy, the theater relied on philanthropy for about sixty percent of its revenue. Local corporations eager to have their name associated with a worthy cause chipped in some. Wealthy patrons like Laura, Sandman, and an anonymous benefactor gave significant gifts annually, and one or two private foundations interested in the arts contributed as well. City support, memberships, advertisements in the Playbill, and ticket sales supplied the rest.

Despite that, they were two million dollars in debt. Building the theater, hiring staff, and getting the first productions up and running with little or no money coming in had put them in serious red ink. The pandemic and two years of lockdown brought their already meager funds to a cold, dead, halt. Could Spider's plan reverse the trend and save the theater? Selfishly, Roxy wanted Glenn to be wrong. She *needed* her theater to live and thrive for years to come. The People's Theater differed from other community theaters. It encouraged people like her—aspiring authors—and gave them a voice on a professional stage. By adding a school, the theater's reach would expand. Roxy pictured it and unwelcomed excitement swept through her again. On the other hand, Glenn and the dissenting board member might be right.

"Every year," Glenn said, "we project increased revenue and each year, expenses outstrip our ability to bring money in." People fidgeted under his steady gaze as if they knew he was speaking the truth.

Sandman shut him down. "A long history of fund-raising failures is not a convincing argument, sir. We require our leaders to have a mixture of optimism, grit, and talent." Without giving Glenn an opportunity to reply, Sandman spoke to Spider. "Good job. We appreciate all you're doing for the people and children of our great city." Then he smiled at the assemblage. "In that vein, as you know, Laura..." he extended his arm toward her, and she tipped her head in response. "... is hosting a special reception in her home Wednesday evening. Our own Ms. Victoria Vega and our esteemed mayor are guests of honor. I look forward to seeing you there with generous checks and enthusiasm in hand."

With that, the meeting adjourned.

CHAPTER 23

No one moved to leave. They milled around, some lining up to speak with Spider, others with Joe. Sheila, the dissenter, spoke quietly with Laura. Several gathered around the rendering of the new school. Spider had backtracked to that slide, letting the fiscal projections fade from view.

"I got to get outta here," Glenn said to Roxy.

Did Glenn mean he had to leave the building or leave his job? "I'm sorry." Perhaps Sandman was right about Glenn's skills, but regardless, he didn't deserve public humiliation.

"Not your fault."

"What will you do?"

"Go home and have a glass of wine." He picked up his overstuffed briefcase. "This will not end well."

"I hope you're wrong."

In a kind voice, Glenn said, "Me too."

"Thank you," she said, her tone packed with emotion.

"Can I give you a lift?"

Although she needed one, she shook her head. "Thanks anyway." In the back of her mind, an unformed idea gelled.

Glenn walked away, leaving Roxy standing against the far wall alone, still unsure what she intended to do or say.

From across the room, Laura stared at Roxy and then smiled. Roxy joined her.

"You're the author of our upcoming play, aren't you?"

Roxy extended her hand and introduced herself.

"I'm quite a fan. Joe let me read it. It's sad, uplifting. Wonderful."

Stunned, Roxy said, "Thank you."

Something swept across Laura's face, a fleeting shiver, and then it vanished. "Rape is an awful thing." Roxy nodded in agreement. "You wrote about it with power and empathy."

"Thank you," Roxy said again, unable to articulate the overwhelming pride and joy Laura's words elicited.

Laura appeared pensive. Roxy waited. "It happened to me," Laura said in a hushed voice. She hiked her shoulders. "A long time ago."

"I was a teenager," Roxy said.

"Me too."

"Did you ever tell anyone?"

Laura shifted in her seat. "Did you?"

"No, but I regret that."

"Regrets are unhealthy."

Roxy's lies by omission pricked... no, stabbed. "I agree. Neither is carrying around a bag full of secrets. They're heavy."

Laura stayed silent for a few beats. "There are more of us than I care to think about. *#MeToo* has revealed legions. I'm hoping your play will inspire more conversation and awareness."

"When I wrote it, I was doing it for me. As I finished, I realized I wasn't alone and maybe the play could help others." But that sounded so grandiose–her little play helping other people.

"One out of every five women," Laura said. "Thirty-three percent of men as well. You've deftly managed a crucial issue."

It was hard to take it in. Praise and recognition were unfamiliar. "Was it hard for you to heal?"

"Yes. I'm not sure I'm fully recovered."

"Depression clouded every day for a long while," Roxy said.

"Understandable. Shame and anger surged at first and then I sank into a deep depression as well."

That sounded like Roxy's experience.

"A friend persuaded me to see a phycologist," Laura said.

"I wrote about it, so I guess that was my therapy."

Laura gave a short laugh. "He got his comeuppance in the play. Did he in real life?"

"No." Spider's words still pierced her. 'You'll like it better next time.' "Not yet."

Laura straightened her shoulders and lifted her chin. "What were your impressions of this afternoon's presentation?"

Surprised but pleased by the abrupt turn in topic, Roxy tried to shift gracefully as well. "I hope it's all true." She amended her comment. "That Spider and Joe are right."

"And Glenn is wrong."

"What do you believe?"

"The jury is out for me," Laura said, her voice once again firm. "I like Glenn. He's far more competent than Otto Sand implied."

"I like him too."

"But I can't let opportunity slip by because I have doubts. I make my good fortune."

Roxy let that sit a moment. Could she make her own good fortune?

"Are you coming to my fund-raiser Wednesday?"

"No one invited me."

"Would you like to attend?"

"Of course." She loved watching the home network on television but that was the closest she'd ever gotten to a mansion like the one she imagined Laura lived in. Since they slated Vicki as the guest of honor, Roxy could escort her to Wednesday's rehearsal, thus ensuring Vicki's attendance.

Laura extracted a card out of her small, flat clutch and passed it to Roxy.

"I appreciate this."

Another possibility was Laura helping Roxy. As a sponsor, it was in Laura's interest to get Vicki's commitment for a seven-day run at a minimum but ideally, the two promised weeks. Plus, Laura wasn't sure about Spider's idea, and Roxy wondered why. Laura's reasons might shed light. "May I drop by a few minutes early?"

Laura raised an eyebrow in an unspoken question.

"I'm seeking a bit of wisdom," Roxy said. When she was little, her mother told her asking for advice was the fastest way to friendship.

"I love gifted writers," Laura said. "Happy to assist if I'm able."

Joe called from the front of the room. "Laura, we need to get to the mayor's residence. Don't want to be late."

She waved in response. "Joe and I are making a private presentation to Mayor Thompson."

"Not Spider?"

Laura looked quizzical.

"Webster Booth," Roxy amended.

"First, we win over the mayor. Prime the pump." She smiled at Roxy. "Until Wednesday." She angled her way around knots of chatting board members and joined Joe.

* * *

Spider caught Roxy's eye and raised his index finger as if asking her to wait. At first, she smiled in acknowledgment but then it spread into a wide grin, not for Spider but for Laura's words. No one had ever said something as positive about her writing. Larry Frome's kind words lacked Laura's enthusiasm, and Dallas and Vicki's praise came with lifelong friendship. Laura had called Roxy's play, "Sad, moving, uplifting." She'd said Roxy was a "gifted writer." Roxy resisted hugging herself. The journey here had been long, littered with rejections. Now, here she was, a playwright with a wealthy patron of the arts backing her. Earlier, she'd decided not to submit *Thunder Snow*, her latest short story, to the contest. Tonight, at midnight, was the deadline. But Laura changed everything. Roxy planned to take a chance.

She watched Spider pack up still smiling to herself. Her buoyed confidence spilled over into her pursuit of the truth. Either he was going to save the theater and city and therefore was worth negotiating with, or he was a low-life liar and Laura might help Roxy corner him.

Everyone left except Roxy, Spider, and Mr. Smalls, the guard, his keys on his packed key ring clanging as if urging Roxy and Spider to hurry.

Spider didn't seem to notice. With deliberate movements, he gathered the last of his papers. Roxy picked up several and handed them to him. Grateful for minor triumphs, she noted her hand wasn't trembling. "Nice."

He laughed, slipping the documents into his briefcase. "Surprised?" He glanced at his Apple Watch. "Let me buy you a beer or some dinner."

"Shouldn't you be with the VIP group meeting with the mayor?" She'd heard Laura's explanation but waited for Spider's.

"Not yet."

"How come?"

"Timing is everything." He finished packing.

"He's not yet convinced of your wisdom, competence..." She paused. "Or honesty?"

"Ouch."

"Well?"

"We have a bit of history," he said with a laugh.

This was interesting news... or was it? "What kind? Bad blood?"

"Let's say, this isn't my first attempt to save Fieldcrest from poor management."

"You came back to town earlier? When?"

"It's been a minute."

Roxy waited to see if Spider would say more. When he didn't, she said, "I stayed because I wanted to ask you something." She was sure he sensed, in fact smelled, her returned angst.

"Let's grab a drink and then we'll talk." His expression conveyed sincerity, trust, no danger at all. As if reading her mind, he said, "I'm not the person you remember."

"Had an epiphany?"

A sardonic laugh. "Give me a chance. Let's be friends again."

Blue eyes, as clear and as bright as she remembered when she had loved him with all her adolescent heart, stared back at her.

"My family is expecting me."

"One drink."

With a decisive no on the tip of her tongue, Roxy surprised herself. "Just one."

A sax player and a woman on a piano played reggae as the rhythmic swish of the drummer's brushes added a steady beat. In unspoken agreement, Spider and Roxy avoided Sandman's establishment. The Banana Bar on North Apple just off East Eighth, decorated in a Caribbean motif, was full. The hand-lettered sign on the door read *Live Music Mondays, Fridays, and Saturdays.*

During the short drive, Roxy stayed quiet, but the conversation in her head was loud and frantic. What are you doing? He sucked you in before, time after time. This is not a good idea. Her mind battled back. Perhaps he's changed. She forced herself to calm down. I won't stay long. I won't drink. We'll have an adult conversation.

A new possibility, one from deep inside a protected place, rose. He'd acknowledge and apologize for what he did to her.

Married to Carl, six months pregnant with Jewel and showing, she'd run into Spider at the Fieldcrest Mall. Both hands holding bags of baby clothes, bedding, and crib decorations, she'd almost knocked him over. "Hey," he'd said. She stopped. Tell me you're sorry for what you did. "You look good." She waited, glued to her spot. Beg me to forgive you. "Boy or a girl?" Unable to speak, she shrugged. "Well, good luck. See ya around." She cried all the way home.

Seated at a table in the back near the kitchen, Roxy tried to work out how to start the conversation. A waitress with multiple ear and lip piercings stood ready to take their orders.

"Iced tea, please, unsweetened."

Spider laughed. "Not taking any chances."

A chill ran down her spine.

"What do you have on tap?" Spider asked. After listening to the list, he ordered Brooklyn Lager.

As soon as the server was out of earshot Roxy said, "This is great—all you're doing for the theater and the city. Must feel good." She used her business voice, the one vendors heard at the salon.

Spider seemed to study her. "I had a chat with Vicki," he said.

"I gather. Is that why she's coming to the fund-raiser Wednesday–because of you?"

"Yeah, he says modestly." Spider laughed at his own joke. "And she's coming to the rehearsal afterwards–going to get back on point."

What was he trying to say to her? That he had some pull with Vicki, like Puzo's Godfather, making offers people can't refuse? "She didn't show Saturday, even though you assured Joe that she would."

"Well, she won't disappoint again."

"Why? What do you have over her?"

"A certain charm."

"Hmm."

"You're welcome."

The music changed to something up-tempo.

"You should come." He still smirked.

"To what?"

"The reception–it's a fund-raiser. Laura Garrison is a passionate promoter of the arts and a fan of Fieldcrest." He retrieved an invitation and handed it to Roxy. "I'm sure Vicki will be glad to see you."

Roxy took the invitation but didn't read it. She considered telling him Laura had already invited her but kept that news to herself. "Why are you interested in my play?" She tried staring him down the way he had stared down Sheila at the board meeting. "What's going on?"

"Here to help," he said. "To be a friend."

CHAPTER 24

Light streamed in from the kitchen as a server came out with a plate of Buffalo wings; their pungent scent infused the air. The door banged shut.

"Are you happy, Roxy?"

The question caught her off-guard.

"No?"

"Yes, of course I am."

"You don't look it."

For a nanosecond, Roxy was sorry she hadn't put on fresh lipstick and a little blush. Then she realized it didn't matter. She wasn't trying to impress Spider. She needed information. Period. In what she hoped came off as confident, she said, "What you see is weariness from working too hard, *not* unhappiness."

"I see someone pretty special." His muscled arms stretched across the table toward her.

"How about you?" she asked.

"Oh. Turn around." His smile reached his eyes. "Fair enough."

Roxy put her hands in her lap.

"Mostly." He fiddled with the saltshaker. "I have many of the things I want."

"And Nadine?" This was not how she'd envisioned the conversation.

"She's as content as someone married to me can be."

"Ha. What does that mean? Are you still unfaithful, adoring but off with other women as well?" Or was he finally self-aware, accepting and acknowledging his failings?

"Why do you care?" he asked.

The amused look on his face annoyed Roxy. Neither her mind nor the conversation was moving in the right direction. "The reason I stayed after the meeting was to speak with you about Jewel."

"Oh, we're done talking about *my* personal life, and we're back to *yours*." His tone was infuriating. "Funny, but I never guessed you and Carl would last this long." He put down the saltshaker and lifted the votive candleholder making the flame flutter. "Wishful thinking, I guess."

Heat crawled up from her breast to her neck. "We love each other."

He set the candle off to the side. "You and I did too."

"Kid stuff."

"I never loved anyone before or since the way I loved you."

Her breath caught in her throat. "You're lying."

"You made me believe I was the person you saw."

Spider used to tell her she made him a better person, but the reality was he stayed the same. "Who were you really?"

"The person my pop accused me of being—never gonna be anyone, never worth the money he spent raising me and my brothers." Eyes down, Spider's speech took on the New York accent of his youth, losing the neutral one he'd cultivated. "The guy my friends knew—the player who always got a hustle going, the shadier the better. But not with you." He raised his eyes and once again met hers. "It doesn't matter now."

"You've accomplished so much. Your father must be proud." Spider stayed quiet. "Who are you today?" Roxy asked.

Their server came with their drinks. "Wanna see a menu?" Spider waved her off.

Roxy waited, but he didn't answer her last question. She shifted the conversation. "How d'you get so—"

He interrupted with an amused sound, a cross between a laugh and a snort. "Rich?" He rocked back his chair. "Hard work and luck. Taking risks."

Roxy sipped her tea.

"Vicki and I had a thing for a while."

Roxy's heart stuttered. But why did she care? "When was this?"

"About ten years back. We were both between spouses."

"Vicki has trouble marrying the right guy."

Spider made his amused sound again. "This time's no different."

"I think they're doing okay–trying to get pregnant." The information wasn't Roxy's to share. Besides, she didn't know if Vicki's husband was a good person, but Roxy felt a need to defend her friend.

"Like the black widow spider, she'll dump him once the deed is done–eat her prey."

"That's awful. I thought you were friends."

He gave a half shrug. "We are."

It was time to get the conversation back on point. "Anyway, I want to talk about my daughter."

"*Our* daughter."

"Mine and Carl's." Roxy heard the angry tremor in her voice. "You are not her father." Even if he was biologically, which he probably wasn't, Carl was and is Jewel's dad.

He took a pull on his beer. "She hates her life, she told me so."

Roxy tried hard to keep her voice steady, but it hitched. "She has enormous challenges ahead of her, but she knows her parents love and support her."

"Absolutely," he said, leaning forward, his eyes wide. "Let me offer some of that support. I can provide the financial wherewithal she needs."

This was true. Roxy knew it. Shouldn't she let him help Jewel? Didn't Jewel deserve every opportunity?

"I'm dazzled by her intellect..." He paused and took another swallow. "Perceptiveness."

Roxy's anger melted. "For as far back as I can remember, Jewel's teachers declared she was crazy smart–gifted."

"The first time I met her, she and Q were coming from a doctor's appointment. I could tell she was special."

All of Roxy's pride must have showed in her eyes.

"You folks have done a fantastic job, raised her right. I can see that." His voice had an eagerness to it, a bounce she'd not heard before–the sardonic, amused tone gone. He leaned in closer. "Together, you and I can help her be everything you hoped for yourself."

Freedom and a home of their own. Until now, she'd seen her play as the vehicle for achieving that dream. And her other, secret goal–success as a writer.

"We used to be a good team, you and me."

"You have different memories than I do."

"I have the funds and connections to help her–to help you. She can keep her daughter, get her own place, and go to school." He eyed Roxy now, a colder look. "And your play can get the attention it deserves."

No one believed Roxy's play would ever make enough money for all the items on her list, much less college tuition for Jewel.

Narrow fingers, as long and as lean as his frame, reached across the table again, this time taking her right hand into his and squeezing. "I never stopped loving you. And when I saw our daughter—"

Oh, sweet Jesus. Roxy snatched her hand away. "She's not yours."

"Of course, she is. She looks like you except for the light hair and eyes, which she got from me. Where is Q in her DNA?"

"One of my twins looks just like me and the other like her dad." She didn't mean to sound defensive. Why was she having this argument? Spider possessed zero claims on Jewel.

"You tell her. She *should* hear it from *you*."

The implied threat was obvious. "Don't. You'll cause her a great deal of pain."

"Cause *you* pain, you mean."

"I never told anyone... ever." Now wasn't the time to mention Dallas.

The left muscle of his jaw clenched and unclenched. "Nadine tried for years to have a baby."

"I'm sorry. But that can't be a reason to hurt Jewel."

"She asked me to get tested but there was no need. It's not me; I *have* a daughter."

"You don't know that."

"We made love. Nine months later, boom, a kid."

"We. Did. Not. Make. Love." A passing server twisted his head in their direction. Roxy lowered her voice. "You raped me."

"Whatever you say. Your version of history."

145

"You can lie to yourself, but don't you dare lie to me. We both know..." She heard the grief in her voice. With effort, she ratcheted down the emotions. "Carl and I are her parents."

"Fine. Have it your way." He picked up the saltshaker again and jiggled it in his hand. "It doesn't matter. Let me take part." The corners of his mouth lifted in a fast, up-and-down smile. "Stop fighting me."

Their server reappeared holding a tray of drinks for another table. "Can I get you guys anything else?"

Spider gave her a big grin. She beamed back. "Just the check, thanks."

How stupid of Roxy to expect an apology. Revisionist history. Tears gathered in the corners of her eyes. He hadn't changed at all. She shook her head, heaved her shoulders, and tightened her mouth. What difference did it make that he didn't acknowledge what he had done? What mattered was Jewel's future. Roxy would tell Jewel and Carl the truth. If, afterwards, Jewel still wanted Spider's help, then fine.

Spider said, "Looks like you're having a conversation with yourself. Want to let me in on it?"

"Okay," she said.

"Okay what?"

"I'll tell them the truth. What and how it happened."

"Nah. Don't do that." His voice was urgent. "How's that gonna help?"

"No more secrets."

His light eyes grew dark, and his jaw muscles clenched and unclenched. "And no more help from me." He paused. "Is that what you want?"

His mood swings dizzied, going from old friend, to flirt, to on her side, and now threatening again. "We had sex. She was born." His salesman voice returned. "Q's or mine? You're not sure. Is that what you'll say?"

"A more accurate version, but yes."

"What parent doesn't need help? Let me be a positive part of her life."

"You already are a part without my permission. Although I'm not sure the word positive applies."

He watched her from under his pale lashes.

"Prove you mean us no harm." Roxy kept her tone soft but firm. "If, after I tell them both and you're still interested in giving her a permanent job with benefits, then I'm good with that." She waited a beat. "If Jewel and Carl agree." She heard her words but were they true?

He didn't reply.

She stood up and called to the retreating server. "Excuse me."

"Yeah?"

"Can someone call me a cab? Is there a company you use?"

"I'll drive you home," Spider said.

"No."

The server lifted her chin toward the front door. "Check with the bartender."

Spider said, "I've got this." He pulled out his phone. "I'll get you an Uber." After punching in numbers, he put his phone down.

Roxy hefted her bag and slung it onto her shoulder. "Give me time to tell them, that's all I ask."

Without looking back, she went to the front of the bar to wait. She sensed his eyes following her.

CHAPTER 25

The Uber driver dropped her off in front of her building. She climbed out, but long after the car drove away, she stood on the street, not moving toward home. Perhaps there was a way forward. Although Spider didn't say he'd give her time to tell Jewel and Carl, he didn't say no.

She walked toward the front door. Time was slipping by. On opening night, when they saw the play, they'd both know the truth. Even if Jewel didn't figure it out, Carl would. Spider hadn't seen the play either. Did Vicki tell him about it? There had to be some way to tell Carl before the play's opening night. Carl always took her side. Every time Spider broke her heart, cheated on her with some college student or cheerleader, it was Carl who told her Spider was a fool. It was Carl who said her curves were perfect. It was Carl who told her she was beautiful.

Once she explained, how might she keep Spider from going back on his word to Jewel? She trudged up the steps and down the hall and turned the key in the door. The sharp bark of the dogs told her something was wrong. Seeing Dallas in the hallway with the twins confirmed it.

"What's happened?"

"Jewel's having her baby," Kia said. She wrapped her thin arms around Roxy's legs. "And Daddy couldn't find you."

Gabriella, arms crossed, scolded Roxy with her eyes.

Dallas put words to Gabriella's accusing stance. "Where've you been?"

Roxy tried to process Kia's news. "Jewel's in labor?"

"Carl is with her; her contractions started around six." Dallas lowered her voice. "I told Carl you were at the board meeting."

"When did he last call? What did he say?"

"About fifteen minutes ago. Said she's fine. The contractions stopped but they're keeping her."

Pharaoh nuzzled Roxy's leg. Absently, she reached down and scratched the top of his head. "Have the kids eaten? Where's Max?"

"Batman, Robin is here taking care of everyone. You need to go."

Roxy's feet failed to move. She'd been with Spider just when her family needed her the most.

Dallas leaned into Roxy's left ear. "Carl looked all over for you—called your cell a dozen times."

Tears bubbled up. Once again, someone else was doing Roxy's job, caring for and comforting her babies.

"Come on kiddo," Dallas said, reaching for Roxy's hands. "You've got to hold it together. I'll stay for as long as you need."

Tears streamed down Roxy's face. "I'll call from the hospital."

"Don't cry, Mommy," Gabriella said in her grownup voice.

Roxy dried her face with her hands. The children shouldn't see her like this. She bent down and opened her arms. Both girls climbed into the circle they made, and Roxy hugged them tight. "Mommy and Daddy will be home soon. You do everything Auntie Dallas tells you." She stood up. "Thanks, Dee-Dee."

Dallas tossed Roxy the keys to the van.

• • •

The minute Roxy left the apartment, her sobs started again, hit flood stage in the car, eased up as she found her way to Jewel's room in the hospital, but then came back full force the minute she saw Jewel, pale and sallow, lying in the bed.

Carl hugged Roxy and stroked her hair. She buried her face against his shirt and slowly her sobs abated.

"The doc said she may have to have a Cesarean. Her pelvis might be too narrow. Just a precaution."

149

Jewel, sleeping fitfully, shifted around as if trying to get comfortable, the crumpled sheet failing to cover her feet.

"When will they do it? If they must, I mean?"

"Dr. Wu just left. Said Thursday or Friday; she'll know better tomorrow." Roxy blew her nose.

Carl stared at her. "What happened to you? Where've you been?"

"At the theater's board meeting." She willed him not to ask any more questions.

"That's what Dallas said." Skepticism tinged his words. "I went by there, but the place was locked up tight."

"I must have just missed you." Why not tell him she was with Spider? He liked him, kept trying to get them to be friends again. Of course, once he knew the truth... "Spider presented his big vision and after bought me a cup of tea."

She sensed his questioning eyes. To avoid them, she walked over to the bed and balanced one hip on the edge. "It all sounds pretty promising," she said over her shoulder.

A few seconds later, Carl joined her and together they listened to Jewel's labored breathing. "Told you he's changed." Carl rested his hands on Roxy's shoulders and kissed the top of her head.

The apartment was quiet. The children and the dogs were asleep. After providing an update and receiving a shower of thanks, Dallas went home.

Roxy and Carl shared a beer at the kitchen table.

"This is probably a good time to tell you something," Carl said.

Roxy was thinking the same thing; now was the time to tell Carl everything.

"I've let you guys down."

"No. You're a wonderful husband and father."

"You deserve better." She held her breath, terrified of what was coming next. "I'm going to make it right." His face became animated. "I found a house."

"Oh, my God."

"Now, it's nothing special."

Roxy said, "I found one too."

Carl frowned, jerked his head back. "What?"

"It's beautiful and just a few blocks from here on East Juniper. Kinda fake stucco with a little deck, three bedrooms, two baths, and a half basement."

The frown lines deepened on Carl's face. Once again Roxy caught herself but too late. "It's just a house that I... tell me about the place you found."

"How can we afford something like that?"

"How can we buy the house *you* like?"

Carl got up, opened the refrigerator door, and grabbed another beer from the top shelf. "It's a three-family fix-up." The beer cap snapped. "With room for a shop–*for our shop*."

"Oh."

"I thought, I mean, I know how much you want a home of your own." His forehead still creased, he said with passion, "And I need to get out."

"How?"

His tone changed back to eager. "We'd have an apartment for us plus two renters and a nice shop in the basement with four or five operators. Not at first, of course."

"Wow." Roxy tried to take it in.

"How much is the place you like?"

"No, tell me more about the fix-up." Roxy got up, put her arms around his waist, and rested her head against his shirt. "I'm sure I'll love it."

"We can't afford fancy."

"Uh-huh."

"I won some money. I've been meaning to tell you."

Spider's words came back about Carl winning big in a high-stakes game. She pulled her head up and looked at him. "Gambling?"

"Twenty thousand."

"Gambling?" she asked again.

"What difference does it make?" He let her go. "We have 20k. You keep saying you want a house, well here's a way."

"Is that enough?"

"B.J. said he'd go in with me and Spider—"

"No." She surprised herself. Didn't she just agree to take Spider's help once she confessed to Carl?

"We'll never put enough money together alone."

"We'll stay here. Make it work."

Carl stared at her, hard. "Is there something I'm missing?"

He'd just offered her an invitation to explain about the rape and Spider's unhealthy interest in Jewel. What was wrong with her?

"Is there something else going on?"

"No," she said. "I don't like being in someone's debt. Look at your father."

The hole she'd dug, the one she swore she'd climb out of, just got deeper.

CHAPTER 26
TUESDAY

Roxy hung over the toilet; both hands gripped the tank as she threw up last night's dinner of soup and crackers. It entered her mind she might be pregnant, but that wasn't right. No tenderness around her nipples and none of the signs she remembered from three previous pregnancies. Plus, they were careful. She stood up, moved over to the sink, ran cool water, and splashed her face. Her reflection in the mirror showed red-rimmed eyes. The LISTERINE bottle was almost empty. She poured the last into a cup and swished.

"You okay?" Carl stood in the hall, his voice sleepy and concerned. "Can I come in?"

She grabbed her toothbrush and squeezed out some Crest. "Sure."

"You throw up again?" He peered into the toilet.

"Sorry." She flushed the mess.

The crowded bathroom included a bathtub with a showerhead, toilet, single sink, and just enough room for one but often accommodated two-squished together, elbows bumping. Six bath towels hung from double racks and multiple pegs behind the door.

"When are you going to the doctor?" Carl reached for his shaving cream and lathered his face.

"Soon." Roxy finished brushing her teeth, turned the shower water on, and waited for it to get hot. She listened to the scrape of the razor against Carl's stubble and the splash of water hitting the tub. How was she going to get through the day?

"You never said where you were last night."

She tugged off her nightgown and climbed into the shower, pulling the curtain behind her. "I did. At the board meeting and tea with Spider."

"That late?"

"Yup."

They finished the rest of their morning rituals in silence.

•   •   •

The family had to hurry, so the silence between Roxy and Carl didn't seem to register. No one asked pointed questions. Instead, Max wolfed his breakfast of peanut butter on toast and a glass of orange juice before bolting out the door with the dogs for their morning relief. The twins dawdled over their Cheerios, bananas, and milk.

"Come on guys, you're going to have so much fun with MeMa today," Roxy said. She downed her coffee, its heat searing her lips and tongue.

The usually cooperative Kia asked, "Why can't we go to the hospital and see Jewel?"

Roxy said. "Finish up. MeMa is expecting us."

Carl dragged two kid-size suitcases into the hall. Kia's, a battered princess roller board and Gabriella's, a Star Wars roller with superhero stickers covering the front.

"Is Ellie in there?" Gabriella asked. The stuffed elephant went everywhere.

"Absolutely," said Carl. "She's excited about the night with Gram and Papa."

They'd asked MeMa, Carl's eighty-three-year-old grandmother, to sit with the tribe during the day and Carl's parents to take care of them at night until Jewel's Cesarean on Thursday or Friday. Dr. Wu would let them know.

Although MeMa used a cane to get around and had trouble hearing, her mind was sharp, and the children loved her. That was hard to tell this morning.

"Why can't Max take care of us, and we stay here?"

Max banged back into the apartment, the dogs yelping behind him.

"He has basketball camp," Roxy explained for the seventh time that morning. "Finish up. Daddy has to open the shop and I have to get to the hospital."

Carl looked grim as he loaded the brood into the car. Roxy suspected his agitation went beyond their brief encounter in the bathroom. He hated asking his parents for help. Although Frank and Celeste adored their grandchildren, Frank would make Carl pay for this favor, but they had no better options.

• • •

It was still morning cool, the August sun low in the sky, the air heavy with moisture as if they were living near the sea or in the tropics. After dropping off everyone, including Carl, Roxy drove to Fieldcrest Community Hospital. On the way, she dialed Dallas's number. Roxy wanted to tell Dallas about the house Carl found, and Roxy's screwup, and the 20k but she only got the answering machine.

She entered Jewel's semi-private room. "Hey, you."

Jewel sat propped up on the hospital bed, a movable tray of untouched cereal, toast, and apple juice on her right. The room smelled scrubbed—a lemony scent mixed with rubbing alcohol. Muffled street sounds came from the closed window and snores from the other side of the partitioned room.

Roxy clocked her daughter's crossed arms and mouth set in a hard line. With a bright, fake smile she asked, "Are you comfortable? Do you need anything?"

"You were snooping." Jewel blinked several times.

"What?"

"You're always going on about trust and respect."

Roxy searched her memory. What was this about? She hadn't been through Jewel's belongings. "Help me out. What are we discussing?"

"You read the text Eddie sent me when we were at the doctors."

Crap.

"Don't lie."

"I didn't read it."

"I can't believe you'd do that." Her voice rasped. "Hmm, I guess I can, because you're a liar."

The contents of Roxy's stomach roiled. "I'm sorry. I shouldn't have pried, but I only opened the message and didn't read it."

"Right."

All this anger had to be about something else, not just the phone. "What's really going on?"

"I *know*, that's what." She turned her face away from Roxy. "I'm Spider Booth's daughter."

Roxy's hands flew up and covered her mouth. This wasn't right. Together, after Roxy told Carl, the two of them were going to sit and explain everything to Jewel. There'd be tears and hugs.

"Is it true?" Jewel continued to speak to the wall instead of looking at Roxy. "Who told you this?"

"It is. That's why you're not answering me."

"Was it Spider?"

She turned back toward her mother, her face scrunched, and shook her head. "Nadine."

"She had no right. Did you ask him?"

"No. I'm asking you."

Roxy's head swam.

"They had a fight," Jewel said.

"More news from Nadine?"

"Spider."

Sweet Jesus. "When did all this happen?"

"You haven't answered my questions." She continued to glare at Roxy. "Either of them."

Roxy searched around for words, for the right explanation, but nothing surfaced. The morning's coffee burned in her throat. She swallowed hard. "I have to go." She needed to compose herself, to figure out how to explain. "I'll be back."

"It's true then." Jewel's voice went back to its normal tone, little-girl soft but now sad as well.

"This is a long conversation. Everything isn't black or white."

"It's a yes or no question."

"We'll talk about this later. Auntie Dallas is coming by and your grandmother and Uncle B.J."

"Sure. Farm me out just like you dump all your kids."

How was she going to fix this? She sniffed and snuffled. "Once I explain, you'll see and understand." You'll forgive me.

"I don't trust you. I guess I never could."

Now, Roxy cried openly, her cheeks wet. "Please don't repeat what Nadine said. Don't tell anyone until you and I can have a proper talk." Carl was waiting for Roxy at the fixer-upper for sale. She checked her watch. "I'm late."

"I'm keeping you from more important things," Jewel said, the anger-infused sarcasm back. "Does Daddy know?"

"Say nothing to him until you and I discuss this."

"You *lied* to him *too*?"

"I'm begging you."

"You're such a hypocrite." Like Roxy, tears streamed down Jewel's face. In a spot-on imitation of Roxy's voice, Jewel said, "Wouldn't you want to know who *your* father was?" She went back to her own voice laced with reproach. "All this time you lied to both of us."

"Your dad, Carl Quinton, he is your father. He loves you."

"But it was Spider's sperm—"

"Stop it." Roxy's voice lowered in direct proportion to the rising timber of Jewel's. "You don't understand the circumstances."

"How could I? You didn't tell me." The sentences came out choppy, choked with tears and mucus. "Everything is always about you. What about the rest of us?"

Roxy's hands shook. Nausea inched up. "I'm so sorry," she said, realizing how inadequate her apology was. "Give me time. I'll be back. We'll talk then. I'll explain everything. I promise."

Jewel dragged her hand across her face. "Don't bother." She snatched the napkin from the meal tray and cleaned her nose. "Stay away. Don't come back to visit me. I don't want you here."

"You can't mean that."

"I do." She angled her body away from her mother.

"Baby."

"You better hurry. *You're late.*"

CHAPTER 27

Carl and Roxy walked around the perimeter of the fixer-upper. Roxy stumbled; her legs sagged under her. He caught her by her elbow. "Are you sick again?"

"No. Clumsy." She tried to keep Jewel's angry, tear-streaked face at bay. How was Roxy going to make this right?

He shifted his left hand under her elbow and moved his right arm to circle her shoulders. He leaned close to Roxy's ear. "What do you think? I mean so far?"

"So far, so good," she lied. Her stomach made a gassy grumble.

Number 923 sat in the southeast section of town in the middle of Second Avenue between East Elm and Fir Streets, near to the hospital and quite close to the commuter train tracks. To the left and right, houses just like it lined up, tall and narrow with fractured concrete steps leading to their front doors. Eloise, the owner, greeted them with an exuberant hello, blowing smoke out of one corner of her mouth, a cigarette held behind her back. Carl introduced Roxy.

"The siding is kinda old, but it'll hold for a few more years," Eloise said in a rough baritone. "The garage can fit two cars easy. It's just filled with a lot my shit if you'll pardon my Korean." She laughed, which got her coughing. "Don't know why people call cussing French. Sometimes I call it German or Spanish, fair to everybody." She laughed-coughed again. "Come on, let's take a walk through."

They entered the vestibule and Eloise opened the door to the first-floor apartment. Roxy examined the walls, floors, and windows, working hard to keep her expression neutral. Dirty beige paint blended into peeling wallpaper that must have once had a discernible pattern. The two bedrooms, full bathroom, and living room were devoid of furniture. A table too dilapidated to make the moving truck stood in the kitchenette. Stained carpeting covered wood floors.

"The living room's a nice size," Carl said.

"Raised five kids here." Eloise smoothed her untucked top. Ashes stained its front.

"Four here." Carl arced his index finger back and forth between Roxy and himself.

"Nice."

"We're about to be grandparents." His tone made it sound as if it still surprised him.

"Listen, I've got some people kinda-sorta interested in renting once you get it shaped up. Oriental–from one of them countries–but nice enough. Do you mind them kind?" She looked expectantly at Roxy and Carl.

Roxy said in an icy tone, "Asian, is the correct term and—"

Carl jumped in. "If this works out, we'd like their number."

Roxy closed her mouth. He was right, of course. What difference did it make what Eloise thought, what her prejudices were? Unless Roxy believed she could change Eloise's mind in the next few minutes, what was the point? Still, it made her crazy when people said stupid, racist things. She didn't want to imagine what Eloise had been calling Carl behind his back.

"Let's look at the basement next. That's where your business will go, right?"

"Wait till you see," Carl said to Roxy. "There's a separate entrance and space for two shampoo stations and four operators."

They had talked about their own shop for years. When they first got married, it was The Plan, starting with Roxy working on her own, part-time, while she took care of the baby, and they saved money. Then Carl would join her after hours and finally, full-time. To distinguish themselves, they'd open Sunday mornings and get the church crowd going and coming. They needed little to make a good life. That was the rub. In fact, they required a lot. Jewel outgrew her clothes as fast as they bought them. Baby food, diapers, a crib, highchair, car seat–the list went on and on. Salon equipment was more expensive than they'd anticipated. Insurance alone was too much for their meager budget. Every month Roxy and Carl tried to save. The dream was always months away. Then Max was born, and the plan became "next year." After the twins, they stopped talking about their shop.

Eloise opened the basement door and led them down a steep set of steps that creaked under foot. She flicked on the light. A single ceiling light did little to pierce the darkness.

"Do you like it?" Carl asked, peering at Roxy sideways. "I mean, can you see its possibilities?" He stood in the center of the basement with his arms stretched wide. "It's kinda hard to imagine, but we'd put four operator stations over here." He swept his arms toward a concrete wall with two street level windows protected from the outside by black wrought-iron bars. "And over here, we'd put the waiting area with a small television and over there the sinks."

With great concentration, Roxy forced her features into attentiveness.

Carl's arms dropped to his sides. "Hard to picture," he said sounding sad.

"No, I see it. I mean, I can imagine..." Her voice faltered.

"You hate it."

"I don't."

Eloise coughed. "Sorry, but I got some other appointments. Can we see the rest of the place now?"

They climbed the stairs to the third floor, Eloise wheezing.

"This one is where I'd live if I were you." Eloise chose a key from the tangle of others. The door unlocked with a solid clunk, and she pushed it open.

Carl took Roxy's hand and tucked it under his arm, humming a nameless tune under his breath. They stepped through the threshold. Carl said, "You'll like this. Doesn't need as much work as the others. Bigger, too."

"Three decent bedrooms." Eloise flipped light switches just ahead of them. "Plus, a small office or fourth bedroom." Eloise and Carl stepped into the kitchen leaving Roxy a few steps behind. "No dining room but the kitchen is big enough."

From the hall, Roxy heard Carl say, "Bigger than the one we've got."

Roxy poked her head into the powder room.

Clocking both her charges with agility, Eloise was right behind her. "Just a toilet and sink," Eloise said, pointing out the obvious. "A full bath is over there between the two larger bedrooms."

This was not what Roxy dreamed for her family. Her house was new, with fresh paint, a deck, and a yard. This place stank of smoke. It was awful, downright ugly, and in a sketchy neighborhood to boot. A train rattled nearby adding to her dismay.

"Come look. Did you see this?" Carl called to her from the living room.

"Be right there." His energy pulled her toward him. Carl hadn't been this excited since... since when?

"Built-in bookcases." He grabbed her hand again. "With a little sanding and varnish, they'll be as good as new."

It was his Christmas morning voice, the one he used when he'd pulled off a wild surprise. One year it was a ten-speed English racer, now rusted and stored in Dallas's garage. Another year, a pair of earrings lay hidden among the Christmas tree branches, an extravagant gift she treasured more than any other. "I love to make you smile," he'd said. It had been many years since the last Christmas surprise.

"I don't know if we can fit all of those books of yours, but surely the best ones." Carl was referring to the plays and novels she loved to read and re-read; literature she held onto from high school stood stacked in boxes next to the bike in Dallas's garage. Roxy eyed the shelves. A real bookcase–something she'd hoped to build or buy for her new house on the little corner lot.

Roxy forced a smile. "It's great," she said. "Perfect."

• • •

Eloise left them to "look around a bit more by yourselves." With his arms wrapped around her from behind Carl said, "The twins will love their room and Max can have the office."

Roxy tried to see the building through Carl's eyes. "He'll be happy just to have a door he can shut."

"This bedroom is large enough for Jewel." He still held Roxy snugly.

She moved out of his arms. "I think she's changing her mind about the baby." A safer conversation to have.

"I'm getting that impression."

"Not for sure yet, but she's come up with a name–Iris." Roxy imagined Iris scooting around this dump. She squelched the shudder that moved along her spine. Bent blinds covered with dust hung from each of the windows. She pulled the blinds up and let the sun in. "How do you feel about it? The baby will be ours to support even though she claims she'll have a high paying job and her own apartment." Would Jewel return home now that she knew Roxy lied?

"College will be out of reach for a while," Carl said, his forehead crinkled in a frown. "Kinda like what happened to you."

On September 23 eighteen years ago when Roxy told Carl she was pregnant, he never hesitated–didn't miss one beat. "I love you," he'd said. "We'll get married." They did it quickly. Pastor Went officiated. The gathering was small–a family-and closest-friends' event. B.J. stood as best man, and Dallas as maid of honor. Vicki read a poem. Roxy's father walked her down the aisle.

"We'd need space for the baby," Roxy said.

"There's always room, no matter where we live." A grin spread across his face. "Remember our first spot?"

For a year, they rented a basement apartment in a private home a few blocks from the shop. A bed, couch, and dresser from the thrift shop, a television from Frank and Celeste, the same Formica kitchen table they still used with six rickety chairs–it had been fun. Roxy learned to cook after her mother left–spaghetti, meatloaf, fried chicken with mashed potatoes, gravy from a can, and box brownies. With time, she added to her repertoire. She even learned to make holiday cookies, which they gave as presents in the early years. They'd both enrolled in the Frank's beauty school. For Roxy, a bitter pill, for Carl, his destiny.

She stepped back into his arms facing front. "We turned out okay, didn't we?"

Carl was quiet for a second or two.

"I mean for the most part?"

"I've tried to do right by you and the kids, but it keeps getting harder." This time Carl broke contact. "I recognize this isn't what you had in mind but it's something we can afford, with tenants to help make the mortgage. We could strike out on our own."

"It's great." Jewel's conversation with Nadine came to mind. "And you're a wonderful husband and dad."

"I'm trying."

"Me too," she said.

He hiked his shoulders. "It's a dump, but with potential, like our lives right now." He gave her a warm-sad smile. "We still have possibilities."

CHAPTER 28

"How will we pay for this house?" Until now, buying a home was part of Roxy's down-the-road plan, giving them time to save once her play started earning money. This place demanded immediate action.

They were sitting in the Taurus. Eloise assured them that despite her other interested buyers, she liked them best. "But you need to make me an offer soon," she'd warned. "They're coming back tomorrow for a second look." Roxy doubted Eloise liked the Quintons or had other buyers, but Carl was nervous about losing the property.

All the car windows were open, but the air that entered was stuffy-hot and leavened with humidity. Roxy's tank top clung to her back and breasts.

"We put in the twenty thousand dollars I won, and B. J. matches it." His lucky casino chip flipped through his fingers like a magician practicing a trick. "That's the down payment. B. J. and me will fix up the first-floor apartment–do it over a weekend, work flat out."

His voice had its old bounce. "B.J. knows a guy who'll spot us materials and paint. Give us a month or two to pay him back."

Roxy's eyebrows shot up. "B. J. has that kind of money?"

Carl made a face. "It's an investment for him and Joanna."

Roxy knew B. J. and Joanna had a lot more money than Carl and Roxy did. She saw it in Joanna's clothes, jewelry, and haircuts she got from an upscale salon and not the family business. The Tudor-style house they owned sat in the middle of upscale Westwood where Dallas's parents lived. Joanna's parents died in a car crash.

An only child, she'd inherited their house, stock portfolio, and cash. But twenty-thousand-unencumbered dollars was another level of comfortable.

"We'll get the first apartment rented—maybe to the couple Eloise mentioned is already interested. Use the rent money to pay the vendors back." Carl's hands drew pictures in the air. "Then we fix up the second-floor apartment with paint and stuff the vendors give us with another sixty days or so to pay. Dallas might help us find the second tenant. You see how it goes?"

The wail and rumble of an ambulance interrupted them as it swayed past. The house was not only close to the commuter railroad but also to the hospital.

"And B. J. is cool with us setting up shop? We'd be competitors."

"He wants out too."

"When would you tell Frank?"

"Down the road." He jammed the casino chip into his front pants pocket. "I don't owe him anything. Not anymore."

"I get it," Roxy said, remembering the horrible confrontation Frank and Carl had on Sunday. "But—"

"I need this." His pleading tone changed to annoyance. "Give me a break."

"Is now the right—"

Carl cut her off again. "You know I'm drowning." He pointed to the house. "This is the only lifeboat I see."

"I understand, I do." She reached out and touched his neck. She stared into his eyes, but she couldn't read them. "How do we pay the mortgage and our rent in the meantime until both apartments have tenants?"

"Don't get mad."

Alarm prickles moved along her spine.

"I'm in a poker game on Friday night."

This was his plan—gambling?

"You've got your pissed-off face going. Listen to me for a minute." He clasped his hands as if in prayer and shook them back and forth. "I'm good. That's how I got the first twenty-thou."

"This is crazy talk. Besides, don't you have to put up money? Wouldn't you be risking our down payment?"

"Spider is backing me."

"For how much?" She heard the screech in her voice.

"A cut of my winnings."

"Gambling is not a strategy," she said, her voice still too loud.

"Ordinarily, I'd agree with you. But I'm a good. I won five thousand dollars and parlayed that into the twenty grand."

As usual, the words rushed out of her before she weighed their wisdom. "You're not good. Spider let you win; he told me so."

Carl's incomprehension showed on his face. "I won fair and square."

It was too late now to take it back. "No."

"You don't know how casinos work. A player can't throw a game like a boxing match."

"Spider is powerful and rich."

Now Carl's expression moved from not understanding to suspicion. "What the hell are you talking about?"

She swallowed hard. "He told me in the kitchen on Sunday that he set it, so you'd win." She knew she'd already said too much. The hole she'd dug was getting deeper and darker.

"How did it come up? This makes no sense."

Roxy tugged on her lower lip.

"What aren't you telling me?" He searched her face. "This is what you do. All your damn secrets. The silent treatment."

"Listen to me, just for a minute."

His hand was on the car door, and he cracked it open, waiting.

"Joe's trying to get money people to come to the play, and if they like it and we get excellent reviews, then we might make it to off-Broadway and earn legitimate money."

"Do you hear yourself? This is a pipe dream that's not gonna happen."

"Oh, my play is a pipe dream, but a poker game is a sure path to success?"

"Only *your* stuff matters, did you ever notice that?"

"Gambling is crazy and that dump...," she waved her hand toward the house, "... will take forever to make viable."

Carl swung the car door fully open, slipped the keys out of his pocket, and threw them on the seat. "I'm playing. We buy Eloise's place or not, I'm playing."

The door slammed shut.

• • •

165

Roxy and Dallas sat side by side in the hair salon. A slower Tuesday followed a crummy Monday. One potential customer wandered in but didn't stay. Angel and B. J. went home for lunch, promising to return in an hour or two. Zoe read at the front desk, talked on her phone, and played a game on her tablet. Outside, the storm that had threatened for days materialized. Thunder cracked as lightning sliced through the black clouds. At first, the drops were so huge a skinny person could slip between them. Seconds later, the rain picked up speed and volume, coming down in sheets, creating miniature streams on the sidewalks and rushing rivers in the streets.

"I'm in so deep, I can't figure out how I'm gonna climb out," Roxy said.

"When's this big poker game?" Dallas swiveled in the chair, braids swaying, bangles tinkling.

"Friday night."

"He has a right to a dream."

"Don't you think I know that?"

"I'm on your side Shakespeare, but Carl needs hope just like you do."

"Of course, he does, and I crapped all over his." Misery dripped from each word.

"You'll fix it."

"He was so angry." Roxy replayed the conversation in her head. Damn it. Why can't she learn to hold her tongue, to think before speaking? "Angry and hurt."

The two friends sat in silence for a few minutes.

Dallas asked, "Have you spoken with Jewel?"

Roxy groaned.

"She was crazy mad about your checking her text messages."

"It's worse." Roxy told Dallas about Nadine.

"That vengeful little..." She stood up. "Why hurt a child?"

"To get at me? If so, why? Or is she jealous of Spider's relationship with Jewel?" Roxy pondered while Dallas paced. "Jewel said Nadine and Spider had a fight, so perhaps that's how it came about."

Who knew what went on in Spider's household? Even as teenagers he showed and shared only what he wanted others to see. Kept the pain of his upbringing from the eyes of fans and competitors. He wore his masks well.

"How d'you leave it with Jewel?" Dallas asked.

"She banned me from the hospital."

"Roxy."

"But how do I explain?"

"Tell her straight up. Period." Dallas's voice rose to an uncharacteristic impatience. "Can't you see how wrong this is, not telling them the truth? What's holding you back? I don't get it."

"If I tell her he raped me, then what? She rejects his assistance? Aren't I denying her a future?"

"She's going to find out about the rape whether or not you tell her."

"Its gonna devastate her. She'll hate Spider and give up everything he's offered."

"Her decision, not yours."

In her heart, she knew Dallas was right. She'd known ever since Spider returned to Fieldcrest. It was stupid. Too often she spoke when she shouldn't, and then, for this crucial thing, she couldn't get the words out.

Roxy's head hurt with such ferocity that her jaw ached as well. "I'll tell Carl first and then Jewel and pray they forgive me. I'll do it today."

• • •

A sopping-wet Zay Adams came through the door. He shook the water off his cap and stamped his feet on the welcome mat. "Got some news."

At first, Roxy thought he meant info about Jewel or Carl, the two people heavy on her mind. It took a second to remember Zay was trying to help uncover Spider's plot.

Zay shed his wet trench coat. "Hi, Dallas," he said shyly.

"Hello." She didn't smile back, but her tone and pitch welcomed.

Roxy took his raincoat and hung it on the rack by the door. "Like a cup of coffee? It's hours old but still hot."

"Nah, only have a few minutes." He sat down next to Dallas in one of the swivel chairs. Even in this heat, he wore a suit. The detective's pistol bulged under his jacket and his shield flashed from his belt.

"Here's the story." He smoothed out a crumpled paper out on the countertop. "This is what you were worried about." He fished out a pair of reading glasses from his inside jacket pocket and slipped them on. "It seems Booth did a similar project in Connecticut and another one in Maryland."

Leaning in closer, Dallas peered at the smudged paper. "What kind of deal?"

"Let me tell it."

She sat back and crossed her ballerina arms.

"First, he identifies a not-for-profit that's sitting on a desirable piece of property or owns a suitable building and wants to expand."

"Like The People's Theater," Roxy said.

"Right. The organization must be reputable, the people running it well liked in the community, just like Joe Dawes. Spider listens to their aspirations and tells them he can help them. He paints a picture of development and promises money-people will make it happen. Next comes the offer–a loan at too-good-to-pass-up interest rates and assurances of increased business that will come their way because of his new development."

Roxy said, "That's exactly what he pledged."

"Yeah."

"How did you find out about these others?"

Dallas jumped in. "Zay knows folks."

Zay popped up from his seat, nodded to Dallas. "Next, Spider and the executive director win over the board chair. That's where Sandman comes into the picture. Between them, they give Spider credibility and entrée to other people in the community who have connections and clout." Zay paced in a small circle as he spoke. "Together, this group of citizens go to the local municipality and gets them lined up. The mayor and key legislators, usually of the same political party, see the opportunity for increased tax revenues, new business, and in-town revitalization. The cities he picks are not too big but are in excellent locations for gentrification–bringing back the middle and upper classes to a working-class town. Just like Fieldcrest. The coalition of citizens, philanthropists, and politicos then go to the state leadership."

"So far, this doesn't sound like a problem," Dallas said. "In fact, I kinda like it. Is there bad news buried in this story?"

"In each instance, as part of the deal, the not-for-profit involved puts up collateral–a building in Connecticut and land in Maryland."

"Why risk their property?" Roxy asked.

"It sounds like a sure thing to the executive director and board chair. They have the support of people with money, like Spider and Sandman, and the backing of the local governments."

"And they hunger for something," Dallas said. "Like Joe and his school."

Roxy asked. "Does it work, or does Spider steal their land?"

"Yes and no. Not theft, but in each case, the organization's property ends up in Booth's hands."

Roxy asked, "How does he do it?"

"Not sure. But I have a name and contact info for a guy who was part of the deal in Connecticut." He handed Roxy a scrap of paper.

"Trey Laws, Executive Director, Children and Family Advocacy Center," Roxy read. An address, phone number, and website URL followed. "Thanks for all of your help, Zay. This means a lot to me."

"What're you gonna do?"

Roxy stared at the paper. "Take a trip to Connecticut."

CHAPTER 29

Dallas drove with purpose. Her GPS predicted they'd arrive in Connecticut, by 5:15. Trey Laws told Roxy he'd be there until six.

The rain let up for minutes at a time but then returned full force. The wipers couldn't keep up. They pulled over to wait until visibility improved. Thunder and lightning slashed the air.

"Now's a good time to tell me about you and Zay," Roxy said.

Dallas groaned. "He's getting married."

"Oh."

"Came over with a bottle of wine and flowers. I misread the entire situation. Confident he planned to propose again."

"He gave signs?"

"*No.*" Dallas made a dismissive laughing sound. "How dumb is that?"

"You've always loved him."

"In my way," Dallas said, looking out the window. "But if I loved him, why push him away every time we got close?"

Roxy kept her thoughts to herself. Glory and Tapp didn't approve of Zay. Even though Dallas was an independent woman of thirty-six, her parents' values and opinions weighed heavily. "Might be you don't really love him."

"He's been my backup guy. Shame on me." She blew out a puff of air. "And now he's marrying someone else."

"And giving the right guy a chance with you."

Dallas stayed quiet for a few beats. Then her face muscles relaxed, and her expression changed. "Want to attend the wedding with me–be my date? That'll cheer you up."

"You're joking, right?"

"Give you a respite." From her bag, she nudged out a taped together white card with gold lettering. "Got the invitation right here." She waggled it in front of Roxy's face. "Says, Ms. Dallas Swan and guest."

"What happened to it?"

"I ripped it up, but then salvaged it."

Roxy examined the once-shredded card. "Why don't you tell him how you feel?"

"And this is good advice from a serial secret-keeper?"

Unable to hold her head up for another second, Roxy slumped forward.

"I'm sorry, Ro-Ro. Lord, I didn't mean that." Dallas put her arms around Roxy. "Once you tell them and the healing starts, things will get better."

"Are you really going to the wedding?"

"Considering." Dallas shifted and drove the van into the slow-moving traffic. Although it slowed a bit, rain continued to batter the vehicle. For miles, the only sound was the rain slapping the windshield and drumming on the roof.

The road ahead had few cars. The rain sped up again. That, plus the spray kicked up from car tires ahead and next to them, made it hard to see.

"How close are we?" Roxy asked.

The GPS voice answered. "Turn left onto Caroline Drive in 900 feet." The speedometer read twenty-five miles per hour.

"Can you see the street sign ahead?" Dallas asked.

Roxy saw a fork on the left. One road was at a right angle, the other sloped at a diagonal. The road signs were small and unreadable. She glanced at the GPS map. "Looks like a sharp left onto Caroline."

"K." Dallas put on her signal.

From the corner of her eye, Roxy saw a BMW barreling toward them. "Dee-Dee, look out."

Dallas jerked her head right and spun the wheel hard. The tires slipped into a slide. One hand over the other, Dallas turned the steering wheel into the skid. "Hold on."

Roxy braced herself against the dashboard, both arms outstretched, palms flat and forward.

Dallas pumped the brakes. The tires screeched. The BMW flashed in front of them as the van shuddered to a stop.

"Oh my God," Dallas said. "You, alright?"

Panting, Roxy nodded. "You?"

"That idiot driver needs to be arrested."

The two women sat, quieting their hearts, and breathing. Roxy glanced at the dashboard clock. "Damn. We're going to miss Mr. Laws."

"Not on my watch." Dallas spoke to the cyber genie, "Siri, call Trey Laws."

After several rings, a male voice said, "Laws here."

"This is Dallas Swan and Roxy Quinton. The traffic is horrendous, so we might be late for our meeting."

Roxy heard both sides of the conversation relayed through the dashboard phone system.

"How late?"

"Minutes. You understand, I'm sure. The rain and traffic. We won't take a lot of your time, but this is super critical."

He followed a loud huff with, "I'll wait, but not too long. My family is expecting me for dinner."

"We're not far." She took an audible breath. "But we're driving slowly."

"Be safe," he said. "Ring the bell. I've locked up."

• • •

Children and Family Advocacy shared space with a community health center and adult daycare facility. Roxy and Dallas made a dash for the front door, found the suite number on the directory, and climbed the stairs to the third floor. As instructed, they rang the bell.

Forty-something, overweight, with a nine-months-pregnant gut, Trey Laws offered them a seat and bottled water. "What can I do for you ladies?"

"Thank you for waiting."

They'd arrived at 6:10, still shaken from the almost accident, but now alert and hopeful. "As I explained on the phone," Roxy began, "we're connected with The People's Theater in Fieldcrest, NY."

"Great organization." Trey fiddled with his pen, rhythmically tapping it on the desk. "My niece did a summer internship there last year."

"Oh, what's her name?" Roxy loved the interns she worked with, but most were on the technical team.

"My brother's kid, Shanna Laws–set decoration."

"I remember her," Roxy said with enthusiasm. "Talented."

Trey beamed. "She's at Pratt now."

"Congratulations." Everyone's teens were doing great but hers. She gave herself a mental shake. No pity parties. Stay focused.

Dallas gave him her ear-to-ear. "I'm sure she learned a lot, and the experience helped her with her college application."

"It did."

"That's why we're here," Dallas said in her professional voice. "About talented children like your niece."

Trey put down the pen and spread his hands, palms up. "How can I help?"

Roxy said, "Does that name Webster Booth mean anything to you?"

"Booth?" Trey spat the name. "Lying sack of shit. Pardon me ladies. I rarely use that type of language, but that's what he is."

"What did he lie about?" Roxy asked.

"His intentions."

Roxy and Dallas waited.

"Painted this grandiose picture of new business development, jobs and neighborhood revitalization." Trey jumped up. His stomach shook. "We owned a nice building with a playground in the back for the kids and a basement filled with computers and stuff for the folks working on job placement." He scratched the top of his balding head. "We wanted to expand, build on our success. Booth said he'd make that happen." Trey banged his clenched fist on the desktop. "We bought the complete package."

Dallas looked around at the cramped quarters. "Did any of it happen?"

"Yeah." His tone was grudging. "We grew from one site to four. Doubled the number of people we served."

Roxy asked, "What went wrong?"

"Missed-payment clause." Trey rubbed the palms of his hands on his bulging thighs. "There was a statement in the fine print. If we missed *one* payment, late by even *one day*, then the property we put up to secure the loan becomes Booth's."

Roxy's voice became a whisper. "And you missed an installment?"

"Cash flow is the bane of our existence. We're always juggling. The expansion increased expenses. Our creditors hang in there with us because they know we're doing good for the community. But not Booth." He paused. "He took our building and land then flipped it—sold it to the city at a reduced price, shared some proceeds with his other investors, and kept the rest."

"The property wasn't his in the first place, but he gets the money?" Roxy asked.

Dallas added, "The city went along with this?"

Trey's eyes squinted, his lips a straight line. "They made out," he said, his palms open and up. He wagged his index finger at them, schooling them on the ways of the world. "The politicians went along because of the expected commercial success from the entire development. By the time we defaulted, the project was well underway, but we were SOL."

"How come your lawyers didn't catch it and fight?" Roxy asked.

"Good question," Trey said. "If you ask me, they were all in cahoots." He shook his head. "One stinking, dung-infested conspiracy."

Dallas, the savvy businesswoman, said, "I bet the lawyers didn't miss the clause. The deal seemed smart. The anticipated rewards outweighed the risks in their minds."

Roxy said, "I'd never endanger the theater for any reason. I can't imagine Joe falling for this. It makes little sense."

"People trust people," Dallas said. "When they see pots of gold under a rainbow of promises from rich business types and smooth-talking politicos, they accept what they want to be true."

Trey nodded his head. "Exactly."

"He did nothing illegal, though, did he?" Roxy asked. It wasn't a question. She knew the answer.

"No," admitted Trey. "Underhanded, but not unlawful."

Roxy rubbed her hands along the nubby fabric of her well-worn slacks. "And the developments are going forward, housing and jobs?"

"Yeah," Trey said, twisting around, his arms sweeping the air, taking in the tiny office, "but I'm screwed and so are the people we serve."

There it was. Spider did good for the town and better for himself. Was the theater in jeopardy or was Joe aware of the missed-payment clause? Roxy needed to find out and warn Joe if he wasn't.

Roxy and Dallas thanked Trey again and headed for the door.

"Be careful," Trey said. "Not just because of the deal. You women be cautious around him."

Roxy turned on her heels as her nape hairs rose. "Why?"

"Two women accused him of sexual assault. I don't know the truth of it, but my wife says always believe the women."

Roxy walked back to his desk. "What happened? Was he prosecuted?"

"Nope." He took a loud breath. "One of them–single mom, struggling–worked for me and acted as liaison between our project and Booth. Next thing I know, she quit, bought a condo and enrolled her oldest in private school." He hiked his shoulders. "Sounded like a payoff to me."

Roxy took a deep breath and pressed her hand against her racing heart. "Are you in touch with her?"

"From time to time."

A confluence of emotions swamped Roxy. Fear, hope, anger. "Can you give her a message for me?" Roxy pulled out one of her business cards from the salon and wrote her mobile number on the back. "Ask her to call me?"

Trey fingered the card. "Seems like she's put it behind her. Might have signed something, ya know. Non-disclosure sort of thing. Booth ain't stupid."

"Please, Mr. Laws. Tell her..." Her voice faltered. She squared her shoulders and lifted her chin. "Webster Booth raped me. I only want to ask her a few questions."

175

CHAPTER 30

Roxy and Dallas drove to the hospital. Torrents of rain continued to pound down. "We have the goods on Spider plus the possible sexual assault angle. You're going to warn Joe..." Dallas peered at Roxy with a quick dart and then returned her gaze to the road. "Right?"

"Right."

"And tell Carl everything." Again, she shot a look at Roxy. "Tonight... right?"

"Tonight?"

"You have run out of time and road to maneuver."

"Agreed."

"Good girl." Dallas switched on the radio to a salsa station. The music filled the car, fast and spicy. Dallas banged out rhythms on the steering wheel.

• • •

Maternity wards are often one of the nicer areas in hospitals. Cheery colors and liberal visiting hours keep the rooms filled with family and friends. Fieldcrest's community hospital was no exception. Tonight, the atmosphere zipped with anxious happiness. When Roxy arrived, her spirits were just the opposite. When she should feel as buzzed as the surrounding air, her mood deflated instead. Nothing was going the way she'd imagined.

Jewel shared her room with another Black woman named Sam who appeared to be a few years older than Jewel. As Roxy approached Room 221, Sam's people were everywhere–in the hall and inside the room. Two men and a teenaged girl slouched against opposite sides of the doorjamb. The level of conversation resembled a party with multiple conversations and ribbons of laughter.

"Excuse me." Roxy slipped past the girl and edged around a couple who had their backs to Jewel's side of the room.

A drawn curtain concealed Jewel's bed. At first, Roxy thought Dr. Wu was examining Jewel, or a nurse was checking her vital signs. An unfamiliar male voice and a giggle from Jewel told Roxy otherwise.

"Hello."

"Mom?"

"May I come in?" Roxy asked with the equivalent of a mom-knock–requesting while entering without waiting for a response.

Jewel glared at her. "We agreed."

Roxy tried for a warm smile, but she wasn't sure what her face showed. Jewel and a young man sat on the bed side by side, propped up against the slanted mattress, earplugs connected to two sets of ears and a laptop between them. He had a slight build and seemed only a few pounds heavier and a few inches taller than Jewel. Curly brown hair, clear rectangular eyeglasses, cargo pants that hung from narrow hips, and smooth white skin. He pulled out the earplugs and jumped up.

"Good evening, ma'am." He thrust his hand toward Roxy. "I'm Ed Coppersmith."

Roxy tried to catch her breath. She took his hand and gave him a limp handshake along with what she hoped was a neutral look. Without taking her eyes off Ed, she took the two steps necessary to reach Jewel's bedside, shifted her gaze, leaned over, and kissed her daughter's forehead. Jewel jerked away. Roxy ignored the slight. She understood.

She coughed and cleared her throat. "How are you? What's the doctor say?"

"I'm fine." Jewel squirmed under the sheet. "What are you doing here?"

Roxy was still Jewel's mother, still in charge. No matter her transgressions, this behavior was not acceptable. She made her tone motherly stern. "When was the doctor here?"

"None of your business."

Ed said, "Hey, Rabbit, maybe cut your mom some slack."

Who the hell was this guy? Rabbit? "How old are you?"

"Mom."

Roxy back peddled. "Sorry. It's been an exceptionally long and trying day."

Ed said, "No worries. Nineteen. I'm a sophomore at Penn."

"Penn?"

"The University of Pennsylvania in Philly."

"Can we stop the interrogation?" Jewel said. "I'm hungry and the food stinks here."

"Perhaps *Ed* could get you something."

"We already checked out the cafeteria–try finding anything vegetarian. It's a hospital. Isn't it supposed to be *healthy?*"

Roxy knew Jewel's petulance was nerves, fear, and whatever else Nadine's accusations elicited.

Ed said, "I'll take a look around the neighborhood."

"Thanks," Jewel said, still not looking at Roxy.

"Is that computer yours?" Roxy asked Ed.

Jewel spoke to Roxy for the first time in a civil way. Excited was a good description. "Eddie bought it for me and downloaded three of my favorite movies."

That took Roxy back. How much did the computer cost and what was he doing spending that kind of money and how did he come by it? She examined Ed's eyes more closely–large, brown, and fringed with short, thick lashes. Drug users had telltale signs. He looked clean and sober.

"Mom." Her tone angry again.

Once again, Roxy responded as if everything was fine between them. "Yes?"

"You're staring." Jewel squinted at Roxy.

Embarrassed, Roxy shrugged an apology to Ed who, to his credit, shot her a generous grin back.

Ed grabbed his backpack. "Can I get you anything, Mrs. Q.?"

Already using an overly familiar name for Roxy. "No, thank you." Except she was starving. It was already eight o'clock and she hadn't eaten since lunch.

"Mommy." Kia dashed into the room. "Is there a baby yet? We missed you. I rhymed today and MeMa said I did great. I'm gonna be a rapper. Where's Daddy? Where's the baby?"

Gabriella and Carl's mother, Celeste, followed.

"How are my girls?" Roxy helped them shed their rain gear. She hugged them tight. "Where's Max?"

The tasty aroma of pasta, cheese, and warm bread filled the room. Celeste said, "I brought along a late-night picnic." She pointed her sharp chin toward Ed who hadn't yet left. "Do you work here? Pull over that movable tray. I can't imagine they are feeding my grandchild anything eatable."

"Grandma." Jewel sounded indignant. "Eddie is my friend."

Celeste gave him an up and down scrutiny. "Well, friend, pull the tray over."

"Yes, ma'am."

Paper plates, cups, plastic forks, napkins, shredded parmesan, olive oil, and a liter-sized bottle of ginger ale emerged from a shopping bag. She pulled containers of pasta, sauce, and two loaves of bread from an insulated bag.

"Where's Max?" Roxy asked again.

Celeste said, "Coming with Carl. They're walking your mangy dogs."

Gabriella threw her grandmother a disapproving look but said nothing.

"What's the doctor say?" Celeste put two paper plates together and flexed them as if testing their strength.

For the first time, Roxy was grateful for Celeste's presence. Jewel now appeared less angry and hurt, but Roxy knew this was a temporary reprieve.

"Probably Thursday, but it could be Friday. We don't know for sure," Jewel said speaking to her grandmother and not looking at Roxy.

"Induce labor or what?" Celeste piled on spaghetti, ladled the sauce, and then sprinkled on shreds of parmesan and Romano cheeses.

Ed said, "Dr. Wu thinks a Cesarean is best."

Celeste gave him a look that Roxy realized was a replica of Gabriella's–the one that made Roxy feel as if *she* were the five-year-old.

"Who are you, again?" Celeste swiveled her head toward Roxy as if to ask, are you hearing this?

"Grandma, don't be like that." Jewel took the offered plate and sniffed the food. "Yum. Thanks."

Was Ed the baby's father? Roxy tried not to stare at him again. Nothing about him was familiar. She tried to recall the young people who used to hang out with Jewel before she got pregnant. They were every color, a rainbow of friends–Asians,

Puerto Rican's, people from the Dominican Republic, and other Caribbean countries.

Roxy handed Ed a plate of pasta.

"Thank you." He took the food, dipped, and twirled his fork, wrapping the noodles around, and then put them in his mouth with barely a drip of sauce.

"How did you guys meet?" Roxy asked.

"Mommy," Gabriella said, pulling at Roxy's shirt, "when can we come home?"

"Soon, sweetheart." She took a napkin. "Here, let me wipe your mouth." Who was going to babysit now? In a few days, they'd all be home. Then what?

"I'm Kia."

Ed squatted down and put his hand out. "Nice to meet you, Kia. I'm Ed."

Kia shook his hand. "I rhymed today. MeMa took us to the lie-berry. We read all these books, and we had to tell what time it was, but the rhyming was the best part. Do you know any famous rappers? Cause that's what I'm gonna be when I get bigger... or a YouTube star. Gabriella's gonna be a doctor or a pilot or... what else you gonna be?"

"An engineer."

"Wow." Ed put out his hand to Gabriella. "How do you do?"

It was rare for Gabriella to take to strangers, but she seemed to like Ed.

Ed said in an earnest voice, "Jewel and I met at a party," in answer to Roxy's earlier question. A smile spread across his face. "I took one look at her and knew I had to meet her." He turned back to Gabriella. "What does an engineer do?"

Roxy watched Ed, Gabriella, and Kia eat and chat with each other. Jewel caught her mother's eyes sending Roxy an obvious message. "Don't ask him another question." She mouthed, "Okay," before settling down on the floor with a plate, but not touching the food. The family ate propped up against the wall or sitting on the edge of Jewel's bed or, like Roxy, squatting on the floor. Ed and Gabriella reached for seconds as Carl and Max walked in.

"Hi, family. I sure hope you saved some for us," Carl said.

Kia leapt up. "Daddy, Jewel doesn't have a baby yet. And Ed plays the drums. He said he'd teach me."

Roxy rose. Max let her hug him—a rare treat. With his arm circling her waist, Carl brushed his lips against hers and then kissed the tip of her nose. She settled back and took a few mouthfuls as she surveyed her assembled family and searched

180

for the right word to describe her emotions. Normal. Jewel had stopped glaring at her. Carl and the kids were laughing, eating, and talking. Even Celeste's and Ed's presence felt good at this moment. She needed to let it last for a few more minutes before reality crashed down on her. A tune Roxy heard Carl singing the other day played in her head. The lyrics eluded her except one line. The singer longed to "turn back the hands of time." If only she had the power to do that. Another line came to her. "Time goes by, and blessings are missed in a blink of an eye." Here were all her blessings, right in front of her. Every day she tried to achieve more for her family, do something different, and find a new path to something better. The wiser goal might be don't blink.

CHAPTER 31

Everyone finished eating. Carl and Roxy cleaned up, threw all the food-smeared paper plates into the trash and brushed crumbs from Jewel's bed. The noise level thrummed at a comforting level filled with familiar sounds of family talk. The twins and Carl played a game Roxy didn't understand on Carl's smart phone. It required thumbs clicking on the screen, and giggles and gasps seem to add to the fun. Max, Jewel, and Ed watched videos on YouTube on Jewel's new computer, Ed on one side of Jewel and Max on the other, their heads almost touching as they tracked the action. Celeste slept in a visitor's chair rolled in by Ed. Her snores quiet enough not to disturb the others.

• • •

Roxy and Carl entered the empty apartment. No dogs, no children, not even white noise from the always-on television. Now the only sounds were the hum of the refrigerator and the steady beat of the rain hitting the windows. She dropped her bag in the hall and hung her raincoat on one of the hooks. It dripped onto a plastic tray on the floor. Carl flipped on lights and hung his jacket next to hers. They walked into the kitchen. Spread across the table were coloring books and crayons, an empty bowl with dried bits of cereal caked along its sides, yesterday's *Daily News*, and a pile of unopened mail.

The peace she felt at the hospital, a bare thirty-minutes ago, already dissipated. Instead, the information Trey Laws shared left Roxy feeling like every nerve in her body was vibrating. "I need a beer." She opened the refrigerator and grabbed a can of Bud. "Want one?"

"Some of yours."

She popped the top and handed him the can. Carl took a long swallow.

Carl asked, "What's your impression of Ed?"

"Nice enough, I guess." She took the beer can back but didn't drink. "Did you like him?"

"Little surprised he's a white guy."

"Me too. He calls her Rabbit. That's funny. I guess because she's vegetarian."

"Is he the father?"

Roxy shrugged.

"If he is, he'd better man up." Carl retrieved the beer and finished it. "Where's he been?"

"Jewel said he's just a friend."

"This guy is into her. No man gonna be hanging around a pregnant woman unless the kid is his." Carl crushed the empty can and tossed it into the re-cycle bin standing next to the alphabet-and-photo covered refrigerator. "My father is going to go ape shit." An almost laugh. "Good."

"Perhaps Jewel never told him, and he just found out."

"He could do the math. The boy didn't act stupid."

So many secrets and lies. "Can I ask you something?"

He looked at her, clearly recognizing the shift in her tone. They'd been together so long that he knew every inflection. "Got something on your mind?"

"Have you ever kept a secret from me, not something little, but a big secret?"

"Are you still worried about last Friday?" He reached for her and put his arms around her. "You've got nothing to worry about from me, baby. I've never, ever been unfaithful, not once. Just got a lot on my mind these days and needed some space. Like I said, it had nothing to do with you and me."

She curled into the crook of his arm. Friday a zillion years ago.

"And don't worry about the house. It's gonna work out."

Roxy nestled deeper.

He tilted her face toward his and kissed her. Roxy responded. He tasted cool and salty from the beer.

Carl switched off the kitchen light. "Let's take a break from worrying, just for the night."

Yes. Put all the pain and anxiety aside. Scrub everything from her mind and get a decent night sleep. Instead, she said, "Things aren't always the way they seem."

"Things are often exactly as they seem." He took her by the hand and led her to their bedroom.

They lay side by side, listening as the rain and jazz from the radio, each adding riffs, played off each other.

Carl asked, "Wanna make out?"

"Hmm."

He pulled her on top of him, shifted around until his penis, growing harder with each second, nestled exactly between her thighs. With confident hands, he caressed her back.

She kissed his neck. "Carl?"

"Yeah?" He nuzzled her, both hands gently rubbing her buttocks.

"If you ever did something bad, something you kept secret from me, I just want you to know that after I found out, after you told me, I'd forgive you."

CHAPTER 32
WEDNESDAY

Music from Wynton Marsalis's trumpet filled the converted Victorian's halls–a bluesy, swing tune–played loud enough for anyone in the building to enjoy.

The hallway was dark and empty. "Joe?" Roxy called, lifting her voice above the music. "Are you here?" She knocked on his office door and it swung open just as the music reached a crescendo.

The glow from two computer screens and the gray morning light from the window were the only illumination in the room. Joe's office was large but didn't look it. Even in the poor light, Roxy took in all the papers, bits of costumes, and posters that covered every available space. Plaques covered the walls, a white board displaying red, blue, and green bulleted notes, some circled, others underlined, and the architectural rendering of the to-be-built school sat on an easel.

The music made her believe Joe would be back in a few minutes. Should she stay and wait or come back later? The last notes of the trumpet died and now the only sound was the rain pelting the windows, making its own tribal music. Without warning, Roxy's legs buckled. She held onto the edge of Joe's desk, inched around, and sank into his chair. A flash of lightning lit up the room.

Roxy closed her eyes, put her head between her legs and tried to still the irregular thump of her heart. Another panic attack? Once she got past opening night, she'd make a doctor's appointment just in case it was something else. Plus, she needed a way to control them.

Seconds ticked by and the nausea and dizziness passed. Roxy opened her eyes, sat up, and glanced around. She dug out a stick of gum from her bag, unwrapped it, and folded the gum into her mouth. After chewing for a few seconds, she relaxed as her stomach settled and her heart rhythm returned to normal.

It wasn't a worked-out decision, just an impulse. One of Joe's laptops was on in front of her, and to her left a file drawer stood partially opened. At first, she scanned the Word document on his screen, but it was ad copy for a new Director of Philanthropy. That was quick. Had Joe fired Glenn, or did Glenn quit? She clicked on the drop-down box and read the titles of other recent documents. None seemed to have anything to do with the new school or the deal with Spider.

She listened for footfalls. Waited. Hearing nothing, the file drawer received her attention next. Feeling guilty and nervous, she thumbed the file folders, reading their titles–Accounting, Costumes, Deliverables, Sales, School. Her fingers stopped. The manila folder labeled "School" slipped out of its spot with a tug. Roxy pulled a lamp from the desk, slid down from the chair onto the floor, switched on the lamp, and opened the folder.

On top were sketches of the new school, similar to, but in more detail than, the ones Joe and Spider had shown at the board meeting. She shuffled through them, glancing at the drawings but not wasting time there. Underneath were several legal documents. Roxy scanned them, looking at the headings in bold. Nothing looked helpful. On the bottom of one of them was a note to Joe. Roxy's eyes dropped to the signature. It was from Otto "Sandman" Sand.

It's a go. We have the coalition together. Time to move. Put the deeds up and let's make this thing happen.

Otto

Joe Dawes's heavy tread caught Roxy in deep thought. "What the...?" He clicked on the overhead light.

Roxy tried to jump up from her hiding spot. The edge of the desk met her forehead with a painful thump, and Roxy groaned as she scrambled. "It's me."

"You crawled under my desk?" Cinnamon freckles and fine red hairs covered his crossed arms.

"I'm sorry. I didn't mean to snoop."

"What *did* you mean to do?"

Joe walked around his desk. Roxy backed up.

"What the hell are you doing here?" He lifted the open folder. "Talk to me or the next person you're gonna speak to is a cop."

"I'm so sorry." She began again. "I have some valuable information." Except the only evidence she had was the conversation with Trey Laws.

"You skulked around so you can tell *me* something?"

"It's about Spider."

Joe sat down and closed the folder, switched off his laptop. "I'm listening."

"A friend of mine, Detective Adams—"

Joe swung toward Roxy, his tone still challenging. "What about him?"

Roxy explained how she'd asked Zay to do some digging. She didn't give him the full explanation of why, but said she had reason to believe Spider was doing something unsavory. She shared what she and Dallas had uncovered from Zay's tip, without mentioning the sexual assaults. Yet.

For several seconds Joe sat there staring at her, his mouth working, his lips closed tight. When his silence got to be too much, Roxy said, "I planned to fill you in so you can protect the theater."

Joe spoke. "How long have we known each other?"

"A long time."

"I remember when you started volunteering here, asking all kinds of questions about the theater, plays, acting, directing, set design. You were like a kid soaking it all up."

Roxy's dismay returned full force. She recognized this technique and knew she was about to be asked to either butt out or go home or both.

"In less than a week your play will open, with or without Vicki. If it's going to stay open for its two-week run, we'll need Vicki for more than opening night. She's due at tonight's fund-raiser and rehearsal. The play will bomb otherwise. You get what I'm saying?"

"Yes."

"Couldn't prove that by me."

"I'm sorry. I really am." She waited but Joe just stared at her. "So, you're not going to say anything about Spider or if this is a surprise or what you're going to do?"

"Do I appear stupid? Street dumb? Gullible?"

She shook her head.

"Spider's deal is solid. Everyone is going to win including you." Joe rose. "Until it comes through, we each have a job to do."

Roxy felt like a little kid facing a stern, disappointed parent. She apologized again. "I shouldn't have nosed around your office."

"I thought better of you."

Her crash was now complete and her play making it to off-Broadway a pipe dream, just as Carl said. Jewel and Carl would hate her. Jewel already did. Spider got to be a hero in the town, and no one would believe anything she said about him. She'd lost Joe's trust and probably any interest in putting on her next play. In her mind, the success of *The Monday Night Murder* would lead to a movie or TV mini-series and maybe to staging her next project. All fantasy. All gone or going to crap.

Roxy stayed put.

"Something else?"

"Laura Garrison invited me to the fund-raiser tonight. Vicki's promised to stay afterwards for the rehearsal. I plan to escort her here."

Joe closed his eyes. Roxy waited.

When he finally spoke, his tone was businesslike. "It's a start, but we're almost at the finish line. We'll have to close after opening night until the financing is approved for the school and renovations unless Laura's crowd comes through in a big way."

There it was. "One night? No backers?"

With a cold edge to his voice, Joe said, "Make sure Vicki shows." He looked back down at his papers, every aspect of his body language asked her to leave.

"Thank you for everything you've done for me."

He waved her words away. "See you tonight. We have money to raise and a show to put on."

CHAPTER 33

Dallas and Roxy sat across from Zay in Crony's Restaurant and Bar, a family-owned business that had been around for three generations. Outside the storm continued unabated. The three stayed quiet as they tucked into their meals of scrambled eggs, bacon, and toast. Dallas looked great. Dressed in one of her favorite outfits from Senegal, she'd twisted her braids around her head in a crown. Large gold hoops and her trademark bangles finished the outfit.

Roxy, on the other hand, looked rumpled and stressed. She'd overslept. Carl must have realized she needed the rest. When she jumped out of bed, and washed up, she only had time to drag on slacks and a short-sleeved blouse and left without makeup or jewelry. The family car waited for her in front of the building. She'd sped to the theater to warn Joe and get back in time for this meeting. Joe. His discovery of her snooping and their subsequent conversation weighed her down.

"Thanks for coming," Roxy said to Zay, wiping her mouth with her napkin. "We learned a lot in Connecticut. Plus, we need your advice on another matter."

"What'd you uncover?"

For the next few minutes, Roxy summarized what she and Dallas heard from Trey Laws about the land deal. "I'm gonna tell Laura. She's on the board and holding a fund-raiser tonight. My plan is to share everything and hope it's enough to keep the theater safe," she said in conclusion. "I warned Joe, but he said he has things under control."

"So why butt in?" Zay asked.

"Joe might be over his head."

"Not the Joe Dawes I remember," Zay said.

Roxy's suspicion, that Joe knew and was going along anyway, niggled. Sandman might be forcing Joe into this scheme. Or he had a plan, but no longer trusted Roxy, so he stayed quiet.

"Sounds like good news and bad," Zay said.

"Where's the good?" Dallas's tone was sharp. She ratcheted it down. "I mean, he's the Lex Luthor we suspected."

"The Connecticut town and folks made out. Only the nonprofit got hurt."

"And that's okay with you, letting Joe and the theater get messed over?" Dallas asked.

Zay pushed back in his seat and crossed his arms. "I'm not the bad guy here."

Roxy squeezed Dallas's hand under the table. The conversation she had with Dallas about setting Zay free flashed through her mind. Dallas had said she didn't love him the way a wife ought to love a husband. Plus, his idea of a family included children, but hers did not. If they stayed friends, it would have to differ from what it was in the past. Now her behavior contradicted both her newfound understanding and intentions.

"I see your point," Roxy said refocusing, "but why should Joe lose so Spider can get richer?" She couldn't take a chance with her theater. She had to protect it at all costs.

Zay sipped his coffee.

"Well?" Dallas asked, her sharp tone back.

He shifted his gaze and spoke to Roxy. "I hope you can pull off a miracle. Save Joe but leave the deal in place. This town needs a break, is all I'm saying."

That logic and wish were hard to argue.

Dallas said, "I'm showing Spider and his wife some of the properties I've identified as good for their business and several houses and condominiums that might meet their needs. During the tour, I plan to dig deeper, hint at what we learned and see if Spider will back off."

Roxy and Dallas had discussed this strategy on the way home from Connecticut. It made Roxy nervous.

"Be careful," Zay said. "Don't overplay your hand. He's savvy and quick, not to mention ruthless."

Roxy considered that, but she and Dallas had agreed to try different avenues. Even though Joe seemed confident, Roxy doubted he understood the extent of Spider's evil ways. "Something else I wanted to ask you," Roxy said.

"Uh-huh."

She told him about the sexual assault accusations and the message she'd left with Laws.

"Did you get a name? Has she contacted you?"

"Not yet."

"Defamation of character is real and NDRs–non-disclosure agreements–are dangerous to break."

For the second time in her life, Roxy said the powerful words aloud. "He raped me, so I know he's capable."

"Shit."

"Yeah," Dallas said. "Exactly."

"Be in touch if the woman calls you," Zay said. "Ask lots of questions including can you tape the conversation, but don't count on that. Call me afterwards." He drained his cup. "And I'm sorry." He shifted in his seat as if uncomfortable. "About what Booth did to you."

They finished their meals. Roxy shook his hand and said goodbye. Dallas stood but didn't move to leave.

"I appreciate the invitation to your wedding," Dallas said to Zay. "I realize I acted the opposite the other day—"

"Tell me about it."

"But." She amended her sentence. "*And*, I've had time to reflect."

Roxy knew how hard this was for her friend.

"I'm happy for you and your bride," Dallas said. "You deserve everything you desire."

Roxy watched Zay look at Dallas with squinted eyes, his expression wary.

Dallas plowed on. "It would be unfair of me to attend your wedding–unfair to both of you."

"I told her I invited you. She's cool with it."

"A gracious lady. But it's odd for your former lover, longtime girlfriend, to show up."

Zay appeared to weigh Dallas words. "I'd like us to still be friends."

"How will your wife feel about us hanging out?" She shook her head in answer to her own question. "You are free Xavier Adams. Free of me. Go forth, be happy, and multiply." With her right hand raised, she made the Vulcan live-long-and-prosper sign from Star Trek.

· · ·

Roxy felt on the edge of everything, as if balancing on a ledge of life-changing answers. When she woke up, late and alone, she prayed for guidance and strength. She knew she had a choice. Keep worrying and watching her world crumble—or change her mindset and take charge.

Everything was in motion. Dallas's meeting with Spider and Nadine, and the woman who accused Spider of assault had Roxy's number. Yesterday at the hospital, Jewel appeared less angry with Roxy. And last night, making love with Carl, reminded her of good days past and what their future might hold.

Jewel's condition was stable. Celeste reported the kids were all fine; even the dogs, which Celeste hated, were behaving. Tonight, Roxy planned to enlist Laura's help, and together they'd save the theater. Vicki was coming. So far, Jewel had said nothing to her father. Roxy intended to tell Carl after the rehearsal tonight. She needed to practice what and how she'd say it. She'd write the script of her life.

Be positive. Count your blessings. Make things happen. Don't blink.

· · ·

"Roxy," Angel said snapping his fingers in front of her eyes, "Violet is waiting at the sink."

Startled, Roxy let out an "Oh." She had been standing still, smiling inwardly. Now she focused on Angel, his brown eyes wide.

"You know how *she* can get," he said in a stage whisper.

"Thanks. On my way."

Roxy trotted to the back of the shop to rinse out the conditioner in Violet's hair. For the first time in more months than Roxy remembered, she didn't have a headache. No nausea or dizziness or oppressive tiredness. And for a second full day, welcome rain came down hard.

Zoe hustled over. "Aunt Roxy, you have a request for a wash and set at three thirty and two requests for four or five."

Roxy glanced at her watch. It was two forty. The fund-raising reception for the theater started at five followed by the dress rehearsal at seven. She hoped to meet with Laura at four. "Sorry, I have to get ready for tonight. Can't take any of them. Maybe Angel or B.J."

The shop buzzed with activity. Unlike most other weekdays, Wednesdays enjoyed a steady stream of businesswomen who came for midweek touchups. Roxy had back-to-back appointments from ten to three with no break for lunch.

She wrapped Violet's hair in a towel. Fifty, polished, successful, Violet worked and lived up-county but came to Frank's because, as she had explained the first day she'd showed up, finding a salon in her town able to care for a Black professional's hair was next to impossible.

Angel said, "Did you hear me?"

"Sorry," Roxy said to Angel who was cutting a man's hair in the chair to her right.

"I asked how rehearsals and ticket sales are doing. Good?" He snipped the gray sides with expert speed. "Big rehearsal tonight, right? Isn't Miss Thing supposed to show?"

"Yep." Roxy rubbed her eyes and lowered her hunched shoulders. "Huge night." In so many ways.

B.J. asked, "Do you have Jewel covered or need more help?" His customer appeared engrossed in an e-book while B.J. styled her hair.

Angel said, "I can run over around three for an hour."

"Thanks, but we're good. Of course, she'd love to see you both." Angel and Jewel enjoyed salsa dancing and he often helped her with her Spanish classes.

B.J. said, "Joanna is going by."

"Bless her," Roxy said. "She's there now."

"How's Jewel doing?"

"Both Dallas and Joanna reported all was well."

"Who's covering tonight while you're at the theater?" B.J. asked.

"Carl's gonna relieve Joanna."

"What's wrong with your daughter?" Violet sounded concerned more than curious.

193

"Nothing," Roxy said and meant it. "She's having a baby."

"Congrats."

This was also new for Roxy, being at peace about the baby. Dr. Wu scheduled the Cesarean for 2:00 p.m. on Friday. So far, Jewel was still ambivalent. The social worker, Annie Long, knew Jewel might change her mind, and she'd alerted the adoptive family. From Roxy's point of view, that was also fine. She pictured Ed's pale skin and bright brown eyes. No matter. A beautiful, healthy, loved baby—that's what was important. Roxy wished her dad were alive for this momentous time in their lives.

If Jewel decided to keep the baby, it would be hard but wonderful. If she went ahead with the adoption, well that would be hard but okay too. Jewel was young, but not too young to make a sensible decision. An inside smile emerged. Where was all this peace coming from?

With swift strokes, Roxy pulled a comb through the remaining tangles of Violet's hair, picked up the blow dryer and brush and began to dry and curl her straightened, shoulder-length locks, the heat and brush making smooth bumps at the end of each handful. Just as Jewel was going to give birth, so was Roxy. Birth to her play, but more importantly, revealing her eighteen-year-old secret.

A petite Black woman dressed in jeans and a loose top walked in the front door. Holding a dripping umbrella, she pulled off her baseball cap and ran her fingers through a short afro.

"Still raining like crazy," she said to the room at large.

According to the weather station, a slow-moving front had settled over the East Coast bringing steady rain jazzed by occasional thunder and lightning.

"I like it," Roxy said. "Better than the heat."

"May I help you?" Zoe held her cell phone in her hand as if she were about to make a call.

"I'd like to speak with the owner," the woman said, looking at Roxy.

B.J. asked, "How can I help you?" He continued putting rollers in the hair of the young woman in his chair.

The guest came over to B.J. "My name is Harriet Jones," she said looking at both B.J. and Roxy. "I'd like to rent a booth. I've got a strong client base but need additional space." Her eyes swept around the salon and then landed back on B.J. "I'm licensed and dependable with strong references."

"I'm sure what you're saying is true, but we're not renting." B.J. made another part and wrapped the lock around a red roller.

"You look like you have enough space, and I can see you've got folks waiting," Harriet Jones said with an accusing tone, her hands thrust deep in her pockets. "I can help. Pick up the slack on full days and bring in folks on slow ones." A drop of rain seeped from her scalp onto her forehead. The woman pulled out her hand and wiped it away, her eyes once again scanning the shop.

Roxy looked at the salon through the newcomer's eyes. Although all three of them–B.J., Angel, and Roxy–were working flat out, empty workstations lined the wall between Angel's space and the sinks.

"Well, sorry, but that's how it is," B.J. said.

The woman made a disgruntled sound but didn't move. B.J. asked his customer if the weather was getting to her. Clearly, he believed the conversation with Harriet Jones was over.

Roxy spoke to her. "Let me take your name and information." She steered the woman to the counter where Zoe was now on her cell phone. "We're not renting right this second." Carl's plan for their new salon came to mind. She lowered her voice hoping no one else heard her. "We will be soon." She handed Harriet a piece of paper and a pen.

"I hope you're not giving me a line to get rid of me." She wrote her contact info on the scrap of paper. "Your guy over there," she lifted her chin in B.J.'s direction, "shut me down hard."

"I'm interested," Roxy said with conviction.

She was getting behind Carl's dream. Joe made it clear. *The Monday Night Murder* was going to have one day on stage with Vicki, maybe a week. After that, the amateur actors took over for the rest of the run. No angel investors. No off-Broadway. The play was *not* her road to freedom. But the fixer-upper held potential. If they brought in someone with existing clientele, getting the salon going became easier. There was room enough for four stations... or was it three? "God presents opportunities disguised as challenges," Pastor Went used to tell her.

Grabbing one of her own cards from the front desk, Roxy gave it to Harriet and took the piece of paper. "Thank you. I'll be in touch." The woman left and Roxy returned to her customer.

"Were you thinking about Carl's venture?" B.J. asked in a quiet voice.

"Yeah." Angel might leave with them. He was great with hair and customers and helped keep the clientele multiracial. Their few white customers came because of Angel, and a loyal group a gay men and Latinas filled his chair.

"Carl said you were against—"

"Things change." She gave him a broad, confident smile.

Angel lifted his head. He must have heard Roxy's last remark. "Not around here."

Roxy gathered another swatch of Violet's hair. "That's true."

For Frank's Beauty Salon, but not Carl and Roxy's.

• • •

Roxy popped into the restroom to dress for the evening bash. Without Jewel to help her, Roxy did the best she could. An emerald-green dress with cap sleeves from deep in her closet. When was the last time she'd worn it? Another charity function, a few years ago–pre-COVID. Dallas, Zay, Carl, and Roxy went together as Dallas's guests. Since then, Roxy had gained a few pounds. Spanx helped smooth the bulges.

"Roxy?" Angel's voice bellowed. "You got company."

"Coming." She fastened her gold hoops, shut off the lights, and headed for the main salon.

Angel whistled as she passed. She gave him a slight bow and a big grin. He pointed to the front door.

Nadine Booth stood there, both hands clutching her leather bag and a dripping umbrella.

Roxy walked up to her. "What can I do for you?" She let ice chill each word.

"Can we speak somewhere privately?"

Anger bubbled up. This was the woman who told Jewel about Spider and Roxy, but not the truth about what happened. "Why are you here?" Roxy asked again.

"If you don't care that your customers hear your ugly stuff, then I don't."

Stiff-necked, Roxy led Nadine to the back. They went into the treatment room where, in theory, they waxed eyebrows and upper lips, but few customers asked for this service.

Roxy turned on the light and faced Spider's wife.

"Leave him alone," Nadine said. She stood an inch or so taller than Roxy. Her tailored jacket dress fit perfectly, and her hair looked freshly coifed. The same diamond-and-gold studs she'd worn to Sunday dinner dazzled from small ears.

"Who?" But Roxy knew.

"You're not becoming his new family. Not happening."

Roxy scrunched her face. "I don't know what you're talking about."

"I'm on to your game. Jewel this and Jewel that. Carl hanging out with him. You and your rabble clan won't get another dime." She'd lost her upper-west-side accent and sounded like street-folk.

Stunned, Roxy tried to decipher what Nadine was talking about.

"I intend to keep my man and every dime. Back up and back off."

Roxy's anger surfaced fast. "Why did you hurt my daughter?"

"Next, I tell your husband and the rest of your family unless you get out of Spider's life. He's not dumping me and he's not giving you any more money and he's not becoming part of your grubby family. Period."

Roxy's anger spilled over. "You can't intimidate me. I don't want anything to do with you or your rapist, swindling, lying husband. So, *you* better back up and back off."

Sweat beaded on Roxy's forehead and nose. Her heart thudded. Perspiration seeped from armpits and ran down her sides. She stomped to the front of the shop, grabbed her raincoat, shrugged into it, picked up her umbrella and rain boots, and without putting them on, stalked out of the shop.

CHAPTER 34

A young woman dressed in a beige suit opened the door. She took Roxy's umbrella and raincoat.

Laura Garrison's home was lovely. Just north and east of Fieldcrest, the hamlet in which Laura lived, was home to many wealthy people–Wall Street analysts and investors, hedge fund managers, and an assortment of doctors and lawyers who practiced in New York City or in the wealthiest parts of Westchester County.

Roxy expected a mansion but felt pleased with the sprawling two-story colonial. Straight ahead, a welcoming living space with a freestanding stone fireplace invited guests in. Overstuffed chairs, loveseats, and several pieces of free-standing sculpture, one a wrought-iron twist of angles and shapes, dotted the room.

In one corner, a telescope pointed toward the sky. The room went all the way through to a back patio and garden, visible through rain-pelted sliding glass doors. Beyond that, the Long Island Sound was a gray haze. Even in the storm, although it was the same body of water, the Sound from this vantage point looked nothing like the Bronx's Orchard Beach.

"May I use the rest room?" Roxy needed to repair her makeup and hair before speaking with Laura. She ducked into the powder room the greeter pointed out and did the best she could with the contents of her makeup bag and the guest towels stacked on the sink. Using her fingers, she twisted her blond locks into place, smoothed her dress, and took a deep breath.

A second woman, her breasts squeezed together and pushed up high, ushered Roxy into a cozy den. Bookshelves lined the walls and thick area rugs covered the squares and rectangles of the hardwood floor.

"Ms. Garrison will be with you in a minute," the woman said. "May I bring you a beverage?"

"Water, thank you," Roxy said, her mouth dry with tension.

While Roxy waited, she tried to calm down. The confrontation with Nadine had left her shaken. What would make Nadine think Roxy wanted anything to do with Spider? And what money? Carl's winnings? Paying Jewel as an intern? Being part of their family was bizarre.

"Hello."

Roxy mentally jumped.

Laura walked toward Roxy in full host mode. Arm extended, smile wide, dressed in a cobalt-blue suit perfectly tailored, neither tight nor loose. "I forgot you were coming. So much going on."

"Of course. I won't keep you."

"No, not a problem. You said you needed advice. Does this involve your play?"

The front doorbell rang in the distance.

Laura's face folded. "People can't be arriving already."

Roxy's confidence faded. The adrenaline rush from standing up to Nadine was now a full crash.

The woman with push-up breasts stuck her head in the doorway. "Caterers are back with the mushroom risotto."

"Thank you." She turned to Roxy. "They forgot a part of my order. What a day." Laura straightened her back and put her smile back on. "Come. Let's grab a corner over here before everyone invades." She used her right hand to indicate the way. "How can I be of service?"

The two women sat in plush wing chairs far from the door. A tall lamp on a round end table stood between them, its light soft and flattering. Laura's smooth skin had only a few faint wrinkles around her eyes and mouth.

Roxy screwed up her courage. "I'm worried about the theater," she began. "There's so much debt. Joe said my play is in jeopardy."

"He knows what he's doing." Her tone belied the confidence of her words.

"I wondered if there was anything I could do to help with fund-raising tonight or..." Roxy's voice trailed off.

Laura smiled and patted Roxy's hand. "Artists should not have to worry about finances."

Roxy tried to judge the sincerity of Laura's words. They were patronizing, but the tone kind. "I have to." She plunged into what she'd learned about the financing for the new school. "We're so vulnerable."

"The board is on top of things." Laura sounded miffed. "We review all the data, are aware of problems and threats, and we address them."

This was news to Roxy. Glenn intimated that Sandman, as the chair, wasn't trustworthy and Roxy held no doubts. "I'm glad to hear that."

"So?"

Roxy sensed Laura was about to dismiss her, but she had to try. "There's something else."

Laura's brow wrinkled. "Yes?"

She told Laura about the visit with Trey Laws and the missed-payment clause. "Joe didn't seem worried, but I thought you ought to know. Spider isn't a good person."

Laura stayed quiet with her head bowed. Roxy waited. Laura said, "What you've told me doesn't make him a bad person, just a shrewd entrepreneur."

"After the board meeting, you and I shared we'd both been raped."

Laura raised her head and looked at Roxy full on.

"Spider was the rapist."

This was the third time Roxy had said this aloud to three different people but not once to her husband. She stood, ready to leave, to run. She'd miscalculated everything.

Laura rose as well. "I'm sorry," she said in a soft voice. "Law enforcement caught and convicted the man who violated me, which is rare. What a terrible thing to endure, seeing your rapist every day."

Tears flooded Roxy's eyes and rolled down her cheeks. So much for repaired makeup. She pressed her hands against her face soaking up the moisture with her fingertips.

"Thank you for trusting me with your secret," Laura said. "You've given me a lot to consider."

"I forgot to tell you one more thing."

"Surely, there aren't more revelations?"

"Sorry. I'm wearing out my welcome, but Vicki hasn't committed for the entire run and—"

"That will hurt our sales and reputation."

"What will?" Spider asked from behind Roxy. She spun around. With just a few strides, he stepped into their space. His hair was as carefully coifed as Laura's. He wore his black, pinstripe suit and white shirt with a silver-gray tie well.

Laura had her host face back on. "We were discussing Vicki's commitment to at least a week."

Roxy exhaled. Laura wasn't going to say anything about the rest of the conversation.

"Not to worry," Spider said. "It's all under control."

"I'd better let you both welcome your guests. Thank you for your time, Laura."

Just as she did in the bar, she sensed Spider's eyes following her as she left the room. What a mess. This morning everything was going to work out and even an hour ago her confidence had soared. But now, Spider was with Laura spinning his tale, pulling Laura back to his side with promises of a bright new Fieldcrest. With sagging shoulders, Roxy joined the growing crowd.

The babble of voices pierced with occasional laughter and throat clearing filled the large room. Roxy craned her neck, looking for Dallas. Instead, she caught Glenn Phillips's eye. She wove her way to his side.

He looked even sharper than usual. He'd brushed his tight curly hair straight back. The navy-blue suit looked new.

Glenn said, "I'm surprised to see you."

"You didn't quit?"

"In my business, you have to have a thick skin. Besides, I love my job and the theater." He glanced around. "We'll raise a lot of needed funds tonight."

Roxy remembered the job description she saw on Joe's laptop. She hoped Glenn wasn't in for a rude surprise.

Dallas waved as she squeezed through the crowd and joined them.

"How are you doing?" she asked Roxy.

Roxy tried to smile but her mouth failed to work. Enthusiastic hand clapping and bravos broke out before Roxy responded.

Vicki swept into the room. Dressed in a black-and-red silk suit, the jacket hugging her curves, the skirt just above her knees, she embraced the assemblage with outstretched arms. The shining column of auburn hair hung exactly in place as if posed by a fashion photographer right before a shoot. Cameras and cell phones flashed.

"This event is lousy with her marketing people." Glenn's facial muscles were quiet. "She's maximizing her moment."

"Look, Dorothy," Dallas whispered in Roxy's ear. "The wicked witch is wearing *your* ruby slippers."

Roxy glanced down at Vicki's feet. The red patent leather shoes had three-inch heels.

"Not a positive omen." Dallas half-laughed. "Did she kill the good witch?"

"Maybe Vicki is the good witch."

"That's why we all love ya, babe, ever the optimist."

Roxy's peripheral vision caught Spider purposefully walking over to Vicki. After two European kisses, one next to each cheek, he took her elbow and steered her toward various guests. While Vicki's laugh carried over the heads and conversations in the room, Roxy was unable to catch anything Laura said to her guests.

Dallas observed, "The mayor arrived–to no thunderous applause, I might note."

Roxy asked, "Isn't he popular?"

"With some. Spider for sure. Tapp told me the city council is going to approve the redevelopment kit and caboodle." Dallas's dad was often in the know.

"Still, no public hearings yet," Glenn said. "I'm surprised he showed up. Coming out for this project at such an early stage could be a bad political move."

"Opportunist," Dallas said. "Like me. Have you looked around? This is a virtual power who's who. I'll be back after I kiss his ring."

The delectable smells of meat, melted cheese, and pastry prompted a stomach gurgle from Roxy just as a server walked by with a tray of red and white wines in crystal glasses. Behind him stood a woman in an outfit that matched his–black slacks, a white shirt and black apron–but *her* tray had an array of delicacies. Glenn and Roxy each took a glass of white wine and accepted several of the proffered morsels along with a napkin.

Deep in worry, Roxy sipped her wine and munched on a miniature quiche. "Do you really believe we'll a raise a lot of money tonight?"

Glenn swung his body toward Roxy. "I doubted at first, but Laura's assembled a moneyed crowd. See the guy with the beard standing next to her?"

Roxy stretched her neck. "Yeah."

"Paul Darby, a multi-millionaire entrepreneur. And the woman standing next to him is Shay Roberts, generous, rich, and into the arts."

Roxy surveyed the room. She nibbled and sipped. Everyone seemed to know each other; even Dallas mingled with the mayor and a small circle of guests. This was a world as far away from Roxy's shop and cramped apartment as galaxies were from each other. Is this what she wanted? No. They'd scrounge up enough money for the fix-up house and start their own business. Vicki starring in the play would help Joe and the theater. Jewel would have a healthy baby girl. Carl and Jewel would forgive her.

Just as she finished that thought, Roxy's skin prickled. She looked up, straight into Spider's hard eyes.

CHAPTER 35

"There you are," Vicki said, her voice trilling. Sweeping past several knots of guests who parted as she approached, she came over to Roxy's spot. Vicki leaned in and gave Roxy a hug. White wine and something Roxy didn't recognize infused Vicki's breath, but Roxy did recognize the behavior. How many times had she seen her mother look exactly like this? Eyes dancing, movements unsteady, and the entire world surprisingly entertaining.

"Big night, Madam Author."

"Yes." Roxy eyed Vicki. "You, okay?"

"Course." She wobbled on her ruby-red heels.

Roxy steadied her friend by holding onto her forearm and elbow. "Let's find a seat."

As if on cue, Spider appeared at Vicki's side. "We have other people to speak to," he said, taking Vicki's other arm. "I've got her." Roxy let go.

Vicki shook him off. With exaggerated slowness, she said, "This is my friend."

His left jaw muscle tightened. "We have work to do."

"You're such a bully." She inched closer to Roxy. "I've invested in his consortium and in return, he's helping me with a..." She lifted her right hand, her index finger and thumb held parallel and close together. "A teeny-weeny problem." Vicki laughed and sent her column of hair over her shoulder and back in place. The toss of her head proved too much. In slow motion, the hair still moving, she swayed, teetered, and fell into Roxy's arms.

"Pull yourself together," Spider hissed under his breath.

To Roxy's surprise, Vicki began to weep.

"I'll take care of her." Roxy put her arm around Vicki's shoulder.

"Can you sober her up?"

"I'll try."

"We *both* need her tonight."

Roxy steadied her grip on Vicki, careful not to squeeze too hard and hurt her.

"Be fine." Vicki straightened, balanced herself, and wiped her eyes with the tissue Roxy gave her.

"You don't seem alright."

"Duty calls." With a limp wave and Spider's hand firmly on her elbow again, Vicki swayed her way across the room.

Dallas rejoined Roxy. "This was fun for about five minutes." She munched on a shrimp coated in a sauce that smelled like curry. "Is she as drunk as she looks?"

"Pretty much."

"What's up with Spider, Joe, and our host?"

"Why?"

"Saw them huddled. I'm guessing a tense conversation."

"Did you hear any of it?" Roxy hoped Laura discussed the missed-payment clause with Joe.

"Nope. A lot of gesturing and finger pointing."

"How did your afternoon with Spider and Nadine go?"

"Nadine has her good points, but she and Spider aren't long for this world as a couple."

"Really?" Roxy's phone vibrated in her purse. She fished it out. A text from an unknown number appeared. *I'm Bobbie. Trey gave me your number. You can call me now.*

Making her excuses, Roxy slipped through the circles of people to the powder room. She latched the door and sat on the toilet cover. Buds in her ears, she punched in the number.

"Hello?"

Sweat coated Roxy's neck. She twisted her gold bracelet back and forth. "My name is Roxy."

"Oh, yeah, hi."

"Thank you for contacting me." Roxy swallowed hard. "I'm at an event where Spider Booth is one of the starring players."

Silence.

"So, I'm wondering what happened to you. With him."

Throat clearing. A cough.

"He raped me and... Did he hurt you too?"

"Look, he paid me off. I have two kids and a mortgage."

"I understand. You signed a non-disclosure agreement?"

"Yes. What the fuck could I do? My oldest has special needs."

"Of course, you had no choice." Roxy wasn't sure where to go from here. "Trey mentioned two women. You and someone else."

"Maria Rivera."

"Did she sign one too?"

"Nope. She quit and walked away. I'm sorry I can't help you, but Maria... I asked her and she's willing to speak with you. Just talk. No promises."

Relief swept through Roxy. "Thank you."

"I'm texting you her digits now. She's expecting your call."

"Who knows how many others are just like us," Roxy said.

"Yeah."

"Thanks again for speaking with me and for Maria's number."

"Shit. We have to fight guys like him, don't we?"

Roxy's head swam. Fight. Stand up. It wasn't your fault.

"If you guys take him to court, let me know. Even though I can't testify, I'd like to be there."

Take him to court. Her heart rate picked up off-kilter speed. "I'll keep in touch." Prosecute him. Roxy Googled the statute of limitations for rape in New York. Twenty years thanks to the Times Up movement and the then governor. Two more years. Roxy's eyes filled with tears for two women she didn't know and for the girl she'd been.

Maria's number arrived on her phone. She started to dial but the screech of a microphone cranked up too high pierced the air. The program must be starting. Roxy left the bathroom.

Joe Dawes stood on a makeshift riser behind a podium. "Hello, hello," he called, working to get everyone's attention. He rapped on the microphone. "I only need a moment of your time."

The crowd quieted.

"Thank you for coming this afternoon, for your support and generosity. I applaud every one of you." He clapped enthusiastically for the crowd, his arms outstretched and moving in an inclusive arc the same way he'd applauded at the board meeting. "First, I'm delighted to announce we've raised over $250,000 this afternoon thanks to all of you and a few extraordinary guests."

Cheers went up.

Joe called out various names and people waved in response to the applause. "This will go a long way toward achieving our dreams, your dreams, for the children and citizens of Fieldcrest and beyond. Thank you."

Another round of clapping and cheers followed.

Roxy looked at Vicki standing on the riser behind Joe, fake smiled pasted on, stoned.

"Now, I'd like to turn the program over to our gracious hostess—the amazing Laura Garrison."

Joe helped Laura adjust the height of the microphone. She put on a pair of reading glasses. In her left hand, she held a piece of paper. "Thank you, Joe, and thank all of you for coming." She paused. Pulled her glasses off, cleaned them, and put them back on. "I grew up in Fieldcrest, the daughter of immigrants grateful to be in this country."

It was obvious she was not used to public speaking. Her voice cracked, and she cleared her throat several times more before continuing.

"My mother emigrated here from the Czech Republic, worked as a nurse's aide while she raised four children, and attended college at night. My father landed here from Poland. Came on a student visa and never left. Together, they taught me to work hard, respect others, thank God every day, and give back, no matter your circumstances. Someone always has less than you, even when you're poor."

Voices murmured in agreement. Roxy heard a couple of amens.

"Thirty years ago, I met a gifted man. We married, began a family, started a business that grew every year. Then Harry contracted cancer, and I lost him two years ago July." She looked up from her paper and scanned the crowd. Her eyes gleamed. "He loved gatherings like this." She bent her head again and returned to the prepared speech. "Today, I find myself with an embarrassment of riches. Both our children are successful in their own rights. I have more than I need. My love of the arts, love for my birth city, and belief in Joe Dawes's vision and leadership, has inspired me to take the step I am about to announce."

Spider, standing next to Vicki, twitched. Something was amiss. Emotions bathed Roxy—fear, anticipation, and hope.

Laura paused again. "For years, I have kept my philanthropy private, making all but my annual gifts to The People's Theater anonymously."

Joe interrupted. "We so appreciate everything you've done. Without you, our doors would have closed that very first year." He started another round of applause.

Laura bowed toward Joe and then held up her hand for silence. "I love all live theater, but I especially love The People's Theater and its mission of giving unheard voices a megaphone, giving budding talent a stage. I adore actors and I especially love writers, like our very own Roxy Quinton." She paused and lifted her hand toward Roxy. "A woman of outstanding talent but also brave; she has given me courage." Again, Laura paused, tipped her head at Roxy. "Her wonderful debut play is opening this weekend, and I hope all of you have purchased tickets."

Roxy flushed. People twisted around and stared at her. She gave a little wave in response to the applause. Her heart thudded.

"But we need more than that. This city deserves additional opportunities for all the talented people who live and work here." Laura turned toward Joe. "Things have transpired that makes going public now the right thing to do. Today, I pledge to pay all the theater's loans made as part of the redevelopment project and building the school."

Now the applause was thunderous with people calling out congratulations. "Wows," and "Ohs" riffed through the air. A male voice yelled, "Well done."

Spider stood to Laura's right—his expression one Roxy recognized. His face a frozen mask of rage disguised as a smile.

Laura raised her hand for quiet again. "In addition," she said, speaking over the crowds' buzz. "I am paying back the two million dollars the theater owes Mr. Sand and providing another one million over the next three years for operations."

Joe gasped. A grin suffused his face. The surprised voices and congratulations from the guests reached a revival pitch.

Laura believed Roxy that the theater was in trouble because of Spider's scheme, and that he was a rapist snake. A sense of pride and relief filled Roxy's entire being. Clapping wildly, she wanted to rush to the podium and hug Laura.

Dallas said, "Brava, kiddo. You did it."

"We did it together. I told her about Trey and the missed-payment clause." Roxy kept her voice low, but no one was paying attention to them, all eyes on Laura. "I told her what Spider did to me."

"I'm so proud of you."

Movement on the riser caught Roxy's eye. Vicki wobbled up to the microphone, inching Laura to the right. "What a beautiful gesture," she said. "What a perfect ending to a wonderful soirée. As an artist..." she swayed but then straightened, head high. "I commend your commitment. As another child of Fieldcrest, growing up poor and without great theater, I stand awed by your gifts." She paused and appeared to search the faces of the crowd as if looking for someone. "And I'm also proud of the talented Roxy Quinton, my childhood friend."

The moment was undoing Roxy. She wished Jewel and Carl were here. And her dad.

Vicki continued. "I too, have an announcement. I'm going to donate as well— a scholarship for the new school tied to the theater. One girl and one boy will receive full tuition every year and..."

Her knees gave way. Joe grabbed her before she hit the floor.

As guests rushed forward to assist Vicki and others to congratulate Laura, Roxy watched Spider's mask crack, revealing a grimace of fury.

CHAPTER 36

Vicki lay on a king-size bed, her eyes closed, breathing heavily. One of Laura's guests, a physician, sat in a chair nearby.

"Is she awake?" Roxy asked.

Vicki answered before the doctor. "Hey." She opened bloodshot eyes. "What a mess." Tears leaked out. "I'm sorry."

Roxy sat on the edge of the bed and took her friend's hand. "Thank you for the shout out and congratulations on the scholarship. That was wonderful."

"Hmm." She sounded wistful. "We could have used that back in the day."

"We did alright." Roxy didn't want to ask about the rehearsal or opening night. Her friend wasn't well. But Roxy had so much at stake. "How are you feeling?"

"Like shit." The leaking tears became a flood. Sobs escaped and then a few burbs. "Kenny wants a divorce."

"Oh no. What happened?"

Vicki waved her hand. "Not his fault. Mine. I can't seem to hold on to anyone in my life."

"You've held onto me." Vicki's smile, a tiny movement of her lips, looked so sad. "How can I help?" Roxy asked.

Vicki closed her eyes again. "I won't let you down. I'll be there for opening night."

Roxy was no longer counting on her, but she still loved her and told her so. "I'll call in an hour to see how you're doing."

The doctor said, "Laura's offered Ms. Vega a room for the night or for as long as she needs." She rose and spoke to Vicki. "I too will check on you in an hour or so."

Roxy and the physician slipped out of the room.

As Roxy headed for the front entrance, Laura pulled her aside. "You were the impetus for much of my gift. I'd promised Joe I'd be there for him, but it was you who helped me see what I needed to do. Thank you."

Roxy grinned all the way to the theater.

• • •

"Five minutes, people," Larry Frome, the director said. His arms symbolically gathering the group.

Tea Rose Washington came on stage dressed in Vicki's costume, the cutoff denim shorts showing off long chocolate legs and a small round rear. Roxy had a private laugh–as if I ever looked that good when *I* was seventeen.

From stage right, Roxy poked her head around the red velvet curtain and looked out at the mostly empty theater.

"Places everyone," Larry said.

The lighting and sets were opening-night perfect. This was their next to the last rehearsal. Despite her concern for Vicki, Roxy's excitement hit like several glasses of wine.

Tea Rose was a strong enough actor to carry the play without Vicki and Tea Rose's understudy possessed fine acting chops as well. In five minutes, it would come alive on the stage. No money people, no critics, and no paying customers but otherwise identical to Saturday's debut. Roxy shimmied a happy dance. Everything was going to work out. She felt sure.

She sat in the audience rather than watch from backstage. It was dark, so she walked on her tiptoes so as not to disturb the actors. Movement came from behind the shadows.

"What's going to happen when he sees it?"

Roxy jumped with a squeal. "What are you doing here? How did you get backstage?"

"He's going to figure it out." Spider's voice, edged with bitterness or anger, chilled her. He stepped closer.

Dressed in the dark suit and white shirt with French cuffs and onyx cufflinks he'd worn to the reception, he still looked pressed and tailored.

"What do you want?"

"Too late; I gave you a chance."

"Listen, Spider—"

"No, I'm done listening. I'm taking my daughter and granddaughter. Period."

"*Taking* them?"

"Jewel is furious with you. You lied to her."

"You raped me."

"She won't believe you. No one will."

"Nadine does."

His jaw muscled clenched and unclenched. "Nadine and I are parting company soon. What she believes doesn't matter anymore."

"What about Laura Garrison? She believes me."

"What did you do?"

"And Jewel will too."

Spider's eyes narrowed to slits.

"Plus, I've located two more of your more recent victims and we're discussing pressing charges." Anger and fear surged through Roxy along with a new feeling. Power. "Twenty-year statute of limitations in New York."

"Your word against mine."

"And theirs. Hmm. Wonder how that will go?" Roxy's newfound confidence buoyed her. "Joe and Laura outsmarted you. I saw your face."

"Shut up."

"And guess who told them? Guess who else outsmarted you?"

She heard his ragged breathing.

"What happens when I go public with your deal and how Joe and Laura got the best of you?"

Even in the dim light, she saw his fists bunched at his side.

"You better step aside and let me pass. I'm not some frightened teenager. You don't scare me." She led with her right shoulder and tried to move past him. He grabbed her and flung her around, his fingers digging into her skin.

"Whatever you suspect, forget it. You're in *way* over your head." He hissed his words in her ear.

Despite the pain, her back straight, she pushed forward. Her body almost touching his, she locked eyes with him. "Remember, you die in my play, Spider Booth. I kill you."

For a few seconds, they stood in a frozen tableau, but then he released his grip.

"You win this round," he said in a normal voice. His breathing quieted. "But the last act of *this* play isn't *me* dead. Not even close."

Rubbing her sweaty palms along her sides, Roxy went out into the empty theater and took a seat. Still shaken, but also elated. She'd stood up to him, the theater was safe, and tonight, before Spider said anything, she'd tell Carl. Together, they'd figure out how to explain everything to Jewel.

Roxy sat riveted. Her story unfolded before her. Her vulnerability, foolishness, and the rape. Larry didn't like the rewrite. Kept the rape scene. There it was. And miraculously, Roxy didn't cringe or cry. She watched, her emotions tumbling, but none of the lifetime of guilt and shame surfaced. She and the play were doing fine. The blame was his. And the protagonist shot the rapist dead. Not something Roxy would ever do but satisfying to watch.

A scattering of applause rose from stagehands. Larry came from behind the curtain. "Well done everyone."

This time Roxy's tears were joyful. Dreams can come true. They can. They did.

CHAPTER 37

Roxy hurried down the ramp to the lobby. She had to get to the hospital. Oh my, what an amazing night. Her theater safe, her play coming together. Tomorrow a new baby. She shrugged on her lightweight raincoat and stepped through the theater door.

Carl stood in front her. His eyes wet and red.

At first, Roxy thought Jewel had given birth, and he came to tell her. She believed he'd arrived a few seconds ago, but then she saw his face scrunched into a fist-like ball.

"Please, let me explain."

He turned away, his head down.

"Wait." She ran until she caught up with him in the parking lot. Rain poured down on them. "Please," she said again.

He twisted toward her in an awkward motion. "How much of that is true?" His dark eyes clouded. "Which parts are real?"

"He raped me." She was openly sobbing now. The rain covered her face, her neck, dripped from her hair and scalp.

"Like that?"

"Yes."

"What were you doing with him? You and me, we—"

"We were."

"And he raped you?"

"Yes."

"Your father—what did he do?"

"I never told him or anyone." She reached for him. "Back then."

"Why didn't you tell *me*?"

"I was afraid."

"Of me?"

"For people to know."

Carl stared at her, as if trying to understand the words she was saying. When he finally spoke, it felt like bullets ripping into her the way they tore through the antagonist on the stage. "And for eighteen years you *lied*? For eighteen years, you were *afraid*?"

"I should have told you."

"Instead, you choose to tell the whole fucking world."

"It's a play," she sobbed, sinking down onto the asphalt. "Not real." The rain soaked through her dress and underwear. Her opened raincoat useless.

Carl stepped closer, looked down on her. "What will Jewel think?" He was no longer shouting at her, his voice a rough whisper. "Did you even consider her reaction?"

"She knows."

"What?"

"Nadine told her." Roxy covered her face with both hands. "Not about the rape but—"

"She knows he's her real father?"

"He isn't."

Carl sat down next to her on the wet pavement. Thunder growled and lightning tore through the sky.

"I wanted to tell you back then, but I was so ashamed. I'd been drinking, and you and I were dating, and I shouldn't have been at the beach with him." Roxy reached out to touch his face.

Carl jerked away.

She tried again. "He punched and attacked me, and I thought it was my fault."

In the twenty-six years they'd been friends, first as children and then as husband and wife, Roxy only witnessed Carl cry twice. Once, when he was twelve, a neighbor ran over his puppy. Carl sat in the street holding the limp dog and sobbed. On the morning Jewel was born, tears of joy and wonder rolled down his cheeks as he described their little girl to his mother on the phone. Now, tears welled in his eyes and rolled down his face mingling with raindrops. His body shook.

"Please forgive me. I never meant to hurt you."

Silently, he wept and trembled next to her. Finally, Carl whispered, "I'm sorry he molested you." His pain was palpable. "You're telling me Jewel isn't even mine."

"She's yours."

"Not my blood."

"I don't know for sure but what difference does it make? You're her father in every essential way."

"You don't get it, do you?" Slowly, he stood up. "What a chump I am, hanging around that smirking pig, all your little unexplained hints. He was playing me, and you let him."

In her head, this conversation was going to be different. He'd understand how terrible the rape was and how awful and isolating it was keeping her pain inside. She knew it was going to be hard, but she never imagined feeling like this—stabbing pain, guilt, and shame flooding back. Confidence and hope gone.

As if he read her mind, Carl said without looking at her, "Everything isn't about you, Roxy. You always..." he stopped as if groping for words. "Lying all these years, telling me like this and Jewel finding out from a stranger." He turned and stared at her for several beats. "Jewel and I deserve better."

Another strike of lightning lit up the sky. The rain soaked through all her clothes; filled her shoes and left her shivering on the curb just as she'd sat eighteen years before at the edge of the Orchard Beach parking lot waiting for Dallas to come and get her.

CHAPTER 38
THURSDAY

Curled in the fetal position on Dallas's tissue-strewn bed, Roxy finally managed to control her non-stop crying, though tearless shudders still ripped through her body like dry heaving. She opened her swollen eyes a crack and, without turning her head, surveyed the room. An empty carton of Ben & Jerry's sat on the nightstand with a circle of melted ice cream on the glass top. The television blasted a message about a gadget that guaranteed painless and sweat-free weight loss. Roxy blinked several times. If she didn't believe the humiliation would outweigh the comfort, she'd put her thumb in her mouth.

"It's Thursday morning." Dallas picked up the remote and clicked off the television. "Four a.m. We have to sleep."

Roxy had lost her ability to process information.

"Even if only for an hour." Dallas put down the remote, fluffed her pillow, slid under the satin sheets, and settled in.

Fragmented thoughts swept in and out. Carl crying, Jewel's angry eyes, and the sound and images of applause at the board meeting, at Laura's house, and for her play by the stagehands and director.

"Later, we can come up with a strategy," Dallas said, her voice muffled by the sheets. "It's hard to plan when you're drunk with exhaustion and ice cream."

Carl had called Dallas and then left Roxy in front of the theater. Dallas was there in less than thirty minutes. They drove to Dallas's house. Roxy's sobs the only sounds in the van. Once home, Dallas pulled off Roxy's ruined clothes, shoved her into the shower, toweled her dry and dressed her in terrycloth sweatshirt and pants. Never once, not in word or action, did Dallas say I told you so.

They watched old movies through most of the night, talked and talked some more, Roxy reliving every decision, every facet of her conversation with Carl. They ate butter pecan ice cream from the carton, drank pots of tea, and prayed together kneeling by the bed like they did as children, hands clasped on the covers. But nothing eased Roxy's grief or guilt.

"Did I tell you Ed, the baby's father, is white?"

"Get out." Dallas, lying on her side, rested her head on her right hand. "Jewel told you it's him?"

"No. But we're pretty sure."

"And?"

"And nothing. Iris is going to be loved, smart, and beautiful."

"No doubt."

From the window, Roxy stared at the orange streaks of sunlight edging the horizon. It was dawn on the day she was to become a grandmother at 2:00 p.m. She moved her pillow closer to Dallas's and closed her eyes.

Sleep finally came.

With a jerk, Roxy's eyes flew open. The room was cool and quiet. A sound or a dream-fragment must have awakened her. With her right hand, she searched the nightstand for her phone. Two spoons coated with dried ice cream fell to the floor. She peered at the screen. It was 10:10 a.m.

The two friends showered and dressed. Roxy's mind rejected the thought of food, but Dallas placed a slice of toast and two hard-boiled eggs on the table. "Eat," she demanded. Roxy ate it all, followed by two twelve-ounce glasses of water.

"We need to hustle," Dallas said. "See Jewel."

Roxy's phone rang.

"Hey. It's B.J."

"What's wrong? Are the kids, okay?"

"Yeah. I left my parents' house ten minutes ago. Everyone was good, but they really miss you guys."

Guilt swamped her. She didn't see them all day yesterday. Max was having a tough time at camp. When she called, the twins asked for their father.

"What's up?"

"It's probably nothing."

She sagged against the wall anticipating more bad news.

"Zoe and I, we dropped by to check on Jewel on our way to the shop."

"And?"

"Spider was there."

"With Jewel?"

Dallas put down her second cup of coffee and crossed her arms, obviously listening to Roxy's side of the conversation.

"I clocked them going over some papers."

"Newspapers, documents, what?"

"Documents. They looked legal. Weird, right?"

Switching hands, Roxy grabbed her bag. "I'm on my way."

"Should I call security?" B.J. asked.

"No."

"What's going on? Where the hell is Carl?"

"It's complicated."

"I'm family. You guys are all *my* family."

"I'll be there soon and explain but watch Spider for me. He's evil. You can't trust him."

B.J. audibly sucked in his breath. "Sorry. I had to open the shop. I left him with her. Didn't know what else to do."

"It's alright. I'm on my way. Thanks for alerting me." She pressed the end-call button. Spider was with Jewel going over legal-looking papers. Could things get any worse? She made a bitter, almost amused sound. The twins liked a story that every time one of the characters said the situation can't get any worse, it did.

Wadded tissues poked out from the folds of Dallas's sheets. Roxy began collecting them.

"Forget it." Dallas handed Roxy a bright orange sundress. "My friend Maggie left it." She added a clean pair of underpants. Roxy would have to wear yesterday's bra because she was a D cup and Dallas an A.

From over her shoulder, Roxy said, "Please find Carl."

"Sure, but we tried so many times last night. Where else can I look?"

"I don't know." She reached for the bottle of mouthwash, poured some into a paper cup, took a gulp, swished, and spat. "Can I take your van?"

"I'll get my keys."

Roxy stepped out of the sweats and into the panties, bra, and dress. Dallas tossed her the car keys.

"Find him."

• • •

Quiet filled the hospital corridor. Several women and one man at the nurses' station sipped coffee, each intent on a cell phone or computer. One of them nodded hello and pointed down the hall.

"Thank you," Roxy said on the run. She reached room 221, Quinton written in block letters under Vaughn, the name of Jewel's roommate.

Sunk deep into the pillows on the slanted bed, Jewel's face was pale and her eyes fever bright. Sheets of typed papers lay scattered across the bed. Jewel held a pen in her right hand.

"Hi, sweet pea."

Although weak, Jewel's voice was clear. "You're not supposed to be here."

Roxy stepped closer. "Of course, I am. Even if you're angry with me."

A sound behind her made Roxy spin around. Spider's sneer chilled her. "What are you doing here?"

Jewel jumped in—her tone defensive. "Mr. Booth... Spider, dropped by to talk about my future."

Roxy arranged her face in an expression she hoped conveyed confidence and control.

"Rough night?" His eyes moved from her face to her body.

Roxy tugged at the sides of the too-tight sundress. "I thought you were leaving town."

Spider came closer, his undertone caustic. "What made you believe that?"

Roxy dug for her own menacing tone. "Since your business dealings clearly fell apart, time to tuck in your devil's tail and run."

Spider laughed aloud. "You *are* a naïve woman."

In her peripheral vision, Roxy saw bewilderment in Jewel's expression.

While every nerve ending in Roxy focused on Spider, she turned her body toward Jewel and pressed the back of her hand on Jewel's forehead. "You have a fever again. Do the nurses know?"

"The mom thermometer, once again at work."

Roxy smiled. That was better than 'you're not welcome here.'

"They didn't act worried."

"I'll pop over to the nurses' station and alert them."

Jewel seemed to be screwing up her courage. Roxy recognized the mix of guilt and rising determination playing across her daughter's face. "We've been talking about college."

"Really?"

"Yeah, Bentley. Spider says it's perfect for me."

"I've been investigating," he said. "They have a special program that lets students finish high school while working on their associate degree."

"There's childcare, so Iris can be with me."

"You're keeping Iris?"

"Yes."

With everything else going wrong in her world, here was something wonderful. "I'm glad." And inadequate word for her relief and joy.

Jewel picked up the papers and wagged them in front of her. "And listen to this part. Spider secured a full scholarship along with a stipend and a part-time job."

Roxy sucked in a shaky breath. College, a job, a scholarship, and a way for Jewel to take care of her daughter. Spider said Roxy was no match for him, and he was right. She had no way to give Jewel any of those things.

"You have to sign the papers. That's the only thing. Plus, you *have to* get Daddy to agree."

"Where's Carl?" Spider's tone came out cruel, as if he knew about the scene in the parking lot.

"Yeah?" Jewel asked.

"He'll be here." Roxy shot Spider a look, half-pleading, and half-threatening. She turned back to Jewel. "Why don't we discuss this later? Right now, you need to concentrate on getting your fever down and bringing Iris into the world.

"It's never too early to talk about the future," Spider said. "School starts in two weeks. We have to hurry, or I'll lose the scholarship."

How might Roxy stop this Spider-flood? Finish high school, associate degree, a full scholarship, a job, childcare–all life-changing. Carl and she had no way of competing. *If* it were all true. Spider twisted the truth and cheated. Would he lie to Jewel?

"As soon as Dad gets here," Roxy said, trying not to sound despondent. "We'll talk about it then."

Jewel sank back onto the pillow. "I don't feel well."

Roxy pushed the nurse's call button.

"Mom."

Roxy swung around.

Jewel curled forward as if doing an abdominal crunch, panted, gripped Roxy's hand to the point of pain. The contraction subsided and Jewel fell back on the pillow. For several seconds she lay there, her eyes closed, huffing.

Another contraction ripped through her body. "What's happening, Mommy?"

"You're going into labor. Not to worry. That's why we're in the hospital." She took some ice chips from a cup on the movable tray. "Suck on these." She fed Jewel the ice.

A nurse, clad in blue scrubs, a stethoscope dangling from around her neck, trotted into the room. Expert eyes took in the scene. With choreographed moves, she checked the monitors, Jewel's IV drip, wrapped a blood pressure cuff around Jewel's arm, stuck an electronic thermometer against her forehead and watched the machine. "Sir, you need to leave now," she said, with authority. "The waiting room is down the hall."

Jewel cried out in pain, bent forward, and let out a long groan.

"I've paged Dr. Wu," the nurse said. She pulled the curtain around the bed. "Please leave us to it, Mrs. Quinton."

Reluctantly, Roxy moved toward the doorway. "I'll be right here, just outside your door, baby."

Jewel disappeared behind the curtain.

Another fever? Something wasn't right. They'd scheduled the Cesarean Section for two o'clock and it was eleven, yet Jewel was already having contractions one on top of the other.

"Carl left you." Spider said, his back to the hall. "He saw your pathetic, fake-news play and ran.

She had no comeback. Spider won.

CHAPTER 39

Jewel moaned. Draped under a sheet with her legs bent and spread wide, she gripped the sides of the bed, her knuckles bloodless pale. A stinky-sweet smell like menstrual blood filled the room. Dr. Wu pulled a rubber-gloved hand from under the sheet.

"What do you think?" Roxy asked the doctor.

"We have concerns." Dr. Wu pulled off the disposable-gloves and threw them into a specially marked container. "The baby's heartbeat has slowed. It should be between 120 and 160. It's still within normal limits but it's dropped. Plus, Jewel's fever is a worry."

Another groan from Jewel, this one not as loud.

"We need to operate now." She spoke to a woman with bright red hair. "Let's prep her."

Roxy stroked Jewel's forehead. It was damp and warm. "Mommy's here. Everything's gonna be okay." She searched Dr. Wu's face for confirmation.

"Absolutely," the doctor said checking the monitors again. "We don't want to take chances. I'll meet you in the OR. Nurses will bring you in a few minutes."

Jewel said to Roxy, "Can you call Eddie?"

It was only right. "Sure." She jotted the number on a scrap of paper.

"Is Daddy here yet?"

Roxy shook her head. She didn't know what to say.

Despite the tremor in her voice, Jewel's iron-determination was still clear. "Tell me the truth, now, before Iris is born."

"This isn't the right—"

"Now. Is Spider my father?"

The truth, even if it meant Jewel giving up the future Spider promised? "I don't know who your biological father is. Not for sure."

Jewel's fevered eyes widened. "You had sex with both of them, with Dad *and* Spider, at the same time?" She sounded incredulous, outraged.

"*Consensual* sex with your father."

Jewel seemed to consider Roxy's words. Puzzlement and then understanding rippled across her face. "Spider raped you?"

"Yes."

So now, everyone knew the complete miserable story. How stupid to have kept it a secret for so long.

"Did you prosecute him? Do something about it?"

"No. I was embarrassed, ashamed, and scared."

Jewel moaned, but Roxy didn't know if it was a response or the baby.

"I'm sorry I didn't tell you sooner." She couldn't turn back time, but she possessed the power to make things right today and do better tomorrow.

Tears rolled out the corners of Jewel's eyes, down the sides of her cheeks to her ears. "I smell so bad."

"Don't worry about it."

"Does Daddy know? Is that why he's not here?"

"Your dad loves you very much."

Jewel, her eyes bloodshot, said, "Daddy has been sad."

"Not about this. I mean not before."

"When did you tell him?"

"He figured it out yesterday."

Another contraction gripped Jewel. She bent forward, groaned, panted, and sank back onto the bed. "Is it supposed to hurt like this?"

"Soon you'll forget all the pain. You'll have a beautiful, healthy little girl, who will fill your heart with as much joy as your dad's and mine was when you were born."

"Truly?"

"Yes."

•   •   •

"We're going to prep her for surgery now. You can come with us and be in the delivery room," the young woman said, green eyes looking professional but, at least to Roxy, concerned. A man with snake tattoos peeking out from under his white smock rolled a gurney into the room.

Together, the woman and man pulled the gurney alongside Jewel's bed and eased her onto it, bringing the IV bag and pole around. Roxy walked next to the gurney holding Jewel's hand. They reached the elevators.

"I'll let the social worker know the good news," she said to Jewel. "You're doing the right thing."

"Roxy."

She twisted around, hoping to see Carl. Instead, it was B.J.

"How is she?" he asked.

"They're doing the C-Section now." The wide elevator door opened, and the nurses pushed Jewel's gurney in. Roxy followed. "Try to find Carl," she begged. The doors closed.

•   •   •

The operating room looked like a set on a television show. Roxy wore a blue surgical gown. They'd covered Jewel everywhere except her abdomen, still a basketball sized mound. With big eyes, Jewel stared at the ceiling as Dr. Wu explained each step.

The anesthesiologist placed an oxygen mask over Jewel's nose and mouth and, to put her under, inserted a drip into the IV.

"Count backwards from ten," the doctor said, checking the stats on his many machines. "Breath normally."

"Ten, nine, eight, seven." Jewel fell asleep before she reached six.

Roxy had trouble watching them insert the catheter and turned her head during the first of several incisions, moving through Jewel's abdomen in layers, scissoring down to Iris. Dr. Wu's voice was calm, its' soft cadence accompanied by the whirring of some machine they were using as they snipped. "Now, I'm cutting through the uterus," she said. "The nurse is suctioning away the amniotic fluid. We're almost there."

Roxy glanced at the white-faced clock on the wall. Less than fifteen minutes elapsed since they started. Must be a good sign.

"Suction," Dr. Wu, said, lifting Iris's little head from Jewel's pelvis.

Oh, sweet Jesus, there she was, her face covered in gooey fluids, reddish-brown hair plastered to her scalp, swollen eyes closed.

The energy changed in the room. Roxy felt it shift and crackle.

"Fetal heartbeat at 100," the nurse read from the monitor, her voice creased with tension. "99."

"We're losing her," Dr. Wu said. She slipped her hands deep into the bloody caverns of Jewel's womb and pulled Iris out all the way.

A nurse took Roxy's arm.

"Wait, what's happening?"

They moved her quickly to the OR doors and with an insistent nudge, sent her into the hall.

CHAPTER 40

The waiting room was too small for the Quinton clan and friends. People leaned against the wall, filled all the chairs, and squatted on the floor. Kia and Gabriella played tag, scooting around the living-room-like chairs, fake-wood tables, and people clusters. Squeals and shouts emanated periodically.

"Behave, you two," Joanna said. "Slow down."

Roxy smiled at her girls. They had no idea there was any reason to be sad or frightened. "Let them play."

With a disapproving shake of her head, Joanna retreated. Dallas, her phone mashed against her ear, paced. Max bobbed his head to his too-loud music seeping out from the ear buds of his iPhone. With her nose buried in *O* magazine, Zoe's flip-flops slapped rhythmically against her bare soles.

Celeste said, "It's taking too long. We should have heard something by now."

"What are you saying, woman?" Frank asked, sounding irritated. His eyes never left the television set mounted on the wall. A CNN anchor reported a tornado leveled a midwestern town of one thousand. "You don't know how much time it's supposed to take."

"Not this long."

"Bah." He put an unlit cigar in his mouth and chewed on its tip.

"All three of mine popped out without a problem." Celeste sniffed.

Frank pulled the cigar from his mouth and pointed it at the television set. "This is why we live in the Northeast," he said to no one in particular.

"We have our share of floods, these days. Even tornados," Zoe said. "Climate change is—"

Frank cut Zoe off with a dismissive wave and turned to Roxy. "Missing fathers–it's not right."

She wasn't sure to whom he was referring–that Jewel hadn't named the father of her baby or that no one had seen Carl for twenty-four hours.

Ed came over and sat beside Roxy, his J. Crew slacks and collared shirt in stark contrast to Max's faded jeans and T-shirt. Roxy had forgotten about Ed until Jewel asked her to call him. They'd been so worried about him hanging around with Jewel in the apartment, drinking up their cans of Bud. How long ago was that? It seemed like months instead of days.

"I found out in May," Ed said loud enough to cause Frank to look at him sharply. Roxy noted Ed's eyes staying on Frank for a meaningful second before shifting to Roxy and lowering his voice. "She never told me. I was away at school, and she acted like she didn't want to go out with me anymore. I called and texted. But she ghosted me. Silence. Nothing. I slowed down, but I never gave up. When I got out of school for summer break, I came to see her."

May. Jewel was six months pregnant then and barely showing.

"Hurt me. That she'd keep a secret as important as this." A chill of guilt swept across Roxy–generational echoes.

He paused and appeared to be thinking or remembering. "But then I understood. She didn't realize how much I love her."

Was that why Roxy kept the truth from Carl–she doubted the depths of his love? Its staying power? She studied Ed. Handsome kid, with bright, cocoa-brown eyes. She thought about Iris's reddish-brown hair. Ed's.

With effort, she tried to look and sound positive, but she knew her face and voice suffered from a day's worth of grief, worry, and lack of sleep. "I'm sorry."

"Me too."

All their avoidable anxiety and fights about the baby's father and adoption. "Glad you're here now," Roxy said, and she meant it. Keeping Iris was more important than everything else–the house, the play, escaping from the hair salon and school. No more abandoning children. And stepping up as a mom was next on Roxy's list. She had to do better.

Ed asked in an earnest voice, "Can I be with her in the recovery room?"

"Sure." Roxy patted his hand. "Plenty of time to work things out."

"Does she know I'm here?"

"She asked me to call you."

Dallas leaned over Roxy and spoke to Ed. "She knows."

He gave Dallas a warm smile. "I called my parents. They live in Vermont. Flying down tomorrow."

"How'd they take it?" Dallas asked. "Must be worried about you finishing college."

Roxy watched Ed's face, looking for truth. This was Iris's father. She'd need a wonderful dad. A man like Roxy's father, a man like Carl.

"I told them last week," Ed said to Dallas. "It was a lengthy conversation, followed by two more, but they're cool now. At least, they're acting that way." He dragged his fingers through his hair. "They're worried about school and..." He heaved his shoulders. "A lot to take in. Tons of stuff to figure out."

Roxy said, "I'm looking forward to meeting them."

"Is Mr. Quinton on his way?" Ed asked. "Jewel's been sad and worried about him."

Roxy slouched in her seat. "Hope so."

Dallas told Roxy she'd called every person she knew trying to locate Carl. Zay did all but put an APB out on him. No luck so far.

B.J. walked into the waiting room with soda, water, and chips from the vending machines. Roxy questioned him with her eyes, but he shook his head in answer to her unspoken query.

Carl was gone.

B.J. divvied his purchases among the children and then sat down next to Dallas. "Who's this kid?" he asked, lifting his chin toward Ed, who was now looking out the smudged window onto the parking garage.

"Who do you suppose?" Dallas said.

"Oh."

"He seems as surprised as we are. Not right. Men know what they did," Dallas said.

"Now wait a minute. Don't go knocking us men."

Roxy listened to the exchange with only half her mind. The other half was far away. Spider. Every time he did something awful, he followed up with a winning combination. How would Carl feel about the new offer, a high school diploma and AA degree, a scholarship, job, and childcare? Roxy stared at her hands and twisted her gold bracelet. How do you stop generational chains of actions and reactions? Were her mother and Jewel just like Roxy, playing out a predetermined dance only God understood?

She shouldn't have told Jewel about the rape. Why prevent life-changing opportunities? Spider was horrible to Roxy, but he was good to Jewel. It was her life, her choices.

Then she thought about Maria and Bobbie, the two women in Connecticut. Their painful stories as graphic as Roxy's. Spider's narcissistic callousness and stated belief that each of the women, girl in Roxy's case, were better off for the experience. She answered her own question. He had no place in Iris and Jewel's lives.

· · · ·

Dr. Wu entered the room smiling, a surgical mask dangling from one ear. Her grin was broad but her voice tired. "You can join Jewel in the recovery room, but only three at a time."

Roxy, her hand covering her heart, asked, "How is she?"

"A little woozy and in some pain, but overall, she and Iris are doing just fine."

Ed sank into one of the chairs and let out a breath as loud as Roxy's. The moisture in his eyes mirrored hers.

"The baby is here," Kia said, jumping up and down, her pink-and-purple sneakers flashing tiny lights as she moved.

"How big?" Celeste asked.

"Eight pounds, six ounces and nineteen inches long." Dr. Wu said. "Gave us a scare for a few minutes, but she's already nursed and has a lusty wail."

Iris... What was Ed's last name? Coppersmith. Or would she be Iris Quinton? It didn't matter either way. Roxy whispered a prayer of thanks.

· · ·

Which of the babies in the nursery was Iris? Roxy had just seen her in the recovery room, but now, as she peered through the glass, she couldn't pick Iris out. All the babies were in diapers, laying on their backs, warming lights bringing up their body temperatures. Some stretched, some cried with fat legs kicking into the air. Last names declared to whom each child belonged.

A nurse's aide walked over to one of the bassinets. The name hand lettered on the back, read Coppersmith. Jewel had given Iris Ed's family name.

The aide lifted Iris. In less than an hour, she'd changed. Amber eyes opened wide, thick reddish-brown hair peeking out from the cap. Roxy remembered when the twins were born, together weighing less than Iris. Every day they morphed, God's miracle unfolding. Now they were five-year-old aunties. Bemused, Roxy speculated about her father's reaction if he were alive.

"Your dad would have been proud." Carl appeared weary, black stubble on his cheeks, upper lip, and chin making him look like B.J.

"I think you're right," she said.

"Dallas tracked me down thirty minutes ago and told me about the emergency C-Section. How's Jewel?"

"Started out a little bumpy but fine in the end." Roxy tried to keep her tone as even as possible. Her heart palpitated, making it hard to catch her breath. "Go see for yourself."

He didn't move or say anything. Roxy reached out her hand and touched his. His hung at his sides. "How are the kids?"

"Missing you." She inched her hand back. With her peripheral vision, she studied his face. In profile, only his puffy left eye was visible, but it was enough. His pain filled her with shame.

Still not looking at her, he asked, "How are you? Got that doctor's appointment tomorrow?"

"I'll go next week. Probably panic attacks."

He didn't respond. Roxy stayed quiet.

"Saw Spider."

"Oh?"

He rubbed his knuckles. Roxy hadn't noticed before, but now she saw bruises.

"You punched him?" Carl never fought except with B.J. back in the day.

"Yeah, gave him back the money too."

"Our shop money?" She'd accepted Eloise's fixer-upper as their home, their future, a fresh start. When Roxy passed her dream house on the way to the hospital, a *Sold* sign sat on the front lawn. She wasn't even disappointed.

"I'll find another way."

He didn't say "We." For eighteen years, it had always been "we," "us," "our" "team Roxy and Carl." No words came. She wanted to say, "Thank you. I'm sorry. I love you and I'll never lie to you again, ever." But she doubted he'd believe her.

They watched Iris wriggle in her bassinet.

"My folks have anything to say?" Roxy knew he was referring to Ed. Frank held biases he offered to anyone who'd listen. All the turmoil and reckoning over social justice roiling across the country underscored his prejudices. Understandable, but still wrong. Carl and Roxy talked about it with all four of their children, separating cruel realities from blanket hate.

"Not yet," Roxy said.

"She's darn cute."

Another stretch of silence, this one several minutes long as they stood side by side but not touching.

Before she opened her mouth, Carl spoke. "I'm gonna go now."

A new pain surged through her body. He was leaving her—leaving them for good.

His eyes flicked to her face, his mouth in a not-quite smile. "To see our girl."

CHAPTER 41
SATURDAY

Joe Dawes flailed his hands and stomped around. The normally calm and measured man was in a state. "She's not coming? *Really* not going to show?"

Roxy shook her head.

"I thought this was behind us. Fixed. The ticket buyers, the press, our members and donors... they all believe she's starring in your play." He enunciated each word. "They. Are. Coming. To. See. Vicki."

The theater was empty except for Joe and Roxy. The stage was dark. In less than twelve hours the curtain would rise.

Roxy had spent Friday in the hospital with Jewel, Iris, and Ed, whom she was getting to know with each hour. She liked him. Even his nickname for Jewel–Rabbit–was growing on Roxy. Carl, staying with B.J., joined them during his lunch hour and returned at five for the picnic dinner with Celeste, Max, the twins, and Dallas. Baby joy kept Roxy's worries at bay for most of the day. No one mentioned Spider or the strain between Carl and Roxy. She felt hopeful.

That ended at the final dress rehearsal Friday night.

"You saw her at the reception," Roxy said to Joe. "Since then, she's been in bed. No calls, no visitors except Laura and the physician tending her." Roxy's shoulders heaved.

"Perhaps I've not made myself clear. In a few weeks Booth's deal will become a reality. Our future–a great regional theater, with a school, lifting this community and the lives of our citizens..." Joe's volume lowered. "You go to Laura Garrison's house right now and persuade your *dear friend* to get off her butt and into this theater tonight." He waved a stack of Playbills filled with notes about the play, the cast, the director, and Roxy, along with paid advertisements. "Don't make us liars."

• • •

Her legs jiggling and her heart racing, Roxy rang Laura's bell. The door swung open. "Good morning," Laura said. "Welcome."

"Thank you for letting me come by."

Laura, dressed in a flowing caftan, shook her head. "We're in this together."

Roxy stepped into the foyer and once again admired the house. Wood floors gleamed. Plush area rugs, their colors rich, covered parts of the floor. A gold and silver vase on a round marble table, filled with an array of fresh flowers, added to the visual appeal.

"As I mentioned on the phone," Laura said. "Vicki will see you." Laura motioned for Roxy to follow. "Let me show you to her room." Laura's dress swayed with each step.

Roxy stopped on the top step to catch her breath. This was her last gambit. Vicki's mental and physical health were important. But. Joe made it clear. If there was anyway Vicki could perform tonight... Roxy had to try.

The guest room walls were a soft mauve with framed paintings strategically placed. Roxy didn't recognize the art but suspected someone famous created each. A vase of white and blue hydrangea decorated the dresser. Vicki, covered and in pajamas, sat propped up by several pillows, a book on her lap.

"Good morning," Roxy said.

The whites of Vicki's eyes shone clear. Her skin, devoid of makeup, was unblemished and unlined. She looked rested. The strain Roxy saw on Wednesday evening gone.

"Hi."

"How are you?"

"Hanging in and hanging on."

Laura said, "I will let you two catch up." She left without making a sound.

Roxy sat in a nearby armchair.

Vicki said in a hurried voice, "I'm sorry for ghosting these past few days. I didn't realize how shaky I was. Needed time to mend."

Hope resurfaced. Vicki had used the past tense. "So, you're stronger now?" Roxy asked.

Vicki looked at Roxy with pity or sorrow. Roxy couldn't tell. She waited.

"I know tonight is your big opening and you're counting on me, but I don't have the energy. I'm still wiped. Somewhat better but emotionally drained."

Joe's voice banged around in Roxy's head. "We've sold out for tonight and—"

Vicki interrupted. "I wouldn't do the part justice–only embarrass myself and harm the theater's reputation." She blinked several times. "Clean and sober for two days and counting. I can't chance it."

"I understand." Roxy did. She wanted her friend to get well. Tea Rose, Vicki's understudy, was excellent. The show would go on. The impact on the theater? Roxy didn't understand all the finances, but Joe's anxiety was real.

"It'll be fine," Roxy said. "Your health is the priority."

Vicki appeared relieved. "Thanks."

"What about your shoot in Boston?"

"The producer said they'll wait, but we'll have to see. There's always someone ready to step in and take your place. Younger, prettier..." She snorted. "Less talented."

"They'd be fools to let you go."

"Thanks pal."

"Do you need anything?"

"Laura is unbelievable. She's taking good care of me, and she said I can stay as long as I want." A sardonic laugh. "I'm hiding out from Kenny and the lawyers."

"You're contesting the divorce?"

"Hell no. I just want to make him squirm and worry." She pushed herself up and adjusted the pillows. "If you can believe it, he's demanding alimony. Good luck with that, the jerk."

Vicki sounded like her old self, but, if she was too weak to perform, there was nothing more for Roxy to say.

"I've got a lot going on today, so I better leave." Roxy leaned over and kissed Vicki's forehead the way Roxy kissed her children goodnight. "Take care of yourself and stay in touch. Let me know when you're leaving town."

"Will do." She placed both hands over her heart. "And good luck, kiddo. Break a leg."

CHAPTER 42

Dallas and Roxy waited. The diner thrummed with conversations–families, older couples, and office colleagues. Lone men read their newspapers as they ate. Outside, the morning air was warm but no longer hot or humid. Inside, the sun streaked through the skylights. It was 1:00 p.m. on the biggest day of Roxy's life.

"She's late." Roxy glared at the front door. She'd booked too many appointments. Her last customer scheduled for a wash and blow dry at four. Opening night began with everyone connected to the production gathering at six thirty before the eight o'clock curtain, but Roxy planned to arrive by five thirty both to help get the cast change typed and into the Playbill, as well as to savor the moment. Her dream, at least part of it, was coming true. No Vicki, but still... Roxy's story on stage to a sold-out house. Would the audiences' disappointment about Vicki take away from their pleasure?

Dallas said, "Try to relax. You look like an old woman about to have a heart attack."

"Ouch." She smiled. "I know. I'm such a wreck." So far, the day was going piss-poorly. First, meeting with Joe and then Vicki. "I'm grateful, but I wish Maria Rivera had chosen a different day." She glanced at her watch again. "And now she's late or not even coming."

"You're making both of us nuts." Dallas poured cream and sprinkled sugar into her coffee.

A member of the wait staff walked by, carrying a tray of sandwiches, burgers, and fries. Everything smelled warm and tasty, but Roxy had no appetite.

"Well, she's late," Roxy noted again, fidgeting with her gold bracelet. "Maria said one o'clock, and it's already..." For the umpteenth time she peered at her watch. "Ha. 1:03."

Dallas laughed. "Whoa, little lady, calm yourself," she said, mimicking a classic southern gentleman speaking to his missus. "You don't want to succumb to the vapors."

That, plus her own foolishness, got Roxy laughing too. One of the qualities she loved most about Dallas was her ability to make Roxy laugh, no matter what else was going on.

"Is that Maria?" Dallas pointed at a woman scanning the restaurant as if looking for someone.

Roxy recognized her from the photo Maria had shared via a text. With a wave, Roxy got Maria's attention.

"Thanks for coming." Roxy scooted over in the booth. "This is my friend Dallas Swan. I hope you don't mind. She's been helping me locate Spider's victims."

"No worries," said the small woman with light brown eyes.

Dallas and Roxy had chosen a spot as tucked-away as possible, but the diner was doing a brisk business, so they kept their voices low.

Maria said, "Bobbie explained what you're trying to do. Just because I'm here doesn't mean yes."

"I understand," Roxy said. "Can you tell us what happened?"

Maria's tale was familiar. First, Spider befriended her. Then he invited her out to discuss the project in more depth. He wanted her perspective. An invitation for a quick drink at the apartment he was using during the project. Then dinner at an upscale restaurant. They never made it out of his place.

"My word against his word, and money, and power." Maria's eyes were moist. "He claimed it was consensual, and he didn't hear me say no." She groaned. "Like my shouts were too quiet and unconvincing." She pressed her fingers against her forehead and rested her elbows on the table. "My struggles, he claimed, were from sexual arousal. He offered me money to keep quiet. Not admitting guilt, he claimed, but to prevent both of us from publicly suffering." Maria lifted her head and brushed away the leaking tears. "I didn't take it."

Dallas asked, "Did you go to the police or the hospital for a rape test?"

Maria shook her head.

"Did you tell anyone?" Roxy asked, hoping someone could corroborate Maria's story.

"Yes, both my parents, Bobbie, and another colleague working on Spider's project."

That was something. Enough? "Would they be willing to testify?"

Maria unrolled the flatware wrapped in a napkin and used the cloth to dab at her eyes. "The defense lawyers make it your fault. Shame you. Plus, I just read an article about how few prosecutors agree to take on rape victims' cases." She crumpled the napkin and set it aside, her eyes downcast. "I don't know if I can testify, much less ask my family and friends."

Everything Maria said was true. And awful. Roxy waited a beat, took a sip of her coffee "We have to try."

Maria lifted her face and eyes.

"For the next woman," Roxy said. "And the one after that."

• • •

The theater was filling up, and it was only seven-thirty. They'd sold every seat except for a few in the mezzanine. Voices buzzed. Ushers led patrons to their seats. Backstage organized chaos ruled. The stage manager, headset covering her ears, bustled from one end of the stage to the other, checking, encouraging, questioning, and instructing. Larry Frome huddled with the actors.

Roxy poked her head from behind the curtain. Cousin Winnie and Carl's sister Yolanda and her husband sat together in the center orchestra. Two rows in front of them, Dallas, some new guy she started dating, Tapp and Glory Swan, and B.J., Zoe, and Joanna sat with two empty seats next to B.J. for Roxy and Carl.

Max, the twins, and the dogs were still with Frank and Celeste until tomorrow. Ed had hospital duty, staying with Jewel and Iris. His parents had arrived and checked into the one upscale hotel in Fieldcrest. Although a bit formal, they were warm and clearly loved Ed. Roxy hoped Jewel and Iris would win their hearts.

Roxy spied Fred Dixon coming down the aisle, the old gentleman looking sharp in a tan suit and bright tie. Angel, holding hands with a handsome younger man, was a few steps behind. She didn't see Laura Garrison, who not only said she was coming but invited friends. And, of course, no Vicki.

It was all out of Roxy's hands–Carl and Jewel's forgiveness and Vicki's appearance. Roxy had done everything she could think to do. She prayed and left it with God. What will be, will be.

Joe came over to her. "The typed cast substitution notices are taking a toll. Several of the press have already left."

"I'm sorry. I let you down."

"Yeah, well, I'm sorry I yelled at you this morning. She's a professional and knows better. Not your fault."

"You said the theater's reputation—"

"This is your big night, Roxy. We'll survive. Enjoy your accomplishment." He patted her shoulder. "Have to comfort our esteemed director."

The stage manager ran up to them. Headphones on, hair in a messy bun, her voice agitated. "She's here. Ms. Vega has arrived."

"Oh." Roxy felt faint.

Joe said, "That's damn fine news."

"And she looks and sounds great. She's asking for you, Roxy."

Joe pounded Roxy's back. "Damn fine," he repeated.

Roxy closed her eyes and tried to compose herself.

"Go, go," Joe said. "I'll let Frome and the cast know. We'll make an announcement to the audience. Where the hell is Glenn? He needs to get those reporters back in here."

She caught up with the fast-moving stage manager and followed her into the backstage dressing room.

There Vicki sat, looking splendid. A wig covered her glossy hair and the makeup artist worked on her face.

"Hey," she said the second she saw Roxy. "Gave you a scare, right? Sorry about that." She waved Roxy over. "Butterflies?"

"Yes." Roxy admitted. Sweat beaded on her nose and forehead. "And bees and wasps."

"It'll be great."

The makeup artist dusted Vicki's face with a fine powder, stepped back, and surveyed her work. "Done," she said.

Vicki tugged the protective cloth from around her neck. "Laura drove me. She's in the lobby waiting for a few folks."

Grateful, Roxy made a mental note. One more reason to thank Laura Garrison.

"But she's not why I'm here." That caught Roxy by surprise. "You, you're the reason." Vicki pulled on the edges of her wig and looked in the mirror before turning back to Roxy. "Since we were kids, every time I got into a jam, or did something stupid, you never judged me. Even bailing on your play, you were gracious. I don't have any other friends like you." She paused. "Too few real friends. After you left, well, I did a lot of reflecting."

Moisture filled Roxy's eyes and throat.

"If you can be kind, brave, and tenacious, so can I. Besides, I know how to dig deep when I must. I'm a professional." Vicki made a little bow from her waist and laughed. Tears rolled down Roxy's cheeks. "There you go getting sappy on me."

The stage manager poked her head in. "They're ready for you, Ms. Vega."

With a squeeze of Roxy's hand, Vicki rose, took another look in the mirror, gave Roxy a thumbs up, and followed the woman.

It was time for the curtain to rise.

EPILOGUE

The family was running late. Max returned from walking the dogs, his hair coated with melting snow. Cleo and Pharoah shook their bodies, spraying the walls. Spring, one week away, had yet to show encouraging signs.

"It's coming down harder," Max said, grabbing a towel, drying first his hair and then the dogs. "Can someone drive me to school?"

Roxy slipped into her parka. The hood covered her platinum hair, longer now and shinning from the carotene treatment B.J. gave her. "No one has time," she said to Max. "Take the girls with you to the bus stop."

Max grumbled. "Come on, you two. We need to slide. Now."

"You can't boss us around," Gabriella said.

"Yeah," Kia agreed. "No bossing."

Roxy grabbed each of the girls for a hug. "Be good in school. Grandma will pick you up instead of the bus." She called to Jewel. "Are you and Iris ready to go? I have to get to court." Roxy spoke again to the twins. "Boots and gloves. Jewel made your lunch. Don't forget it."

Kia sprinted to the kitchen. Gabriella strolled.

Carl came in from the basement salon. "I'll get to the courthouse as soon as I can. Harriet, B.J., and Angel are busy, and we have two walk-ins. I'll get the customer flow organized and join you."

The minute the new salon was operational, Roxy had contacted Harriet Jones, the woman who inquired about renting space in Frank's. She turned out to be a lifesaver, with a loyal clientele and a great work ethic.

Carl stopped and took a few quick steps to Roxy's side. He circled her waist. "Nervous?"

"Scared."

He kissed the tip of her nose. "Me too. But I'm also proud of you." He stepped back, still looking at her. "And you're looking mighty good lady."

Roxy didn't shrug off the compliment. She'd be working on hearing nice things and believing them. "Thanks."

He dashed out the door with a wave.

Jewel walked into the living room, carrying Iris in her car seat, its plastic snow-cover already snuggly in place. Roxy pulled it away and kissed Iris's chubby cheek. "How's my sweet girl?"

"We gotta get moving. Big test today," Jewel said to Roxy. "You gonna be, okay?

"Sure." Except her heart was rocking again and cold sweat popped out on her forehead. Panic attack control was now among her new skills. She took several deep breaths, counted to ten backwards in her head and reminded herself she was fine.

The living room, crowded with her family, also helped, and made Roxy smile. Their old sofa bed was now accompanied by two upholstered chairs she found at the Goodwill store. A kid-size table with matching stools, a smattering of baby toys, and Jewel's rocking chair filled the remaining space. The built-in bookcase held Roxy's favorites—the complete works of Shakespeare and August Wilson, long-ago gifts from Carl. Plus, books by Toni Morrison, Maya Angelou, and the poetry of Langston Hughes and Amanda Gorman. Stacks of library books borrowed by the children and Jewel's community college textbooks—the ones not available electronically—covered the bottom shelves. Roxy's eyes filled with happiness tears. They'd accomplished a lot over the last seven months. Still hanging on the edge of disaster, but also on the cusp of good fortune.

The family thundered down the steps from their third-floor apartment in their fixer-upper. An older couple lived on the second floor. They never complained about the noise the Quinton crew made. So far. The first-floor apartment stood vacant again. The last renters found a place "in a better neighborhood" and broke their lease. They also left a mess for Carl, B.J., Angel, Harriet, and Roxy to clean up. Angel turned out to be true to his name and invested in their startup—money and sweat equity–adding to the cash B.J. invested, and what Carl and Roxy borrowed from the bank.

Roxy kissed everyone goodbye and waited for Dallas. Her van pulled up and Roxy hopped in.

"Sorry I'm late. The snow is piling up and slowing traffic." Warm air blasted from the vents. "My daffodils poked their heads up, clocked the cold and snow, and retreated."

Roxy laughed. "They'll be back." Smooth jazz filled the vehicle. Roxy felt her panic leveling but not yet subsiding. "Appreciate the lift and support."

"You seem more stressed than usual, and that's saying something," Dallas said. She pulled away from the curb and headed toward the Bronx River Parkway on their way to the county courthouse in White Plains.

Roxy hadn't had a panic attack in months until this morning when she felt one building. "I'm good."

"Not."

"The jury's been out for three days. That can't be a good sign."

"What does the prosecutor say?" Dallas slowed. Snow coated the windshield as fast as the wipers swiped it away. She turned on the defroster.

"What if they find him not guilty?"

The friends stayed quiet for a few seconds.

Dallas said, "You spoke your truth. That's what matters, right?"

"I guess."

Roxy had taken the stand, adding her story to witnesses Maria Rivera and Tanya Wilson from Spider's Baltimore venture. On a tip secured by Detective Zay Adams, Maria, Roxy, and Dallas located Tanya and persuaded her to join the case. They each had witnesses who testified that the victim told them about the rape immediately afterwards. Dallas spoke on behalf of Roxy, describing how she found her bloodied friend at Orchard Beach, curled up with an Army blanket around her shoulders. She described the bruises and Roxy's account.

Three rape victims and corroborating witnesses made it harder for Spider to deny, but he did. Venom, charm, anger, and victimhood poured out during his two days of testimony. He used his superpowers on the jury. Roxy watched him suck them in.

Although she'd agreed, she was unsure if voicing what happened was enough.

Spectators, members of the press, and those involved in the case filled the courtroom benches. Carl, Roxy, Dallas, and Zay sat on the prosecutor's side. From her third-row seat, Roxy watched Spider. Motionless, his hair cut and styled, his suit tailored. Each day of the trial he wore a different one.

Her robes flowing, the judge swept in. "All rise," the bailiff said. The judge, a woman in her early to mid-sixties, motioned everyone to be seated.

Next came the jury. Five men and seven women. Four Black, one Asian, one Latina, and six Caucasian, including a man in a wheelchair.

"Excuse me."

Roxy looked up. Vicki made everybody scootch over one to make room. She wagged her fingers in Roxy's direction and sent a quick peck to Carl's bearded cheek. She'd missed the trial but came to town when Roxy told her the defense was wrapping up their case. As she did last summer, she bunked at Laura Garrison's place. Yesterday, she hosted Roxy there for dinner. The four of them, Laura, Vicki, Dallas, and Roxy, had become good friends. With Vicki, it was friends *again*.

After days of deliberation, they'd summoned everyone to the courtroom. The jury was back and the verdict in.

Laura touched Roxy's shoulder from behind. "I'm proud of you," she said in Roxy's ear, echoing Carl's words. She'd been steadfast during the six-day trial, not missing a day.

"Thank you." Roxy felt pleased with herself as well. Scared and stressed, but still, she did it. Funny thing, but watching her play night after night last August, seeing the rape reenacted, took some of its power away and gave her courage on the stand.

The judge said, "Quiet please." She turned her hard stare on Spider. "Will the defendant rise?"

Spider stood, his head high and shoulders squared.

"Madam Forewoman, have you reached a verdict?" the judge asked the tall, slim woman standing with a piece of paper in her hand.

"Yes, we have, Your Honor."

"On the charge of second-degree sexual assault, what do you say?"

"Guilty, Your Honor."

A buzz rose from the spectators.

The judge rapped her gavel. "Quiet." She turned back to the forewoman. "On the charge of aggravated assault, what do you say?"

"Guilty, Your Honor."

Carl reached for Roxy's hand and held it tight.

Spider's shoulders slumped forward, a tiny movement, but otherwise he remained still. His chin stayed lifted and his arms hung at his sides.

Gasps, groans, and a scattering of applause broke out, including Dallas and Vicki. Some of the town's leading lights were hoping for an acquittal and a return to the development project Spider and the consortium began months earlier. Construction stopped in December, both because of the weather and Spider's legal problems. The theater's school was only an excavated foundation, fenced off and covered.

The verdict left Roxy both glad and sad.

Over the last seven months, she was able to persuade two women to step forward—Maria and Tanya. Bobbie, the first survivor Roxy found, attended the trial in solidarity as she'd promised. All three sat in the row in front of Roxy. Maria turned in her seat. "We won," she said. "Thank you."

"Yes," Roxy said. Guilty. She let their collective accomplishment sit for a few joyful seconds. The happiness came from vindication for three women, including Roxy, who stood up for themselves, and, as Dallas said, spoke their truths aloud.

But she was also sad thinking about the women, known and unknown, who he hurt during her eighteen years of silence. Dallas and Carl assured her times were different, and it was her word against his back then, without the moral force of the #MeToo movement. She accepted that. Even so, she should have tried.

• • •

Snow blew and piled up in drifts. Standing under the portico, Roxy waited for Carl to bring around the car. She hugged the three women goodbye and congratulated the prosecutor. He said there would be appeals and months if not years of work ahead. But assured her he'd stick with it. She knew it was not a promise he could necessarily keep. Too many rapists got off because prosecutors cut their losses and moved on. Roxy's research showed how fortunate she was to have come this far.

Many survivors never saw the inside of a courtroom. Especially Black women. She was grateful and still hopeful, despite the long odds.

Vicki, who did an amazing job on opening night of *The Monday Night Murder*, leaned in with a quick hug. She had to get back to the set in Boston where they produced her TV show. No Kenny and no baby, but her new show received strong ratings every week and there was already talk of season two. She followed through with her scholarship for Joe Dawes's new school whenever it became a reality. Now, her driver hurried up the steps with an umbrella and escorted her to the waiting car.

Dallas stood next to Roxy. "Way to go, girl."

"I can't tell you how much your support these last months—"

Dallas cut her off. In her singing voice she said, "That's what friends are for." They hugged. "Have a meeting I might make if I hurry. You going to be, okay?"

"Better than that," Roxy said.

Dallas dashed off.

Roxy wrapped her arms around her torso. Windblown snow swirled at her feet. A day of reckonings and closure. Time was no longer her enemy or something she needed to rewind to fix her life.

She thought about her dad. He'd be proud of her too. With the birth of Iris, and Ed and Jewel's wedding months away, she'd been thinking about him a lot. You're a great grandfather, Dad. Images of her mother and father dancing in the kitchen flashed through her mind. The voices of Mariah Carey, Jay-Z, and Destiny's Child echoed. When did their relationship go wrong? How? She shook her head. No more repeating generational history. I'm not my mother. She pictured the gold bracelet she no longer wore, tucked away in her jewelry box. Her mom chose to leave and not return. Roxy didn't need to wear a reminder every day, a message of not being loved enough.

Thinking about the trial and the last seven months got her heart thudding. She breathed in the cold, moist air. You're fine, she told herself, and took another deep breath. The panic quieted.

Carl pulled up in front of the courthouse in their raggedy Taurus. She watched him park in the waiting area. He'd kept his new beard, grown to mark his freedom from Frank. Roxy liked it. Plus, beards were fashionable and brought in extra business at the shop.

Although Celeste still babysat for her grandchildren from time to time and came by to visit Iris often, Frank stopped speaking to Carl, B.J., and Roxy. No more Sunday dinner invitations. Winnie reported the tradition was dying. More no shows and canceled meals.

Carl and Roxy started dating, which was odd to say but accurate. Once a week they went out together, no children, even if only for a beer and pizza. Never to Sandman's.

Roxy had learned a lot since August. Healing took time and work. Trust lost in an instant required a slow rebuild. Roxy was all in.

Careful not to slip on the wet steps, she hurried down, opened the passenger door, and slid in next to her husband.

"Where to, lady?" Carl asked in a jokey voice.

"Home," Roxy said. "Let's go home."

The End

"For there is always light."–**Amanda Gorman**

"All you need in the world is love and laughter. That's all anybody needs. To have love in one hand and laughter in the other."–**August Wilson**

ACKNOWLEDGMENTS

With gratitude, I thank Black Rose Writing, Reagan Rothe, and his gifted team for this opportunity.

Thank you to my early and final readers for their keen eyes for details, patience, and encouragement—my husband Robert Osborne, Sr., my friends, and fellow writers, Marianne Haggerty, Elizabeth Herman, Willa Hogarth, and Dorin Hart. Thank you to author and teacher Russell Rowland and his band of workshops participants who weighed in.

A very special thank you to my son, Robert Osborne, Jr. who gave me excellent advice.

As always, I'm grateful for my family whose love, support, and enthusiasm means everything—Bob, Sr., Bob, Jr., Alicia, Suzy, and J.P. Osborne and Adam and Aidan Quallo. I know my late brother, Carlton Quallo, is happy for me, smiling down.

About the Author

Karen E. Osborne's novels followed a forty-year career, first as an academic administrator and then co-owner of The Osborne Group, serving as a consultant, trainer, and motivational speaker. She is the author of three suspense/women's fiction novels. *Getting It Right* (Akashic Books) June 2017. It was featured in Poets & Writers and Essence Magazine as a Best Read. *Tangled Lies* (Black Rose Writing) July 22, 2021, BestThriller.com finalist. And *Reckonings* (Black Rose Writing) June 16, 2022. Karen hosts a weekly video podcast, *What Are You Reading? What Are You Writing?* where she interviews authors about their artistic journeys and book recommendations. Karen and her husband, Bob, have two grown children and three grandsons. They live in Port Saint Lucie, FL.

Note from the Author

Word-of-mouth is crucial for any author to succeed. If you enjoyed *Reckonings*, please leave a review online—anywhere you are able. Even if it's just a sentence or two. It would make all the difference and would be very much appreciated.

Thanks!
Karen E. Osborne

We hope you enjoyed reading this title from:

BLACK ROSE
writing™

www.blackrosewriting.com

Subscribe to our mailing list – *The Rosevine* – and receive **FREE** books, daily
deals, and stay current with news about upcoming
releases and our hottest authors.
Scan the QR code below to sign up.

Already a subscriber? Please accept a sincere thank you for being a fan of
Black Rose Writing authors.

View other Black Rose Writing titles at
www.blackrosewriting.com/books and use promo code
PRINT to receive a **20% discount** when purchasing.

CPSIA information can be obtained
at www.ICGtesting.com
Printed in the USA
BVHW031626140523
664015BV00021B/305